Fear

the

Silence

IAIN CAMERON

To find out more about the author, visit the website:

www.iain-cameron.com

Dedication

To those who made my first two books so successful, my heartfelt thanks, you know who you are.

ONE

Voices were raised and it took several seconds before he realised the loudest was his. 'Brad was crap in *Ocean's Thirteen*. There's no story and he couldn't act for toffee.'

'Of course he can act,' Jack Monaghan said in his soft Dublin drawl, more pronounced than ever after numerous glasses of red wine. 'He and the rest of them only made the film so the studios would let Clooney direct *Good Night and Good Luck*. It was a bloody put-up job.'

'I loved him in *Fight Club*,' their host Brian Langton said, the wine glass engulfed in his big hand. 'I went to a couple of bare knuckle fights and I think they caught the raw, aggressive atmosphere about right.'

Ricky Wood sat back and lifted his glass; he'd said enough. He'd probably drunk enough as well, but what the hell. From across the table his beautiful girlfriend, Celia, looked radiant in a summer dress, revealing plenty of cleavage. He found it an arousing spectacle, in spite of the distance and range of obstacles between them: empty and part-empty glasses, candles, plates, a roll basket and a large plant thing, more suited to a garden centre than a dinner party table. She gave him 'the look' and mouthed something, but if it was a criticism of his drunken behaviour, he didn't care.

While the men dissected the movie careers of Brad, George and Matt with a fine toothcomb or a ragged fence brush, as they were all too pissed to think straight, the women talked about schools. Correction, Brian's wife, Kelly, talked about schools while Celia and Jack's girlfriend, Olivia, listened with a little more interest than was good for two single women.

In so many ways, Kelly and Brian Langton were a modern, 'post-celebrity' couple. He used to be the rude television interviewer who shoved a microphone into the faces of gang bosses, corrupt police officers and drug dealers, exposing their dirty deeds to the nation. Less than a decade later, he had been pushed aside by perkier and scruffier lads who were said to relate better to their younger audience. He now owned a television production company with a number of successful shows under his belt and was making way more money behind a camera than in front of it.

Since the age of seventeen, 'Kelly,' as she was known then, was a constant presence in newspaper and television ads as the jilted woman in a stylish car advert, the body for a well-known maker of tights, and the main model for a high street store's clothing collection. She gave up her career for much the same reasons as Brian and now spent her time managing her fashion and perfume businesses under the 'Kelly Kreations' brand name.

Despite the intervening years, their fame remained undiminished. Rarely a week went by without her face adorning the weekend magazines or appearing in a feature in the Sunday supplements talking about her dogs, make-up and children, or the pair of them being photographed at the races or watching polo at Goodwood.

'So what do you do, Ricky? I don't think Celia mentioned it.'

He turned. For the first time, he looked closely at Kelly Langton and even though the lights in the dining room were dimmed, he could see tanned skin, straw-coloured hair, all neatly trimmed and curled, with deep green eyes twinkling in flickering candlelight. Bloody gorgeous for a 38-year-old mother of two, but how did a rough diamond like Brian Langton, twenty-odd years her senior with a pockmarked face and bags under his eyes, manage to snare such a beauty? His mother used to say attraction was more than skin-deep; here was the living proof.

'I'm a journalist.'

'What kind of things do you write about?'

'Oh, I investigate respectable people with dark pasts or those openly involved in doing something illegal.'

'You won't find anything like that around here.'

He laughed. 'I didn't think I would and anyway, I'm not on duty.'

'When people say 'journalist' to me, I assume they must be a feature writer or a gossip columnist, as that's the only sort I ever seem to meet.'

He picked up his glass; good food, good wine, and chatting to a beautiful woman, what more did a man want? 'I couldn't do it, I'm not empathetic enough, according to my editor.'

'Maybe not, but I bet there is a good book in some of the subjects you investigate.'

'You think so? I've often thought of writing one.'

'You should. I read a lot, especially when Brian's away and the children are in bed.'

'What type of books do you read?'

'Everything and anything,' she said, laughing and showing two rows of even, pearly white teeth; amazing. In early pictures of her, at about the age of eighteen, he remembered she had a noticeable gap between the two top incisors with a protruding lateral incisor on the left side.

'I like romance and crime novels, but now I'm into relationship thrillers, although some people call them Domestic Noir.'

Celia was trying to attract his attention above the hubbub and this time her demeanour seemed warm, evidence perhaps that he had not yet disgraced himself in front of her friends, but on turning back a minute or so later to resume his conversation with Kelly, the seat lay empty.

She was on her feet, clearing away plates with the assistance of Irish Jack, who was not only helpful, handsome, and ruggedly unshaven, but also the owner of an IT business. He didn't know what he did but obviously it paid well as he had arrived at the Langton house tonight in a Porsche and wore a gold Rolex.

Ricky missed his chance to help the delectable Kelly, perhaps just as well, as he could be a clumsy sod when it came to crockery, and instead went to the loo. Like everything else in this house, set in its own grounds in a beautiful location on the fringes of Hurstpierpoint, a village to the north of Brighton, the 'smallest room in the house' was large and well appointed, down to the well-stocked bookcase and thick towels which could double as pillows, useful if he couldn't make it all the way back to the dining room.

Ablutions complete, he walked into the hall and for a moment he felt disorientated, or that's what he would say if anyone asked him why he was snooping around. The study was the size of his lounge with a substantial light oak desk, leather chair and an Apple iMac with a massive screen, making his pokey alcove with rickety Ikea desk and old laptop seem poor by comparison.

He ignored the sitting room, as they all had sat in there earlier, and since the conservatory appeared unused he headed for the kitchen. With the door closed, he decided to open it slowly, as he didn't want to scare anyone and cause them to drop those big, fancy dinner plates. He looked in, and looked again to make sure his eyes did not deceive him.

Yes, Jack Monaghan was in there helping Kelly, but not in the way he expected. The Irishman's arms were around her waist, his hands fondling those famous breasts and his tongue exploring the deep recesses of her throat.

TWO

She guided the car between two stone pillars either side of the entrance to Williamson College and drove above the 10 mph speed limit up the long drive. To Kelly Langton it felt as if she had been doing this all her life, as not only did she take her own kids to this school, she used to be a pupil here too, starting in Year 2 and leaving after her GCSEs.

There was nothing wrong with the place, how could there be, with such caring teachers and excellent sport and music facilities? Either she was in one of her black moods or suffering the effect of another Monday morning.

She parked and got out. She buttoned her coat and tied her scarf but still no movement from Ben, Josh or Ollie, sitting inside the car and doing God-knows what.

'Out you guys,' she said. 'You'd think we were half an hour early the way you boys dawdle.'

Josh got out and stretched, as if reaching the end of a long journey in an old, uncomfortable jalopy instead of less than nine miles cocooned inside the sumptuous leather interior of a six-month-old BMW X5.

'I'm tired,' he said, just in case she didn't spot his lethargic movements.

'Well, you wouldn't be if you didn't stay up all hours playing your PlayStation game. You should get to your bed earlier.'

'Wouldn't make any difference,' he said, hauling his sports kit, school bag and water bottle out of the boot.

'What wouldn't?'

'Going to bed early. If I go early, I don't sleep and I would feel even more tired in the morning.'

'Don't talk wet.'

Her son Ben, and Ollie, a boy who lived nearby, as Kelly shared driving duties with his mum, dragged rather than lifted their stuff out of the boot before she closed it, and at last they walked towards the school. She tuned out as morning-person Ben tried to get a response from his brother, who at thirteen displayed the surliness, laziness and strange sleeping patterns of older teenagers, it would only end in bickering. Oh the joys.

Goodbye from her kids amounted to no more than a wave of the hand, like the queen from the deck of the Royal Yacht, the days of hugs and sloppy kisses long gone. She walked back to the car and despite owning and managing a couple of businesses and having what most people would regard as a busy job, this often felt like the lowest point of her day.

Her phone pinged. She fished it out to find a text from Jack Monaghan asking if she would like to go out for a drink. She texted back: 'No, not a good idea.' He came back, seconds later with, 'Why not?' Oh, because she'd drunk more than intended on Saturday night and regretted all her actions the next morning? Standing beside the car, trying to compose a suitable reply in her head, a familiar voice called her name.

'Ah Kelly, I'm glad I caught you.'

Stefan Pearson strode towards her, the perfect embodiment of a modern man: self-made, confident, handsome, with a thick head of black hair and straight, white teeth. He might have been a model and to look at the clothes he wore and the way he carried himself, it was easy to think he was, but instead he chose the arcane world of mercantile financing.

'Hello Stefan.'

'Kelly, it's great to see you. Did you give any more thought to the weekend away I mentioned?'

'I did and Brian's all for it.'

'The dates are ok, both of you can get away?'

'Yes.'

'Excellent news. I'll call Sebastian and get it all fixed up. He's looking forward to meeting you... and Brian of course. Why the glum face earlier? It's not because of me or something I said, is it?'

'It could never be you, Stefan. No, I'm being hassled by someone.'

'A woman in your position should be used to it.'

'My friends say the same but I hurt like everyone else.'

'Well, a weekend away at a top spa hotel might be just what you need.' He glanced at his watch, a thick, chunky timepiece, well-suited to his broad, hairy wrist. 'Must go, train to catch.' He leaned over and kissed her on the cheek. His face felt smooth and warm with the strong scent of sandalwood. If they were not standing in the school car park, but under the porch outside her house, in a cinema or inside her car, she would stroke it and kiss him on the lips, but seconds later the conversation ended and soon his sports car disappeared into the distance.

She drove to Burgess Hill with the radio playing loud, a reflection of her renewed enthusiasm for the day ahead and a method of drowning out the wicked thoughts swimming around inside her head like a tank of tropical fish. What she could get up to while relaxing in the Jacuzzi and the steam room at this spa hotel with only Stefan for company was the stuff of fantasy, but it needed to be put on the back burner for the moment if she didn't want to have an accident.

Arriving in Burgess Hill, she turned into Albert Drive and moments later, into the Sovereign Business Park. She stopped at the second building along, the one bearing the logo, 'Kelly Kreations' in squiggly, pastel-coloured writing, and parked in a space reserved for the Managing Director. She felt a sense of pride whenever she saw the name of her company, her idea and vision, encased in concrete and glass, but running a business was a lot harder than it looked from the outside.

The building consisted of only two floors but it was modern with large rooms, which suited the needs of the business. The ground floor housed the showroom and provided hanging space for finished articles such as dresses, skirts, blouses, and jewellery. Upstairs, it accommodated a small number of seamstresses to take care of alterations, her 'style guru' Jacques who designed all the clothes, and at the back, the Accounts team and her office.

'Good morning, Mrs Langton,' receptionist Katie Ogden said as she pushed open the front door.

'Morning Katie. How are you? How's your brother?'

'I'm fine but Harry's taken a bit of a downturn. The chemo's knocking him for six.'

'It gets worse before it gets better, from what I understand. Tell him I'm thinking about him.'

'Will do.'

'Is Jacques in?'

'Yes, he's upstairs.'

'Thanks Katie. Catch you later.'

She could listen to other people's problems as much as the next woman, but Katie's family were the world's worst for falling into manholes, walking into doors, getting knocked over by cars, and now her brother with cancer. Dwell too long at her desk, and the litany of her family's troubles could easily eat away the following half hour.

She walked into her office. She didn't come here every day, as there were many other things requiring her attention, mainly the licensing agreement with L'Oréal for the fragrance range, a job she could do from her home computer, the swimwear collection, also produced under license, and a book she was in the process of writing for which she needed perfect peace.

'Good morning, Meess Kelly,' Jacques Fournier her deputy and chief designer said, breezing into her office without knocking, on a cloud of expensive

10

shaving soap and aftershave and without giving her a chance to sit down. He spoke flawless English but for some reason could not pronounce the words 'Miss' or 'Mrs'.

'Morning Jacques. How are things today?'

'The delivery from China of all our summer dresses is expected today–'

'They'll need to hurry up, or before we know it, they'll be telling us it's Christmas and nothing's moving.'

'I agree, I'll chase them up if it does not arrive by lunchtime. The new seamstress started this morning and I think she is good, she is going to work out.'

'At last some good news, we've been short-handed for too long.'

So he went on, a long list of systems, people and product issues. It never ceased to surprise her as it was only a small company, but as Jacques never failed to remind her, they were in the fashion business and it moved quickly and if they didn't move with it, they were dead. He departed ten minutes later, and as her accountancy night school teacher often said, he left his monkeys with her, as all the problems he brought into the office with him belonged to her now.

She worked all morning, ate lunch at her desk, and a few minutes after two called Chief Accountant, Ed Hardacre into her office.

'Af'noon Kelly,' he said, sitting down and placing the ubiquitous blue folder he always carried with him on the desk. Aged the wrong side of forty, with wonky teeth and untidy hair, he was bolstered by a gregarious personality and generous spirit, but for all the women he claimed to have bedded, he didn't seem to like them much and resented having a female boss.

'Afternoon Ed.'

'What's the big issue today then, margins or sales?' He reached for the folder.

'Neither.' She leaned forward, composing her words with care. 'Ed, there are discrepancies in the accounts.'

'Wh'dya mean discrepancies? I run a tight ship.'

'I mean the accounts don't stack up. Since the start of the year sales have been increasing fast and Jacques is forever telling me about all the new customers he signed up, so by now I would expect to see profits and cash rise, but instead they fell for the third month in a row.'

'I told you before, London Home are slow payers, they—'

'I've looked at them, but they're too small to make such an impact.'

'Well it must be...'

She listened to his lame excuses but she was expecting them. This conversation could not take place a couple of weeks ago, but ever since, she'd spent many evenings poring over the numbers, forcing her accountancy-averse brain to understand, and she'd even roped in Gemma Ferguson, the FD of Brian's business, who'd examined the details and concurred with her conclusions.

'Listen to me, Ed. I crunched the numbers and I know you're stealing.'

He leapt up and leaned over the desk, trying to intimidate her, but at five-foot nine and weighing about seventy kilos, it didn't have the same impact as her husband or Stefan Pearson.

'You fucking liar, I never stole a penny, why would I steal? My girlfriend's in a good job and I've worked solid for twenty-odd years without a break. Why would I need to do it, eh? Eh?'

'Ed sit down and stop shouting.' Unlike her children, he did as he was told.

She waited a moment or two for his hot head to come off the boil. 'Why does anybody steal? It's usually to fund gambling debts or an expensive drug habit.'

'What the fuck are people saying about me, eh?'

'Nothing. I'm only asking the question and—'

'For your information I don't do any of that crap.'

'Everybody knows you bet on horse racing, isn't that a form of gambling?'

'Yeah, but it's nothing, a few quid, here, a few quid there.'

'Only last week you boasted you'd won three hundred pounds. How many bets do you need to place to win that much?'

He shrugged. 'It's easy when you know what you're doing.'

'I'll take your word for it, but what I'm talking about here is a serious matter.'

'I stole nothing. You hear me?'

'I hear you. I hoped you'd come clean and admit what you've been up to—'

'Why the hell would I? I didn't do nothing!'

'Ok, we'll do this the hard way. Let me show you the proof.'

She placed the invoices in front of him, one after the other. The company involved, the same on every one, 'BH Temporary Staff,' all authorised by the man facing her with the stony stare.

'What's this? Temp invoices? We've needed temps ever since I started working here.'

'I know, but this agency, 'BH Temporary Staff' is owned by you and if I do the numbers it gives us on average, five temps a day for over a year. I think someone would notice, as only fifteen of us work in this building and–'

'What the fuck are you trying to pull? You gonna sack me?'

'What choice are you leaving me, Ed? Count yourself lucky I don't call the police.'

The chair flew back and hit the wall as he got to his feet. He placed one hand on the desk and pointed with the other at her face. 'You fucking bitch. I'll get even with you, see if I don't.'

He stormed out of the office, thumping the door against its stopper and brushing past a startled Jacques, who came over to see what all the fuss was about. Hardacre grabbed his jacket from the back of his chair and headed to the stairs. On the way past her office, he turned his head towards her and mouthed something she could not hear but going by his thunderous glare, he wasn't wishing her a good day.

THREE

Detective Inspector Angus Henderson walked away from the conference room after the press briefing in a sombre mood. For the last two weeks, he'd been leading a large team of officers from Sussex Police in tracking the movements of a gang of drug smugglers using the South Coast to bring in consignments of marijuana and heroin from Pakistan.

The latest intel suggested a sizeable shipment was due into either Shoreham or Newhaven harbours at some point over the next two weeks and he was putting together a couple of surveillance teams to watch both harbours and intercept it. The prize was not only the seizure of the dope, but by arresting the participants they would soon put a name to the person financing the operation. With the large sums of money involved, his chips were on Brighton villain Dominic Green and my oh my, what a mighty triumph it would be to see him go down. Alas, he wouldn't be there to see it as he had been pulled off the case.

At first, he was convinced he'd done something wrong or upset his new boss, Chief Inspector Lisa Edwards, but the more he got to know her, the more he realised she feared the wrath of the media as much as he feared the same from an armed and dangerous criminal. It was something he needed to get used to, but a welcome change from her predecessor, Steve Harris. A few months back, Harris moved to Manchester to join his accountant wife after she started a new job there. With him in the chair, the conviction of a crook brought great pleasure, not for removing another low-life from the streets and leaving Sussex a safer place, but for improving the look of his arrest stats.

It would have cushioned the pain a little if Henderson's removal from the drugs case had been to undertake something of equal importance, but the media going gaga about a missing woman didn't rock his boat. The conference room for the third press briefing of the week couldn't squeeze another body inside, as it contained all sections of UK press and television, satellite broadcasters and web-based magazines, and a smattering of teams from all over Europe and the US. The sage who'd once said, 'sex sells,' got it damn well right.

He pushed open the door to Interview Room Three and walked in, DS Carol Walters following in his wake. When they both sat down in the sparsely decorated room with only a desk, four chairs and austere grey walls, she labelled the tapes and switched on the recording equipment.

'Present for this interview is Detective Inspector Angus Henderson,' Henderson said.

'Detective Sergeant Carol Walters,' the DS said.

Henderson nodded towards the subject sitting opposite. 'Can you please state your full name and date of birth, sir.'

'Richard David Wood, 6 February 1977.'

'Thank you for coming in this evening, Mr Wood. I do hope PC Davidson has made you, if not comfortable, at least relaxed.'

'No complaints but I'm sure glad I didn't book me a room for the night.'

'Mr Wood, as you are no doubt aware, we are investigating the disappearance of Mrs Kelly Langton and are in the process of interviewing anyone who knew her.'

The investigation into the mysterious disappearance of the former model 'Kelly', now plain Kelly Langton, was to be called Operation Condor and he hoped the system-generated name wasn't prescient, as in his mind at least it conjured up images of a large carrion bird picking over the bones of a dead woman.

It wasn't Henderson's job to try and understand the psychology of the press or even the police, but it was curious to note how the majority of missing persons cases were handled by a local bobby who could conclude without too much investigation or shoe leather, that he or she buggered off as they were sick of being treated like a doormat, while others were elevated to the front pages of every newspaper and all available police resources thrown at them.

A cynic might suggest it was influenced by the amount of media coverage and in this instance, it was considerable as a decade's worth of 'Kelly' pictures were accessible from photographic agencies and newspapers, and not only was this catalogue more voluminous than most, the subject in question was beautiful, often wearing little, and better to look at than pictures of a pasty politician or a pubescent pop star.

For the moment, he would do as his boss requested and assume CI Edwards saw something in this case beyond a simple disappearance, making her think it might involve criminal intent. If true, it would make his transfer worthwhile, and not, as he suspected, a case better conducted in private by the Family Liaison Officer, away from the glare of all this publicity.

'Is there any news?' Wood asked.

Henderson shook his head. 'I'm afraid not. Nothing has been heard from Mrs Langton since dropping her boys off at school three days ago.'

'It's awful but I read as much in the paper.'

'If I can make a start, Mr Wood. You're a journalist of Lower Rock Gardens in Brighton. Is this correct?'

'Yes.'

'Who do you work for?'

'*The Sunday Times*. I'm what's known in the trade as an investigative journalist and spend anything from a couple of weeks to a few months getting to know drug gangs or criminal families and then writing an exposé in the newspaper.'

'Does this type of work put you in any danger?'

'Not really. Like your surveillance guys, I dress the part, dye my hair, grow a beard, anything to change the way I look at the moment.'

'What are you working on now?'

'I can't tell you, but last year I investigated two Romanian gangs involved in bringing in people from their homeland, often kidnapping young men and women on country roads to work on vegetable farms in Norfolk and Suffolk. They treat people like slaves, and all the money they earn goes straight to the criminals in repayment of a loan they are told is for transport and lodgings but no matter how much they work, they can never pay it back.'

In his spare time, Henderson liked nothing better on a Sunday morning than to head over to a coffee shop in Seven Dials and read the thick weekend newspapers. If he was trying to forget about work, he would avoid the serious articles and seek out quirky stories about mobile phone usage or acceptable etiquette on the Underground, while at other times he would read the sort of stuff Wood talked about, half-hoping it offered some insight into the problems he was trying to solve.

Wood's hair was fair, grown to collar length and parted in the centre. He had sharp eyes but despite the well-scrubbed face and an absence of stubble, he wasn't what the ladies would call handsome, but craggy in an outdoor way. He wore blue jeans and a white t-shirt and by its prevalence at the press conference earlier, the closest thing media-types could claim as a uniform.

'How well do you know Mrs Langton?' Henderson asked.

'I've met her a couple of times. Let me think. Yeah one time when we got together at a pub for someone's engagement party. I can't remember who, but sometime in July on a hot day, upstairs in a pub called the King and Queen. The other time at a dinner party at their house, last weekend.'

'I'll come back to the dinner party. How would you characterise your relationship with Mrs Langton?'

'A relationship?' Wood said, smiling. 'How could I have any kind of relationship with Mrs Langton when I hardly know her? It's Celia Warren, my girlfriend who knows her. They've been mates since school.'

'We are aware of that sir. We have spoken to Ms Warren.'

'Well, if you've spoken to her, you would know Kelly was her friend, not mine. So don't ask me if I know her well, because I don't.'

'What I think Inspector Henderson means,' Walters said, 'is if Mrs Langton is a close friend of Celia, we might expect you to have met her on more than two occasions, especially as she's quite the celebrity.'

'I see your point, but I understand they're not what you might call bosom buddies. Celia lives in Brighton and they live out in the country, and I know Kelly's got her own business and can work as she likes, but Celia's a nurse at the hospital and works shifts. I guess you could say they move in different social circles and don't see one another so much, but they talk on the phone a couple of times a month.'

'If we can come back to the dinner party,' Henderson said, 'the weekend before Kelly disappeared. How did she seem to you then?'

'I suppose the same as the rest of us, as we were all well pissed by the end of the night. I talked to her for a bit and she seemed fine, happy even. I mean, hosting a dinner party can be stressful but if she was feeling the strain, I couldn't see it. To me, she was enjoying herself.'

'How would you characterise her behaviour?'

'Come again?'

'Did she seem tense or worried about anything?'

Wood shook his head. 'As I said, she seemed happy.'

'How about her husband, Brian? How well do you know him?'

'The same as Kelly, really. Celia got the invite, not me and let's be frank, you wouldn't invite a journalist to your dinner party if you could help it, would you? In popularity surveys, we rank lower than estate agents and it you must know, it really pisses me off.'

Henderson smiled. His girlfriend, Rachel Jones was a journalist with *The Argus*, Brighton's main local newspaper but as much as he would like to leap to her defence, he did not.

'How would you describe Brian, based on the short time you've known him?' Henderson hoped he didn't sound as bored as he felt but this witness was obviously useless. How he made a living as an examiner and inquisitor of modern life he would never know, as he sounded half asleep at this dinner party. Perhaps he was drunk before it started.

'I know he used to be famous in the nineties for door-stepping drug dealers and rogue builders who were ripping off pensioners. Now, he produces documentaries and political programmes for the major networks and by all accounts he's making more money than he ever did standing in front of a camera.'

21

'Interesting,' Henderson said without much conviction.

'I mean, he's a big man and rough looking, which I imagine is an asset when dealing with criminals and the like. He's older than Kelly by about fifteen years but they look to me like a together couple.'

'How so?'

'Ach, you know, helping her serve food, he made coffee the way she liked it and he always made a point of touching her shoulder when he walked past, as he topped-up the wine and the coffee, you know the sort of thing.'

'Would you describe them as a loving couple?' Walters said.

He forced a smile but it sounded more like a snort. 'They've been married for what, ten years? In my case, I was married for five and you would never describe me and my ex as 'loving' and certainly not in public, but the Langton's looked happy enough to me. I mean, they own a big house, got two kids, pots of money in the bank; what else do you need?'

'What do you think happened to Mrs Langton, Mr Wood?' Henderson said.

'I was going to ask you the same thing.'

'I asked first.'

'Police station, primary school, what's the difference? I really don't know her well enough to speculate whether she would or would not run away with someone, but I talked to Celia and she couldn't think of anybody who's shown a particular interest in her, or knew someone with a grudge or a stalker or anything else. She was, she *is* a nice person and not the type to attract enemies and in my line of work, I've met plenty who do the opposite.'

'So you don't think she's been kidnapped, as some newspapers are speculating, or any harm has come to her?'

'I don't think so but it's too early to say, although if she doesn't show up in a few days, it's a distinct possibility, don't you think?'

'We will look at all possibilities,' Henderson said.

'So what is it you guys are thinking? Do you think she's been kidnapped?'

'I'm sorry, Mr Wood,' he said. 'You're an experienced journalist and you surely don't expect me to share my thoughts and conjecture at this stage of the investigation? Your colleagues in the media do enough of that as it is.'

Henderson left the interview room, more glum than after the press conference. Ricky Wood was the last of the dinner party guests to be interviewed and the hoped-for breakthrough hadn't materialised. With not much more to go on, he had a bad feeling they were now in for a long haul.

FOUR

'How long has it been here?' DS Walters asked, raising her voice over the din of a dodgy exhaust rattling beneath a dirty white van as it drove past.

'The woman in there,' PC 2357 said, nodding towards a row of terraced houses nearby, 'thinks it's been sitting here nearly a week, and by the look of the grime on the window, I would say she's about right.'

She turned to look at the copper for the first time and an acne-marked complexion met her gaze. Aged no more than twenty, about the right level of experience required to stand around on a chilly Sunday morning guarding a car that wasn't going anywhere, but she was in no mood for smartarses.

'Constable, carry on watching this car and make sure it doesn't get tampered with and I'll get on with making all the assumptions and deductions. In my book, we leave the detective work to the professionals, if it's all right with you?'

'Yes ma'am, sorry ma'am.'

She walked towards the car. She could have pulled him up about calling her 'ma'am' as she was only thirty-seven and too young to be mistaken for his mother, granny, or elderly aunt but she didn't want to be here all day.

The call informing her Kelly Langton's silver BMW X5 had been found in the car park beside a parade of shops in Pound Hill, Crawley, came through as she lay in bed. While it wasn't unusual to find her still in bed at quarter to eight on the morning of her day off, as a lie-in wasn't so much a luxury, as an essential component of her well-being, it *was* unusual for her to be suffering from a thumping hangover.

Single and without a boyfriend, an active social life, no hobbies and with a job impacting on all three, she didn't often go out on Saturday nights, but as she had been working long hours all week she needed to get out to let off some steam. After cajoling the two biggest boozers she knew, her neighbour Sarah and her friend Evie to accompany her, the bars of Brighton didn't know what hit them.

Making her way to the scene, she made three calls. The first to the DVLA, confirming the car did indeed belong to Mrs Langton, as she couldn't trust the plods around here to do it. Next, she called Brian Langton who was now on his way to meet her with the spare keys. Her third call was to DC Khalid Agha, the young detective she was supposed to be mentoring, who wasn't best pleased to be called out after loading the car with all his kids' things, all set for a day out in Watford to visit his brother.

She tried to see inside Kelly Langton's car but with tinted windows, dull and dirty with road muck, a couple of dead bodies might have been in there for all she could see. Due to the high profile nature of the case, she was in two minds what to do with it, either to send it off for forensic testing or let Mr Langton drive it away.

She pulled out her phone. With her memory of last night a tad hazy, she was convinced someone had been making calls on it while she was in the loo or playing some games when she wasn't looking, as there wasn't much oomph left in the battery. She called Henderson.

'Hello sir, how are you this cold morning? I hope I didn't disturb your beauty sleep.'

'Sleep? I should be so lucky. When I finish work, I spend the next hour fielding phone calls and questions from journalists. The only place they haven't tracked me to is here at the Marina.'

A vision came into her mind of him cowering deep in the bowels of his little boat, waiting until it got dark before he emerged, but no, that wasn't his style.

'We've found Kelly Langton's car.'

'She's not in it?'

'Not as far as I can see.'

'That would make it too easy, wouldn't it? Where is it?'

'Pound Hill shopping parade in Crawley.'

'Pound Hill?' Henderson went quiet for a moment. 'Yeah, I know where it is, up the road from Three Bridges Station, a place with good connections to the South Coast and London.'

'Right first time.'

'The hallmark of a fleeing woman, perhaps?'

'Could be, or to throw us off the scent.'

'Maybe. Did you find anything of interest when you looked inside?'

'I haven't done it yet. I'm waiting for Brian Langton to turn up with the keys. What should I do with it?'

'What, after you've searched it?'

'Yes.'

He paused. 'Nothing. Let him take it away.'

'Don't you think–'

'We should send it for forensic analysis?'

'Yeah.'

'What for? She's been missing less than a week and what will we find? The dabs of two dozen kids, mums she ferried to coffee mornings, some of her business associates? It'll take two officers a fortnight to eliminate them all. No, give it back to Mr Langton.'

She wandered over to the pool car, refusing Agha's offer of a cigarette as she stopped six months ago and only succumbed to temptation when drunk. Her face reddened when she remembered last night. Wasn't it Oscar Wilde who said giving up was easy, he'd done it hundreds of times? Join the club.

'So what do you think, Sherlock?'

'I'm thinking about what a nice afternoon I'm missing with my brother and here I am freezing my bollocks off in a dump like this.'

Four years on the beat in South Wales and another three as a trainee detective in Portsmouth before becoming a sergeant at Sussex, her colleagues would say she 'had served her time.' This know-nothing rookie, fast-tracked on the promotion ladder to the top, spent no time buckling down and learning his trade and wasted more time and energy acting the belligerent and moody bastard with a permanent chip on his shoulder. If the chip was about his colour as his family came from Pakistan, or because he used to live in a scruffy part of South London, she could understand and deal with it, but it seemed to be about anything and everything and his constant whining was starting to piss many people off.

'Listen mate,' she said, turning to face him. 'If you want to make it as a detective, and speaking from my own experience it's a good place to be, but you've got to accept that shitty things happen and when they do, they have a nasty habit of buggering up what you're doing. It doesn't matter if you're at work, sleeping or heading off to Watford to see your brother as murders, suicides and burglaries don't magically occur between the hours of nine and five to suit Mr Khalid Agha.'

'Yeah, but–'

'Yeah but nothing, mate. If you shut the hell up, pack in your moaning and knuckle down, you'll get along fine but if you don't, I guarantee you won't last six months, fast-track or not.'

He thought about it for a moment or two before shrugging. 'I suppose so,' he said.

She was about to head into one of the nearby shops for some heat when she spotted Brian Langton, waiting to turn into the car park. At least she thought it was him, it was a big bloke driving a look-at-me light-blue Mercedes CLS, equipped with low-profile boots, Xenon LED headlights, and a booming sound system playing Sheryl Crow and 'All I Wanna Do'.

When the car stopped, she waited until the engine was turned off and walked over, rubbing her hands together to keep warm.

'Good morning, Mr Langton,' she said, when he opened the car door. 'I'm Detective Sergeant Carol Walters from Sussex CID.'

'What's good about it?'

'I called you earlier. I've checked the car with the DVLA, it's definitely Mrs Langton's.'

'Good, I wouldn't thank you to be dragged over here on a false alarm.'

They shook hands and her dainty digits were enveloped in giant shovels, reminding her of school bully Alice Rounds who liked to stick the hands of fellow pupils in a vice during woodwork.

'You were lucky to catch me. I was about to take the boys to football. Who spotted it?'

'A woman in one of the houses nearby,' she said, jerking a thumb behind her. 'She read about Kelly's disappearance and the missing car in the paper and when this one didn't move for a while, she called us.'

'Good job she did. What the hell is it doing here?'

'How do you mean, sir?'

'Why would she leave the car here, in Crawley? Kelly never comes here.'

'I don't know.'

'I mean there's nothing in Crawley she couldn't get in Brighton and we live a lot closer to Brighton than here.'

'Maybe she came here to meet someone.'

'I doubt it. Where is it?'

'Over there,' she said, pointing towards Mr Acne Fizzer who was picking his face. Every mother knew that touching an acned face was the worst thing to do, as it only caused the infection to spread, but one piece of lifestyle advice was enough for one day.

Without so much as a 'Thank you detective, you've been so helpful. I'll mention this good work to your superior officers,' he brushed past and strode off towards his wife's car. When he got closer, he stopped and examined the rear before walking around it slowly, like a prospective purchaser looking for scratches.

He fished the keys out and pressed a button, making the doors unlock and the lights flash. He opened the driver's door and climbed in and sat motionless for several seconds, an impassive expression on his big, rough face. It was either a good act or he was trying hard to maintain control of his emotions, but from where she stood, it seemed genuine enough.

The outside of the car looked grubby but the inside was clean and inviting with sumptuous leather seats, a complicated dashboard and elaborate steering wheel full of buttons, requiring the driver to digest the handbook before it could be operated.

'Mind if I take a look in the boot?' she asked.

'Be my guest.'

The boot unlocked with a click and she stood there for a moment and took a deep breath. A woman went missing in Portsmouth, the place where she started her ill-fated married life, and she was discovered dead two weeks later in the boot of her car. She didn't work on the case as she had moved to Sussex by this point but knew the officers involved and could imagine the looks on their faces when they opened the boot and found her, as they were probably expecting to see no more than a toolkit and an old can of de-icer.

Up went the tailgate on a pair of sturdy hydraulic arms to the accompaniment of a deep swishing noise, and to her relief it lay empty, save for a window scraper and a litre bottle of oil, tucked away in a handy little side pocket.

'How does it look to you, sir?' she said, as she closed the tailgate. 'There's nothing here.'

He didn't say anything and so she walked around to the driver's door and tried again.

'Do you notice if anything's missing? I didn't spot anything unusual when I looked in through the windows.' In fact, she couldn't see anything much at all through the windows but it sounded a reassuring thing to say.

He shook his head. 'No, nothing yet.'

She turned and scanned the neighbouring shops: an ironmonger, Co-Op mini-supermarket and hairdresser; and the houses close by, but didn't see any CCTV cameras. There were also no sanctimonious signs proclaiming, 'Residents Only,' 'Stay Restricted to One Hour,' or her pet hate, 'Clampers Operate Here,' as appeared all over her adopted home town of Brighton and Hove and spreading to outlying areas faster than the Ebola virus.

He opened the glove compartment and dipped hands into door pockets before checking behind the sun blinds. He sat there, no doubt wondering where else to look but his bulky frame sagged and his face seemed deflated somehow. If he or one of his mates drove the car there, he did well to hide it, as he seemed disappointed not to find anything. Or perhaps he was annoyed because Old Mother Hubbard in a house nearby spotted it so soon.

'Did you find anything, sir?'

'No, there's nothing here.'

'No sign of her handbag, credit cards or something else of a personal nature?'

'No, nothing much at all, a couple of CDs, AA book, sunglasses and de-icer. No more. Nothing added and nothing taken away.'

'Do you mind if I take a look?'

'Carry on,' he said. A moment or two later, he climbed out and she got in.

There was little point in doing another search but she did so as he watched her. Her interest was in the condition of the interior and whether any scratches were visible on the leather seats to indicate a struggle, or clumps of hair or blood spots on the seats, doors, or carpets, the presence of which would give reason to go back to Henderson and force him to put it through forensics.

She bent down and peered under the driver's seat, feeling for anything that someone might have dropped, an earring or a ring, maybe, before shifting seats and doing the same on the other side. The carpets were clean and free from hairs and dust, with no obvious finger marks on the facia or dashboard, suggesting the car had recently been cleaned and wiped of fingerprints or Mrs Langton was a fastidious person, as this car often carried the two main culprits of a messy interior, dogs and children.

'Do you have your cars washed regularly, Mr Langton?'

'A mobile service comes to our house every couple of weeks.'

She stepped down from the car and turned to face him.

'Everything's fine sir, you can take it away.'

'What the hell d'ya mean?' he said, his face changing from pale and cold to red, hot and bloody indignant. 'Aren't you going to comb it for fingerprints and DNA and all that stuff? What if she's been abducted by some psycho or something?'

'No. Until we find evidence to make us think different, this is still a missing persons enquiry and to undertake a forensic examination of the car at this stage would be pointless and a complete waste of public resources.'

FIVE

Ed Hardacre lived in Plumpton Green, a village a few miles southeast of Burgess Hill. It was a small place with a shop, pub, garage, railway station and little else. With so few amenities to choose from, it amused Henderson to find Hardacre's house directly opposite the only shop.

His was a red, sandstone terraced house set back from the road and shielded in part from a range of garish signs declaring 'Open 'Til Late,' and 'National Lottery Sold Here,' by a tall Leylandi hedge. The garden was small and tidy and even Henderson could stretch to mowing a tiny patch of lawn and weeding a narrow flower bed, but 'tidy' was not a word he could use to describe the house, as a rancid smell greeted him and DC Sally Graham on opening the door, and magazines, cups, glasses, and empty plates were strewn around the lounge.

'You wanna cup of coffee or tea?'

Henderson hesitated but being early, the lack of a caffeine kick in his veins overrode any queasy feeling he had about kitchen cleanliness.

'Coffee for me, sir.'

'Nothing for me,' Graham said.

When Hardacre disappeared, she leaned closer.

'A couple of friends of mine are students and live in this big, old place off the Lewes Road with five others. I used to think their place wasn't fit for human habitation and threatened to report it to Environmental Services, but this place takes it to a whole new level. Pest Control should be involved.'

Henderson laughed. 'I know what you mean but I've seen way worse than this and I'm not referring to my own place.'

A few minutes later Hardacre returned bearing two mugs, which appeared to be clean but if they weren't, he was sure the piping hot liquid would do a job on any harmful bacteria.

'What do you wanna see me about?' Hardacre said as he cleared some rubbish from a chair and dumped it on the floor before sitting down.

'Do you live alone?' Henderson asked.

'Yeah. My missus left about six months ago and as you can see, I'm finding it easy to live on my tod. My girlfriend comes round now and again to tidy up but I haven't seen her in a while.'

The personnel file at Kelly Kreations gave his age as forty-two, but the careworn corduroy trousers, wrinkled denim shirt, unshaven face and untidy hair put ten years on the poor sod.

'Was it a mutual separation?' Graham asked.

He lifted his chin and scratched his beard. 'I suppose so, she wanted to go and I didn't do anything to stop her.'

'We're here in connection with the disappearance of Kelly Langton,' Henderson said, 'and interviewing everyone in her social and business circle, trying to build up a picture of what she is like.'

'Well, I can tell ya she was a fucking bitch to me. Had it in for me right from day one. Couldn't hack it in business, could she? But what d'ya expect from a fucking model, they're all a bunch of air-heads.'

Henderson noted down 'air-head' in his notebook. It was stereotypical bullshit from an aggrieved and wounded ex-employee but it would lighten the mood of the next team meeting.

'Why were you dismissed from your job?' he asked.

'How the fuck do I know? She said something about some dodgy invoices but they were nothing to do with me.'

'C'mon sir, it must have been a bit more than you're making out.'

'She said I was nicking from the company, aw right, but did she bother to check who else might be responsible? Nah, she blamed it all on me.'

'From what I understand after speaking to Mr Fournier, a number of invoices were paid to a business owned by you.'

'Do I look rich? Eh? I'm down to my last.'

'We're not here to discuss the rights and wrongs of a fraud, although we will investigate further if Mr Fournier decides to press charges, but I would like to talk about the threats you made to Mrs Langton.'

'Yeah, well I'm not proud of what I said but how the fuck would you feel to be chucked out of a job a couple of months after your missus upped sticks and fucked off? Eh?'

'You're telling me what, you made the threats in the heat of the moment?'

'Yeah. I went out to the pub at lunchtime for one or two beers and lost a few hundred at the bookies so I didn't feel best pleased when she called me into her office.'

Henderson shifted in the lumpy seat as a spring or something else seemed to be sticking into his bottom. 'Have you been back to Kelly Kreations or been in contact with anyone from there?'

'Nope and I don't intend to, but her disappearing is the best news I've had all week.'

'How so?'

'Well, I always wanted her out of my face so whether some bloke's run away with her or her husband's done her in, either way, it gets her out of my hair and I didn't need to lift a finger.'

They left the Hardacre pigsty a few minutes later. It didn't take long for Sally Graham to start bending his ear, insisting she needed to go home and take a shower and wash her hair, but they got into the car and he pointed it in the direction of Brighton.

'What did you think of him, Sally?'

'Not a lot. Scruffy, rude, more bad habits than a wake of buzzards.'

'However, while he doesn't have the property or much intelligence to kidnap and incarcerate our missing woman, he does posses a volatile temper and who knows, maybe he confronted her on the day she disappeared and lost the rag.'

'Could be, but I think he's all talk and no trousers.'

'You could be right.'

'Where are we going now?'

'Back to Brighton, to see Jack Monaghan.'

'He's the guy who didn't tell us much when we interviewed him the first time but Ricky Wood's girlfriend, Celia told us Ricky saw him kissing Kelly.'

'Yes, but it's not the sort of thing I think many men would blurt out in a police interview, so I might let him off.'

DC Sally Graham was twenty-three, a natural blonde with a pretty face and shapely figure, but ditzy blonde she wasn't, despite having every Essex blonde joke thrown at her in the two years she had worked in Serious Crimes. She didn't join the police straight from school but started off in a bank and brought some of that experience with her, as she dealt with witnesses, suspects and victims calmly and impartially and with a good eye for small details.

JM Data, a systems development business owned by Jack Monaghan, was housed on the third floor of a modern, brick-built office block in Trafalgar Place, Brighton, an area adjacent to the main railway station 'regenerated' a few years before Henderson came to Brighton.

At one time, it was a decrepit collection of old houses, abandoned warehouses, decaying train carriages, and redundant shunting yards, many dating from Victorian times, and the sight greeting millions of tourists as they arrived by train for a day at the seaside. Now its replacement, a forest of anonymous office blocks, left passengers searching for the station name board to ensure they hadn't boarded a train to Reading or Basingstoke by mistake.

They were shown into reception by a smartly dressed young woman with the grace and style to feature in the colour pages of a Sunday magazine. They sat there only for a few minutes, before Jack Monaghan came out to meet them. He wore a smart charcoal-coloured suit, white shirt, no tie and brown expensive-looking brogues. Henderson expected no less from the owner of a fifty-person software business, designing and integrating major software systems for the oil and gas industry, or so it said in the company booklet he'd looked at.

Monaghan's office avoided soft furnishings in favour of hard pieces of technology, with a laptop, oversized desktop pc, and various bits of kit winking and flashing atop cupboards and small filing cabinets.

'It's a terrible business, Kelly disappearing like she did, so it is,' he said, from a seat behind a large desk, big enough to accommodate all his electronic toys and still giving him the space to work. The accent sounded Irish but softer than those in the North and probably from Dublin or further west.

'You haven't heard anything from her?' Henderson asked.

'No, and neither has Brian. Absolutely nothing. I tell you Inspector,' he said, leaning forward, 'it's so unlike her. I send her texts every couple of days and she texts me back almost straight away. If I look on Twitter, there's something new there every day and photos of her and the kids are always popping up on Facebook. Look.' He tapped something at lightening speed into the keyboard and turned the screen to face them.

'This is Facebook. The last post she wrote was on Monday, the day before she disappeared and here on Twitter,' tap, tap and up came another screen, 'the last Tweet she did was on Tuesday morning, about the MP caught on a camera phone feeling up one of his interns.'

'Thank you sir, but we have seen it.'

'I don't want to over-egg the pudding,' Monaghan said, turning the screen back to face him, 'but I can't tell you how uncharacteristic this is for her not to be in touch.'

'What do you think has happened to her?'

'She's been taken by someone.'

'You seem quite sure.'

'There's the evidence if you need it,' he said, pointing at the screen. 'If she ran off voluntarily, I'm 100% sure she would have sent me a text or posted something on Twitter to say she was ok.'

'Mr Monaghan,' Henderson said, 'when we saw you last week and talked about the dinner party–'

'Yep, I remember.'

'You told us nothing of interest happened.'

'It was a normal dinner party, everyone got drunk and talked rubbish, same as usual.'

'Information passed onto us by a witness, suggests you were seen kissing Mrs Langton in the kitchen.'

'What? How the hell? Do you have pictures or video? Brian will go ballistic if he finds out.'

'No pictures or video, but a witness statement.'

'Who saw us? Who was it?'

'I can't tell you, sir but perhaps you can tell us what happened?'

He ran trembling fingers through thick, black hair. 'What happened? I'll tell you what happened, nothing. She was pissed off with Brian about something and I gave her a hug to try and cheer her up and it turned into a kiss. It was nothing.'

'Was this the first time for you and Mrs Langton?' Graham asked.

He stared into space for a moment. 'Second I suppose,' he said, blowing out a puff of exasperated breath. 'It happened about two weeks ago. I gave her a lift home when she called me to say her taxi didn't show up. Naturally I assumed she fancied me. Don't get me wrong, I'm not a home breaker but I'm a single bloke and she's a grown woman so she can decide about these things for herself.'

He looked over at the screen for a moment, probably distracted by an incoming email. 'All the time I'm thinking it's about me, but in reality, I'm catching her on the bounce after a bad argument with Brian. She didn't want to progress it and I didn't push her.'

'If she was having such a bad time with her husband,' Graham said, 'why didn't she leave him?'

'I don't know. I suppose she assumed it was a sticky patch and they would soon get over it. Hey, you're not suggesting that after a quick snog in the kitchen I kidnapped or killed her or I've got her living in my flat, ready to scoot off as soon I sell my business or something?'

'Do you?' Henderson said.

'Don't be daft. Olivia stays at my place a couple of nights a week and I'm getting two new bathrooms fitted and the builders are there all day. I think they would notice if someone else was living there or tied to a chair, wouldn't you? In any case, this business is not up for sale and it won't be until they carry me out in a box.'

'You might also consider, sir,' Henderson said, 'that you may not be responsible for Kelly Langton's disappearance, but what would her husband do to her if he suspected something was going on between you two?'

SIX

He nodded to fellow First Class passengers as he took his seat. Brian Langton saw most of them every day, but typically for commuters in the South, nobody spoke to him unless they wanted to borrow one of the three newspapers he carried. Sometimes he was recognised, not as the pugnacious television interviewer he used to be, but either as the disgraced ex-cabinet minister who liked to bugger young boys in public toilets, or the guitarist of an eighties rock band who died twenty years ago of a heroin overdose.

If they did speak to him, it was unlikely they would receive much of a response, as he had been in a black mood ever since his wife went missing. He couldn't escape it, even if he wanted to, as every newspaper carried her picture on their front pages. He didn't even need to buy three newspapers to know this, as they were in his eye-line as he approached the newsagent in the morning, and his every step was dogged by reporters and photographers, flocking like farmyard geese looking for food.

Today, *The Daily Telegraph* were running a taster on its front page, 'Glamour Model Disappearance Latest P4' and on said page, a whole spread about his wife and plotting her career, alongside several stylish photographs of Kelly's younger self with an old picture of him when his hair was thicker and darker – well done DT. *The Times* ran a similar story, but moving away from the bland reporting of facts and instead, compared her 'case' to other high profile missing persons cases and starting to speculate about what might have happened.

His third newspaper was often *The Argus* or the *Guardian* but today, he bought *The Sun* as Kelly had been a permanent feature on page 3 throughout the late nineties and as expected, they went to town with their former 'Babe of the Week.' They ran two full pages of pictures, dating back to her modelling days and giving them the chance to display twelve pairs of boobs rather than the usual one or two, and a few of her clothed and walking across the South Downs with their dogs.

They also launched an appeal for information with a telephone number to call for those with something to share, but he suspected all they would get were cranks and perverts saying they did it, and some saying they wished they'd done it. This number would multiply ten-fold if the editor did his usual stunt of offering a substantial reward if they didn't get a result in a week or two.

It was a short walk from Victoria Station to his office in Francis Street and even though he wanted to take his time as he couldn't stand the empathetic looks, hushed conversations and the endless expressions of sympathy from his own staff, an icy wind whipped down Victoria Street chilling his bones and instead of slowing down, he walked at his usual brisk pace.

Creative companies were often located in Soho, Docklands, or in Uxbridge where they used to be, close to Sky Television one of their biggest customers; but after a shaky start for the company when they started out on making dramas and comedies, he found his mojo working with politicians. He shifted the focus of the business to political and current affairs and moved their offices to Victoria, to be close to the Houses of Parliament and government departments, a decision he'd never regretted.

He called a gruff 'good morning' to those who deserved it and gave a cursory nod or ignored those who didn't and walked into his office. Having spent ten years facing eighteen-stone, scarred roughnecks from Manchester and skinny, knife-wielding thugs from Essex and everything in between, he'd never perfected the mainstay of actors, producers, and even lowly sub-editors, the 'luvvy kiss' or a 'television smile,' but he could produce an impassive mask or an aggressive snarl any time they wanted.

Five minutes later his personal assistant, Melanie Knight, came in bearing two mugs of coffee and a folder under her arm, forcing her to close the door with her foot. Following a recent trip to the hairdresser, her hair was short and dyed jet black, complimenting her rounded face. Perhaps the white blouse and navy skirt matched her hairstyle better than some of the outfits she wore over the last few days but whatever the reason, she looked great, a welcome sight in a sea of gloom.

She placed his mug on the 'BBC TV' coaster, sat down and opened the desk diary on her knee, revealing a tantalising hint of black nylon.

'I take it there's been no news, Brian, or I suspect you wouldn't be in here today.'

'Yeah, I'd either be cracking open a bottle of bubbly with a house full of well-wishers or warming my arse in a police interview room. The cops don't have a clue and neither do the papers, despite putting the cream of Wapping on the case.'

'They haven't exactly been models of restraint, have they? Her picture is on every newsstand with tales of every indiscretion, no matter how minor.'

'Some of which I'd forgotten about but when are they ever?' He lifted the mug and took a drink. It was black with nothing added; a straight dose of caffeine to keep him going, but piping hot and he only managed a sip. 'What's in the diary for me today?'

She glanced at her watch. 'It's the second Tuesday of the month so in ten minutes time in will come Damian and his team for an episode update. What else? You're seeing Emilio at eleven, and this afternoon from two, you're at Television Centre for a meeting with your favourite BBC producer, Tony Blacksmith.'

'Fucking hell. I hate dealing with that odious little twerp. He squeezes me down to the last cent as if the bloody licence payer's money came out of his pocket, and a couple of days later, calls me up, 'can you add this,' 'can you put in that' in his stupid, squeaky voice.'

'Such are the colours of life.'

'I'd like to wring the colours of life out of his bloody neck.'

'You mustn't say those things, Brian, even in jest. You never know who might be listening.'

He sighed. 'You're right. Subtlety is not my middle name. What else?'

'That's about it for the diary as you told me you wanted to go easy on meetings for the next week or two.'

'So I did, carry on doing it.'

'The next thing I need to talk to you about is the arrangements I'm making for the *Newshound* launch party. Now I've booked the–'

The office door flew open and Damian and the rest of his team trooped into his office. 'C'mon Mel,' Damien said, 'out you go. At ten he's ours. You know the rules.'

'Yeah, when it suits you, as any time I ask you to come to a meeting, you arrive late.' She turned to face her boss. 'I guess we can finish this later.'

'Yeah, no problem.'

Mel departed to the sound of Damian's people rearranging Langton's office, bringing in chairs, cups of coffee, thick running schedules, and a storyboard on a stand.

The television programme which had made him rich, bought the house in Hurstpierpoint, and pushed his company high above a slew of young, arrogant, and thrusting independent production companies, was *Prime Minister's Questions*. A humorous, satirical political show, now in its fifth season, it poked a sharp stick at Downing Street and the Government. Viewed through the eyes of a jaundiced PM, played by Peter Grainger, it drew six million viewers, although he suspected many men tuned in to gaze at the PM's beautiful press secretary, Rebecca Watts, who wore skirts way too short and blouses much too tight.

The paranoid members of several Cabinets accused them of having a mole in the Government, as the programme was always so topical and at times prescient. If so, why was it still cutting-edge when there had been a change of Government six months before and the last lot were now in opposition or working as highly-paid consultants for large corporations?

'Picture this,' Damian, the show's current producer said without introduction or formality, an urgency Langton liked. 'The Home Secretary's ratings are falling like a stone after he refused to give a pay rise for the police and banned musical instruments in prisons, very topical. While on holiday in Newquay to lick his wounds and to consider his political future, he dives into the sea to save a drowning woman. The papers are full of the story and his ratings soar but one lone voice, the friend of the woman he saved, is telling anyone who will listen that it was his companion who saved her life while the Home Secretary stood on the beach looking at his phone. This will–'

'Hang on Damian,' Langton said. 'Two things. First, why not set the rescue somewhere a little more exotic and warm than Cornwall, as not many people are swimming in the sea down there in late September; and second, wouldn't it be better for him to rescue a pet because, as we know, the Brits go gaga for an animal lover?'

'See, I said it should be a pet,' Production Designer Stu said in a shrill, theatrical voice. 'It would be easier to film and it would resonate with our core target audience.'

'No, no it works better with a woman as we can use a sexy bathing costume to spice things up and make the Home Secretary appear racier, but I take your point about Cornwall in September. I fancy the Azores.'

And so it went on. To an outsider it resembled the sort of angry shouting match you could hear in any city centre bar at midnight on a Friday night, but meetings like this generated creative energy and often a raft of new ideas poured out. It proved its worth yet again, as the PMQ team left an hour later with more ways of developing the script than before they came in.

He didn't have time for more than one phone call and to grab another cup of coffee, before his business partner Emilio Levanti appeared in the doorway, his generous bulk blocking the view of the outer office.

'Good day to you, Brian.'

'Come in Emilio, take a pew,' he said, a touch more warmly than he felt. 'Would you like some coffee?'

'No thanks, Lucy gave me one twenty minutes ago,' he said, closing the door before he sat down.

Born of an Italian father and Irish mother, he didn't resemble either and looked a man who liked to lunch, leaving him with a big gut and an insatiable appetite for food and drink. With a deep, sonorous voice, sounding as though it came from the bottom of a mine, he had soothed the ears of Radio 4 listeners for many years, and more recently his Radio 2 regulars enjoyed a treat on Friday nights when he hosted his 'oldies' show.

He and Emilio had set up Camino House Productions over a drink, as everything with Emilio is done over a drink, with Langton as Managing Director and head of production and the man in the visitor's chair as the Development Director, a powerful creative force to open television network doors and encourage them to open chequebooks and sign lucrative contracts. To date, their partnership worked like a dream, as good as any blockbuster TV serial and at times, it meant more to him than his partnership with Kelly.

'I take it you've heard nothing new?' Emilio asked.

'Nothing at all. No ransom demand to bring her home, no boyfriend demanding I start divorce proceedings, nothing.'

'I thought as much from the paucity of new information in the press. What do the police say?'

'Their main message seems to be it's still early days. I mean it's only been a week, although to read the papers you'd think it was over a month. She could be in a hospital somewhere or away visiting someone I'd forgotten about or...ach, I don't know. I don't think there's any point in second-guessing.'

'Not likely though is it?' Emilio said picking some fluff from the trousers of his Savile Row suit. He dressed sharply no matter what he did, even for late-night appearances on the radio. 'Kelly wasn't the forgetful type. Quite the opposite in fact.'

'I know, as I've often found to my cost.'

'You see,' he said, moving his overweight frame to a more comfortable position in a chair he dwarfed, 'I've been thinking about this. There's plenty in this industry who would like nothing better than for you and me to take our eyes off the ball and for this business to fail.'

'What? They'd kidnap my wife just to get their name and poxy programme on the box? Do me a favour, Emilio.'

'There's some I know, and you know them too, who would sell their grandmother to a group of Jihadists to get a slice of the on-air time we get.'

'Like who?' he said, but he knew the names well enough.

He opened his hand and counted out on his fingers. 'One, Mat Hannah; two, Jasper Costain; three, Baz Kinghorn. That's three off the top of my head. I could conjure up a few more with a drink in my hand.'

Langton fell silent for a moment, Emilio was right. Mat Hannah's company, Fortuna Infiniti made a mini-series about a group of political journalists, which aired on prime-time but he and Emilio persuaded the BBC it contained too much swearing and alienated audiences, and in time, they replaced it with a similar programme made by them, called *Truth and Lies*. The incident happened nine months ago and Hannah swore revenge and had even reiterated the

51

threat when they attended the International TV convention in Dubai the previous month.

Jasper Costain, an up-and-coming documentary producer, made a brilliant programme about criminals making money from refugee camps in Syria. They took an option but all the big broadcasters turned it down, judging it too harrowing, and four weeks ago Langton told him he could no longer help and advised him to tout it around more sympathetic markets in France or Spain. His disappointment was palpable and after much shouting and hand-wringing, he went ballistic and had to be thrown out of the office. On the way, he threatened to shoot Langton and set fire to the building.

Baz Kinghorn was a successful freelance photographer who sold pictures of film and pop stars to publications around the world, but three months ago he'd taken a picture of Langton in the arms of a young starlet, wearing nothing more than a sheer, short dress and a smile at a TV awards dinner. It caused an almighty rumpus at home and Kelly had never let him forget it.

Langton had confronted him in a quiet side street and given him a sound beating. He hadn't heard anything from him since, but he knew the Essex snapper was friends with some unsavoury characters and he wouldn't put it past the vindictive little sod to be behind Kelly's disappearance.

There it was. Three enemies and a missing wife. Was there a connection? And if so, what was he going to do about it?

SEVEN

The television in the corner was tuned to Sky News. The dignitaries waited a few minutes until the British Prime Minister arrived at the Brussels summit, and on each occasion on the looped newscast his beaming smile never faded and the greeting he received from the diminutive French prime minister, who didn't quite reach to the knot in his tie, was still as cold as a filleted halibut.

DS Carol Walters' companion for the day was once again DC Khalid Agha. He was born in Pakistan and brought up in Stockwell, aged twenty-three, bright with a degree in criminal psychology but with all the policing know-how and nous of a blind traffic warden. It was either a sick joke by DI Henderson because she forgot to bring him his coffee one morning, or a genuine attempt to give the boy some experience, but whatever the reason, why her? DS Wallop was capable of talking the hind legs off a donkey and would tell him everything he needed to know, including a lot of the things he didn't, while DS Hobbs was more circumspect and everybody's idea of a decent copper, and working with him Agha would learn a wealth of good habits. So why her?

'Detective Sergeant Walters?'

She looked up. An eager young woman with short, elegantly styled hair, expensive make-up and a purple dress that must have been sprayed on and probably cost twice her weekly wage, stared back. 'Miss Egger will see you now. I'm Mandy.'

They walked to a glass-walled lift, which whisked them up at breath-taking speed to the seventh floor in a blur of glass and retracting London street scene. Passing a large open area filled with predominately young people tapping something into computers, they walked into a massive office, the size of which didn't exist in Sussex House, the building where she worked, or Malling House, the Grade I, 18th Century mansion in Lewes, the headquarters of Sussex Police.

The room was divided into three areas: an informal seating area with two large black leather settees and a coffee table, its only embellishment a bowl of fruit; a chrome and glass desk from behind which Liz Egger came striding over to greet them; and a long conference table beside the window, looking out over the street below.

'Hello. I'm Liz Egger, so pleased to meet you Detective Sergeant Walters,' she said, shaking her hand, 'and you must be Detective Constable Agha. Please, come and sit down.'

Normally in police interviews, the fretful interviewee would now retreat behind the desk and put a big lump of wood and metal, or in Egger's case, glass and chrome between them and the forces of law and order, as if somehow this scant barrier would save them from uncomfortable questions or charges of corporate misfeasance and money laundering.

It therefore came as some surprise when Liz led them to the informal seating area and she instructed Mandy to fly off and make some coffee. Just as well, as Mandy's skimpy dress and VPL were starting to make Agha a little too hot under the collar.

'You found us ok?' Egger asked.

'It took a couple of attempts,' Walters said, giving a withering glance in the direction of her companion. He was about as much help at navigation as a three-legged guide dog and too easily distracted by the sight of pretty girls or the rumbling of Maserati and Ferrari engines, the owners cruising the streets near Portman Square, looking for a parking space.

'I still don't find it easy,' Egger said, 'as most of the buildings around here look the same and more often than not, don't display the company or building name.'

'So what happens here?' Walters asked. 'What is steel trading?'

'Stibert and Henkel are one of the oldest steel stock traders in the world, but the business has changed a lot over the years. Way back, we used to own steel mills, forests, and warehouses in Bavaria and Norway, but nowadays all the work is done by computer, by all the people here,' she said, indicating the tappers they saw on the way in.

'We buy steel on the spot market,' she continued, 'which may be on a ship heading out to Yokohama or lying at the dockside in Antwerp, and we in turn sell it to stockholders, who perhaps require the entire consignment for one of their customers, or directly to end users such as oil, gas, and car manufacturers.'

'I see,' Walters said, and meaning it as Egger made it sound so simple.

'Now I know what you're thinking, we're just a bunch of gamblers, buying and selling shiploads of steel we never take delivery of, but no. Our job is to match producers to buyers, as steel producers want long production runs and standard sizes while end users require smaller quantities in a variety of steels. The clever trick is balancing these two very different needs. Ah, here's the coffee.'

'Shall I pour?' Mandy said.

'No, leave it Mandy and I'll do it. Close the door on your way out, please.'

Walters let out an inaudible sigh. She was in the wrong job. For the money Mandy earned, she could greet people with a smile at the door, make them a cup of coffee, carry it into the office and close the door. Mind you, without losing a stone or two, she wouldn't look as pretty in such a tight dress.

'Enough of the corporate speak,' Egger said handing her a cup, 'what did you want to talk to me about?' If the coffee tasted as good as the aroma wafting towards her, she was in for a treat; it was such a shame boy wonder didn't partake.

'As I said on the phone,' Walters said, 'we are investigating the disappearance of Kelly Langton, now missing for almost a week and interviewing people like yourself who knew her and trying to build up a picture of what Kelly is like.'

Her affable face took on a serious note. 'It's a terrible situation, it really is. I feel for those lovely boys and Brian. I can't imagine what they must be going through.'

'How well did you know Kelly?'

'Better than anybody, I should think. We were at primary school together and in the same class at Williamson College until she dropped out to become a model. I stayed on for my 'A' levels and went to university like most of the girls from my year, but I used to wonder who made the right choices. I get this,' she said, waving an arm around her office, 'which pays the bills and all the rest but she's travelled the world, hobnobbed with lots of famous people, made a pile of money modelling and doing a job she loved.' She shrugged and sipped her coffee.

Walters didn't wonder. She didn't have the legs or the face for modelling but she would take this office in a flash. Liz was being a little disingenuous about her lot, as she worked in a nice office, she wore smart clothes and expensive jewellery, and a fat salary came thumping into her bank account each month to cushion any pain. Throw in London with its Michelin-starred restaurants, West-end shows and all the places she ever wanted to visit, she would sign up in a trice with no misty eyes for a facile modelling career.

'Even though we went our separate ways and our paths didn't often cross, we've always kept in touch and only last month I went down to their place in Hurstpierpoint.'

'Do you live in London?'

'Yes, in Notting Hill.'

'Does Kelly ever come and stay with you?'

'No, she hasn't done that since the boys were small. Nowadays, if they're not at school, they need ferrying back and forth to football and tennis camps or training, and so it's easier for me to go there.'

'Has she been in contact with you since she disappeared?'

'No, and I check all my phones and my home and office computers every day but I've received nothing. It makes me sad and I have to say, a little suspicious because if she was in trouble or running away from something, she knows she can call me and there's a place for her to sleep and I would give her money or anything else she needed to tide her over.'

The Condor team were now considering the possibility that Kelly's disappearance was not a consequence of her infidelity, as they suspected right from the start, but her husband's. With Liz a regular visitor to Manor House Farm, it created the opportunity for her and Brian to spend time together but so far, his name was barely mentioned. It could be the sign of something going on between them, or quite the opposite. She needed to probe deeper.

'What do you do when you stay there?'

'I usually drive down on Saturday morning and join Kelly, ferrying the boys to football and afterwards, into Brighton or Haywards Heath for lunch. In the evenings, Brian would come back from watching the Albion or work or whatever he'd been doing all day and we'd all sit down for a family dinner. After dinner, and when the boys were both in bed, we would watch a DVD and chat until late.'

'Does Brian join you?' Walter asked.

'Not usually. Sometimes he has work to do or more often than not, he's in the kitchen or study watching Match of the Day.'

'And on Sunday?'

'You don't get a long-lie with two young boys around, so after breakfast, we take them and the dogs and go for a long walk down to the river or over to the old mill and try and tire them out. I head back to London after lunch and depending on how far we've walked, it will be me who's worn out and if not for the radio, I would probably fall asleep. Although it's not something I should be admitting in front of a police officer.'

'Count yourself lucky I'm not in Traffic. Where is Brian during all this activity? He sounds a bit peripheral, if you don't mind me saying.'

'No, it's true, he often is. He says it's so Kelly and I can spend some time together, but I think he's avoiding me.'

'Why?'

'I'm not the sort of person to keep my mouth shut, and not when my best friend is involved, and as Brian knows my views, he keeps out of my way in case I air them.'

'Your views about what?'

'Oh, about the way he treats Kelly. I hate the way he talks to her and his philandering.'

'How does he talk to her?'

'You're too young to remember him as a television presenter but he got results by bullying people. It's in his nature to be a bully and he does the same with Kelly, you know the sort of thing, 'when's dinner I'm starving?' 'This place is a tip, why don't you clean it?' As if he is the only one working. I don't know how she puts up with it. I know I wouldn't.'

'Is he having an affair?'

'I heard rumours when I went to football with the boys and Kelly was away doing something else. Other mums would come up and talk about a picture they saw in a magazine or how a friend saw him with a woman in a pub or restaurant. After a time, you start to think, it can't all be about business, but I never saw anything. Have you heard about his secretary?'

'No, I haven't.'

'It's the same again, I'm afraid. I heard rumours about an affair with his secretary, Melanie Knight, but I dismissed it as tittle-tattle. You know how some women like to gossip and snipe.'

Walters nodded in agreement, as she had been on the blunt end of malicious gossip herself.

'Gemma Ferguson, the Financial Director of Brian's television production company, called me up and told me it was the talk of the office and asked me to speak to him as it was affecting business and the atmosphere at work. Believe me I tried, several times, but it always ends the same way, in yet another argument and I didn't want to press it and get Gemma into trouble. Maybe I should have and things would have turned out better.'

It was an interesting revelation and if she was not mistaken, the first real glimpse of a motive to appear in this case.

'The thing with Melanie Knight is different you see,' Egger said, 'as I understand it all the others were brief flings and were over before the rumour became established, but I think this one has been going on for a while. Kelly knew about it, as some people were only too happy to tell her, the ones jealous of their marriage and success, if you ask me. She once told me if she ever found firm evidence, she wouldn't hesitate to leave him.'

EIGHT

He parked the car at Brighton Racecourse and walked towards a line of buses. It was a still, clear night with temperatures a little higher than of late, making it feel to Ricky Wood more like the end of summer than the start of winter, and an ideal night for football.

During a lull in drunken banter at the Langton's dinner party a week or so back, Brian mentioned he was a season ticket holder at Brighton and Hove Albion. There followed a lively conversation about the Albion's mixed fortunes this season, footballers' wages, transfer fees, and the impact of foreign players on the national game, to add to a long list of topics which would wake the children if they weren't already staying with their in-laws, or out-laws as Brian liked to call them.

To Wood's surprise, the big man had called him a couple of days ago and told him he didn't get to many games at the moment, as he was too busy working and looking after the boys, would he like to borrow his season ticket for the Tuesday evening match against league leaders, Sheffield United? Would he? Was the Pope a Catholic? He gladly took it, although if he was being picky, he would have preferred the Emirates as he had been a 'Gooner' since childhood, but hey, a live match was a live match.

Brighton Racecourse was set high up on the South Downs and on a fine day, visitors were treated to a clear view of the South Coast from Newhaven to Worthing and across the English Channel where the outline of France was sometimes visible, but now it was dusk and all he could see was a murky haze. The area was well known to thousands of race-goers who flocked there for race meetings from April to October and on Bank Holidays, when it was packed to the rafters.

To those of a literary bent, Graham Greene's dark novel, *Brighton Rock,* featured a memorable scene here, when Colleoni's men, armed with razors, attacked twisted killer Pinkie and his friend Spicer. No such gangs plagued Brighton now, thank God, but the place never ceased to evoke memories of that great story whenever he came here.

The huge car park lay unused between race meetings and became an ideal Park-and-Ride facility for Albion supporters on match nights. Moving closer, buses looked jam-packed with upbeat fans, all wearing team-coloured scarves, hats and replica shirts and despite looking like an interloper or a spy, as he didn't possess any such insignia, he managed to squeeze aboard one.

The bus pulled into the car-park at the Amex Community Stadium twenty minutes before kick-off, leaving him enough time to find the area of the ground containing his seat, buy a meat pie and a pint, before settling down to watch the pre-match build-up.

Brian said the seat beside him belonged to Jack Monaghan, the Irish guy he met at the dinner party, and when someone else sat down, he felt confused and a little annoyed. He'd looked forward to meeting Jack again and getting his take on Kelly's disappearance, and finding out if their kitchen sink dalliance was the sign of an on-going relationship or a consequence of too much wine.

The game kicked-off and even though he was reluctant to get involved in a bun-fight with a fellow supporter and a couple of stewards all because one stupid prat couldn't be bothered looking at the seat number on his ticket, he leaned over and said to the interloper in his best non-threatening voice, 'Jack couldn't make it tonight?'

He turned to face him. 'Oh, hi there, mate. Sorry, you must be Ricky Wood,' he said, sticking out a hand for him to shake. 'I should have said something earlier as Jack told me you'd be here. I'm Brendan Osborne.'

He knew Jack and Brian were good mates who socialised with one another regularly, but didn't realise they were so close Brian would tell Jack he couldn't come tonight and he was taking his place.

'How do you know Jack, Brendan?'

'I work for him. I'm a computer programmer.'

He nodded, as if he knew what it meant, but he suspected the sum of his knowledge could be written on the back of a season ticket.

The standard of football was good, the occasional slips and mistakes inevitable with players who weren't as skilful as many of the international class players at clubs like Arsenal, but they didn't cost their club the best part of thirty-million pounds either.

At half-time, the Albion led 2-0 and he joined a happy, buoyant throng heading for the exits, many of whom seemed to be in desperate need of a drink, as they immediately started to queue at the nearest bar, while others like him headed for the toilets. When he came out, and risking the ire of his bladder in the second half, he purchased another pint and caught up with Brendan, as he watched highlights of other matches being played this evening on one of the big screens strung from the ceiling.

'How long have you worked for Jack?'

'About nine months.'

'He must like you to give you his season ticket.'

'Could be, or he's so relieved to find someone in the office who likes football, as most of the people I work beside don't follow any sport at all.'

'What's he like as a boss?'

'He's fair, I'll say that. If you do something good, he tells you but if you mess something up, you'll get a bollocking, or if you do something really bad, you get fired.' Osborne shrugged. 'It happens a lot in our business, an occupational hazard, you might say, but there's plenty of other jobs out there.'

'Do you know Brian Langton, the guy who sits in my seat?'

'Sure, he's been in our offices a few times and he's been here a couple of times when I've been to games.'

'He's quite the successful businessman by all accounts.'

'There are so many people who've been on telly and you never hear of them again but this guy and his missus keep popping up in the papers and those celebrity mags you see in Tesco, every other week.'

'I suppose he's still on the telly, but now all you see is his name in the credits.'

'I saw the programme he used to front on YouTube,' Osborne said, 'the one where he challenges criminals by sticking a mike under their noses and asking them if they murdered this guy or paid for a stack of drugs. The funniest one I saw was when he got punched in the face by this ugly bruiser from Liverpool. What was the show called again?'

Wood was trying to think, a difficult thing to do as his usual sharp memory was clouded with beer. Moments later, it came to him. Wasn't it called *Criminal Watch*?'

'Yeah, that's it.'

With only a few minutes to go before the start of the second half, fans started streaming back to their seats. He deposited his empty beer glass on a shelf and joined Osborne in the throng. Further conversations were impossible now as a tremendous roar rattled the roof when the teams came running back on the field and since he came there to watch a football match, he put all thoughts of Brian Langton and Jack Monaghan out of his head and concentrated on the spectacle in front of him.

After the game, which Brighton were lucky to win 3-2, he said goodbye to Brendan outside the stadium, declining his offer of a lift back into town, as the stadium car park was choked with cars and buses and he would be fortunate to get home this side of midnight. The buses back to the racecourse were also busy but the people standing there reassured him that plenty were running and so he didn't mind waiting.

He knew little about Brian Langton other than he was married to a beautiful woman, he set up his production company just as television networks such as the BBC began clamouring for independent content, and with a reputation as a hard bastard. So why did his wife disappear?

Was it possible Brian was up to his neck in something illegal and maybe Kelly found out and threatened to blow the whistle, or was Kelly having an affair with Jack Monaghan and Brian exacted some form of terrible revenge?

It was all speculation as he didn't know any more than anybody else, but he possessed an advantage not enjoyed by other media hounds because in a small way, he knew the main protagonists and if he wanted to interview one, Celia could organise it. However, in order to write something newspapers would want to publish, he needed to dig the dirt on some of her friends and he wondered if she would still be his girlfriend after he did all that.

Fifteen minutes later, he squeezed his thin frame into a tiny gap between three uber-fat blokes who reeked of sweat, half-time beers and a recent intake of chips. Mercifully, the trip didn't last long and by the nature of his immovable position, he didn't get thrown about as much as some other people when the bus hit a pothole or sped around a corner.

They pulled into the racecourse, the bus stopped and as soon as the doors opened, several men with jowly faces and fat guts who looked as though their only exercise was picking up a burger or reaching for a pint, exited the bus in double-quick time and ran to their cars in an attempt to get out of the car park before everyone else. There was little point in him doing the same, as he'd arrived late and parked at the back and so took his time walking to the car in the hope that by the time he set off, most of the traffic would be gone.

Even under sparsely spaced sodium lights, brighter in some areas than others, he could see his Honda Civic in the distance, a metal and glass oasis in a desert of grass, as many of his near-neighbours were gone. He was twenty yards away and searching for his keys when he felt a mighty thump on the back of the head, forcing him onto his knees. Before he could understand if he had been struck by lightning or a piece of space junk, hands grabbed his collar and arms, and dragged him into a gap between a couple of high-sided 4x4s.

They threw him to the ground and before he could make a move to get up, boots and fists came raining in. The suddenness of the attack forced him into a curled ball to protect his head but the ferocity of the blows thumping into his torso one after the other convinced him they were trying to kill him.

He moved his hands away from his face and a groin faced him. Without hesitation, he struck out as hard as he could. The punch made a sound connection with someone's balls and the guy yelled and doubled up in pain, distracting the others from their work for a moment. Seizing on this momentary lapse, he forced himself upright and drove a punch into the guy's face. When his fist made contact, the guy's nose flattened.

He turned to be confronted by two other heavy-set guys who didn't hesitate to wade in. A fist came out of nowhere and crashed into his head, turning his knees to jelly and causing him to black out for a second. He tried to protect his face but they kicked at his hands and when that didn't satisfy them, they kicked him in the balls, leaving him breathless and groaning in pain and exposed to whatever they wanted to do.

It was obvious they were trying to hit his face and stamp on his hands, as they did it whenever they could. It stopped as suddenly as it started as someone grabbed him by the neck and hauled him to his feet. A face met his but he could only peer at him through slits, as his eyes were swollen, with blood and a throbbing head clouding his vision.

'This is for Kelly you hack scum,' a fat, dark face with a thick northern accent said.

He felt a blow to his stomach and only when his knees buckled and he collapsed on the ground, did he realise his shirt was soaked with blood. A glint of steel came towards him and hit him again, again and again, until he felt no more.

NINE

He drummed tunelessly on the steering wheel, waiting for the traffic lights on Lewes Road to change. When DI Henderson brother's band lost their drummer to a road accident all those years ago, he'd volunteered to stand in as the unfortunate incumbent, Donny Sands, was a nice lad but a farmer's boy and thick as a haystack and anything he could do couldn't be so difficult, could it? Henderson could keep a basic rhythm, fine for a couple of tunes, but he couldn't master more than a quarter of the songs on the evening's playlist. Chastened by the whole experience, he went back to being a roadie.

Before being called out by Lewes Control, DI Henderson was sitting in his flat at Seven Dials in his favourite spot, a seat by the bay window, reading the transcripts of all the interviews done with Kelly Langton's friends and associates. Fortunately for the operator at Lewes Control, and for him, his stock of his special tipple, a ten-year-old Glenmorangie was exhausted otherwise he might be on his second or third by now, and he didn't hold back with the measures as they did in local hostelries. A drop of the hard stuff always helped with his thinking, evidenced by this evening's effort, as he couldn't find anything in the interviews worthy of further investigation.

None of Kelly Langton's business colleagues, friends or the people who attended the recent dinner party, had spotted anything untoward about her behaviour or anything to suggest she would jet off without telling anyone, or needed to get away from something. Her friend Liz Egger told DS Walters that Kelly suspected her husband was involved in an affair with his secretary, but even though this had provided the motivation for many murders in the past, he wasn't yet convinced it was a big issue in this case.

Other witnesses commentated on how happy they looked together and suggested Brian often acted like the cat with the cream and no wonder, as Kelly was a successful businesswoman and in his opinion, as attractive now as the days when she was modelling, or perhaps this was a feature of the ageing process and admiring women of a similar age.

His new boss, CI Edwards, was a keen media observer and demanded regular briefings and updates and she had taken a close interest in the Langton case from the start. He tended to take a more chilled approach and rarely looked at newspapers or television unless provoked, like an actor ignoring critical reviews for fear of denting his confidence, but he suspected it would become a source of tension between them in time to come.

Despite the man-hours expended, neither Edwards nor anyone in the Condor team could understand why Kelly left without leaving one clue to indicate her intentions or whereabouts, not one of her friends or acquaintances had received a text from an unknown phone number, there were no strange transactions on her credit card from bars in Marbella or Puerto Rico, and her husband hadn't found a creepy envelope full of newspaper cuttings or murderous messages made up from words cut from a children's reading book.

Newspapers had outshone themselves this past week with new glamour shots from Kelly's early career, details of her business activities, and their current obsession, offering a new theory every other day, the latest being that the book she started writing would harm the reputations of some important and powerful people. There were no stories yet of alien abduction or her falling into a sinkhole but in time, he wouldn't be surprised to see such suggestions in print.

A few minutes later, he turned into the car park at Brighton Racecourse. On match days, it required time and patience to find a parking space, but at this time of night it was deserted, save for a small knot of people in the distance working under bright arc lights.

It was a couple of hours after the final whistle of a match Brighton won, so it wasn't a surprise to find it empty, as he would imagine a good proportion of them were in pubs now, toasting the team's success or sitting at home and watching the highlights on television.

With the choice of places to park, he didn't suffer from 'empty car park syndrome' and park beside the only car for miles around, and instead drove past the glare of lights and stopped in the distance. He wasn't unaffected by the police activity going on behind him, but he needed some fresh air to clear his head of all thoughts of a missing woman and a pile of unsatisfactory interview sheets, and concentrate on finding who murdered this poor soul.

When he got closer, he spotted Pat Davidson, the Crime Scene Manager at the back of the group, holding a clipboard and writing up notes. He headed towards him.

'Evening Pat.'

'Evening Angus. How are you?'

'Not best pleased to be standing here. We're stretched as it is. You?'

'Me neither as it buggered up a cosy meal I was having with my new woman. I could have picked any night of the week but I had to go and pick this one, didn't I?'

'C'est la vie.'

'Do you think I can make a claim for emotional impairment as there's a fair chance she'll never talk to me again and bad mouth me on Facebook?'

'Pat,' he said, putting his hand on his shoulder, 'you can make all the expense claims you like, getting anyone to sign them is a different matter. What do we have here?'

Pat walked towards the group of SOCOs huddled around the body, the scene lit up by occasional flashes from the photographer's camera and Henderson followed behind him.

'We have a male,' he said, 'aged about forty, white, lower than average weight, average height with extensive bruising on his face, arms, hands and legs and multiple stab wounds to his stomach and chest. He has no ID as his wallet and phone are missing, assuming he brought them to the match with him. The pathologist is on his way. That's all I know at the moment.'

'Please don't tell me he was wearing a Sheffield United shirt.'

'No, he didn't have a Sheffield United shirt, scarf or anything else, but nothing from the Albion either.'

'Thank goodness for that, it's all we need right now is a war between Albion fans and some other outfit to add to the aggro we get from Crystal Palace and Portsmouth. Mind you, doesn't it strike you as a bit odd when everybody going to a match nowadays wears something bought from a football shop?'

'I can see you in a replica strip.'

'Not on your life, but I do have a hat and scarf.'

Henderson stepped back and climbed into the paper suit and overshoes he carried to prevent contamination of a crime scene, before bending down to look at the body. The victim's back was to him while a SOCO examined the ground underneath the body, and when finished, he turned him over.

Henderson recognised him immediately as his photograph was in the file, one he had been looking at before he came out.

'His name is Ricky Wood,' Henderson said. 'He's a reporter.'

'What sort of reporter?' Davidson asked. 'Was he covering the match?'

'No, I don't think so. His interest is in criminal investigations.'

'How do you know him? Is he under investigation?'

'No, he's a witness in the Kelly Langton missing persons enquiry. He was one of the attendees at the dinner party that took place at the Langton's house a few days before she disappeared.'

Henderson stood, and through the glare of the bright lights spotted DS Walters standing close by. He walked towards her.

'Evening Carol. Have you just arrived?'

'Evening sir. No, I got here about forty minutes ago and since then I've been interviewing our so-called witnesses.'

'I guess from your tone they didn't see anything.'

'Got it in one. It was dark, there was a lot of movement of cars and like all men, those who might have passed the spot where our victim was attacked were too wrapped up talking about the game to notice anything else.'

'Touchy tonight, aren't we?'

'You know what I mean.'

Walters had been going out with a guy for a couple of weeks, but the first time work intruded on their relationship, a five-hour stint a few Saturdays back when she was called in to interview suspects in an armed jewellery theft, he'd dumped her.

'I've identified our victim.'

'Who is it?'

'Ricky Wood, the journalist we interviewed in connection with the Kelly Langton case.'

'I remember him. Was that a bad luck dinner party or what? I'm glad I wasn't invited.'

'Give me a flavour of what the witnesses did tell you.'

She pulled out her notebook and turned it towards the light.

'I found five people who parked near to where the murder took place and stayed back to try and assist us. Three heard and saw a scuffle but not much else and I've got their contact details if we need to speak to them again. Another watched the beating until an angry shout by one of the attackers forced him to move on, but he couldn't describe them beyond 'big guys and wearing dark clothes', while the last one I would reckon is our only real witness.'

'You can't see it now,' she continued, 'because the vehicles are gone, but Ricky Wood was attacked in a space between two high-sided 4x4s, one of which we know was an Audi Q7 belonging to our main witness, Darren Hinckley.'

'Where was Mr Hinckley while the attack was taking place?'

'He was walking back to his car, which was on the left side of the attack area, and about to press the door opener when he saw the fight. He thought of wading in himself, but he could see four gorillas and common sense prevailed. He walked past and called us.'

'A smart move for sure otherwise we might be looking at two victims. Did he see any of the attackers? Can we get a description?'

'No,' she said, 'it was dark and he only glanced up as he walked past. A few minutes later the men ran off and he attended to our victim.'

'Did he see how the attackers left the racecourse? Were they on foot, did they use a car?'

'No, Hinckley said they melted into the night and there were so many cars around, they could have been in any one of them.'

'It's not much to go on, is it?'

'No, it's not, but what would you expect from a crowd of football-obsessed blokes?'

'First thing, call *The Argus* and get them to put out an appeal for witnesses. The usual thing, the date, the time, the incident, you know the drill.'

'Sure, will do,' she said.

'Next, put a board and a couple of PCs here on the racecourse for Brighton's next home game and flush out any witnesses we missed, it won't help us much initially as the game isn't until a week on Saturday.'

'In that case, I'll also try and get an announcement over the tannoy for the next away game.'

'Good idea, see if you can sort it out.'

'Right-oh.'

'Is there anything else we can get our teeth into now, otherwise I'm going home and back to the interview sheets I was looking at before coming out here. There's not much else for us to see until Pat's crew have finished their bit.'

'Ok but there is one other thing,' she said, 'although I'm not sure how relevant.'

'Try me.'

'Our main witness, Darren Hinckley, thought he heard one of the assailants say something to Ricky a few seconds before they left the scene. I quote, 'this is for Kerry'.'

'This is for Kerry?'

'Yeah.'

'Could be a person, what's it short for, Kieran?'

'It might be a girl's name, a surname, or the place in Ireland where butter comes from.'

'Fancy a trip to Ireland, do you? I thought your family were from Wales.'

'They are.'

'Mind you, it sounds not unlike, 'this is for Kelly.' In the heat of the moment, our witness might have been mistaken.'

'Could be, but what does 'this is for Kelly' mean?'

'I don't know,' Henderson said, 'but we'll think about it later as I've just thought of something. Now, tell me I'm wrong, but Ricky got jumped and then they pulled him into a space between two 4x4s?'

'Yep.'

'The attack would have been shielded from sight by these 4x4s, one of which was Mr Hinckley's Audi Q7 on the left. Who or what was on the other side?'

'I don't know, they left without leaving details.'

'What colour is it?'

'The colour of what?'

'The car, Carol; Hinckley's Audi.'

'Black.'

'Ok. We think there were four assailants?'

'Correct. Where are you going with this, you putting together a pub quiz?'

'Four guys in a confined space all trying to get a kick at Ricky Wood,' Henderson said, demonstrating the movements as he spoke. 'He's lying on the ground, squirming around, trying to get out of the way, so they move here and here, trying to find a better angle.'

'Yep.'

'What if one of the assailants, for leverage or because he fell back and tried to stop himself falling, left a paw print on Mr Hinckley's black paintwork?'

TEN

He arrived late at the office, a bad start to the morning, as Brian Langton hated being late for anything. Since his wife disappeared, a neighbour, Gina Jamieson with a child at the same school as his boys, drove them to Williamson College, a job she used to share with Kelly. Today the Jamieson lad was sick and he had to do it.

He worked without a break for a couple of hours on a new proposal while ignoring a flurry of emails and Post-it notes sprouting around his desk like mushrooms under an old oak tree, before his P.A. Melanie Knight guided a reporter into his office.

She was a reporter with *The Argus*, the main newspaper in the Brighton and Hove area and the place he went for the latest on local news and sport. When she started modelling, Kelly joined a Brighton talent agency and her picture frequently appeared in the local paper and even now they were still interested in running stories about her and whatever she was up to. If he owed one newspaper a story, it was *The Argus*.

'Good morning, Mr Langton,' she said, shaking his hand, 'I'm Rachel Jones from *The Brighton Argus*.

These are nice offices you've got here, not what I was expecting at all.'

'Good morning, Miss Jones. I suppose because it's an old building on the outside, you'd expect to see mahogany panels and Chesterfield sofas on the inside, but we're in the media business and not only do our people like to work in a place that is interesting and modern, and perhaps even a bit quirky and inspiring as well, our visitors do too. Otherwise they'd think we were a bunch of old fuddy-duddies who can't communicate with our target audience.'

The inside of the building had been ripped out before they moved in and the floor laid with fancy-patterned wooden tiling, black desks arranged at random angles, the white walls lending a clean, utilitarian air, broken up by bold primary colours painted on panels hanging from walls, multi-coloured chairs, and large cushions scattered all around.

'It makes sense.'

'Now if you think this is modern, you should see the editing suite downstairs. It resembles the offices of a Californian computer games developer more than a place where we make television programmes, all soft seats, soft drinks, and high tech.'

He guided her to the conference table near the window. It was black and the seats were striped with a multitude of primary colours, a ray of sunshine when there wasn't any outside. She sat down and removed a notepad and a digital recorder from her handbag and placed them on the table.

'So what can I do for you Miss Jones? You said something on the phone about wanting to hear my side of the story.'

'Yes, I did.' She lifted the recorder. 'Ok if I put this on?'

He shrugged. 'Sure.'

She fiddled with a few buttons and laid the little electronic device between them. 'First thing, let me offer my sympathy about your missing wife and I do hope, for everyone's sake, she is found soon.'

He grunted something appreciative but in truth he was sick of people offering tea and sympathy and wished they would cut to the chase.

'In cases like this,' she said, 'the media concentrate on what the police are, or are not doing, and publish stories based on press briefings and press releases, but they seem to forget there's a family left behind who are often confused and traumatised about what's happening and fearful of what the future might hold. Your wife, Kelly, has been missing for eight days now and I just wanted to get your perspective on what life is like and how you and your boys are coping.'

He watched her face as she spoke, as he was wary of journalists, even before his wife disappeared: not only after his run-in with Baz Kinghorn, but about a year ago protestors were outside the building, complaining about their depiction of Islamic people in one programme and an incident of wife-beating in another, and the coverage they got was less than favourable, despite issuing an apology and offering to meet the protestors to hear their grievances.

Jones was mid-thirties, tall and elegant with short, shiny, black hair and a finely-boned, round face which was photogenic without being overly pretty, but facial features were not the only method by which he made judgments about women. Her legs looked long and skinny with small boobs barely registering against the light material of her white blouse. He preferred legs a little thicker, ones to fill a pair of stockings and large boobs to get lost in. His mind was wandering and only with luck did he catch the end of her question.

'...and considering all of those things: do you think enough is being done to find your wife?'

He puffed a blast of air, feigning frustration. 'How much is enough? I don't think you can ever say enough has been done, as they haven't found her yet, have they? On the other hand, her picture is in all the papers, including yours, there's been an appeal on the radio, the police are interviewing all her friends and neighbours and they've poked around our house and her car so...' He shrugged, 'I'm not sure what else they can do.'

'What do you think has happened to her?'

'I wish I knew, it's not like I haven't given it a lot of thought.' He paused, searching for the right words. 'At the start, I assumed she went off to see someone like a relative or an old friend and perhaps forgot to tell me about it, even though she's never done anything like it before.'

'She hasn't?'

'No, never. Then I'm thinking maybe she suffered a seizure or something and is lying in a hospital bed, unable to tell anybody who she is or where she lives but she's such a well-known face, somebody in the hospital would have recognised her and called us by now, wouldn't you think?'

'You would think so.'

'Since none of them are coming up with the goods, the only other thing I can think of is she must have been taken by some psycho.'

'I would imagine the police are considering such a possibility with no activity on her credit card or mobile phone since she left.'

'It's the clincher for me as she's always on the phone calling people in her business, her book agent, or the bank to check on her money. She's always on somebody's case.'

'Did any of your friends or anybody else in the past show a strong interest in her? Perhaps there is someone she mentions a lot or spends time talking to at parties or on the phone?'

He sat back in the chair and stared at the piece of modern art behind her head. It was by Picasso and if he viewed the face one way, it was a single person but if he half-shut his eyes and glanced at it another way, it became two people. In some respects, it summed up his thinking, as he was confused too.

He leaned forward. 'I've been thinking hard about this, don't think I haven't. Sure, we've attended dinner parties, gone out for meals, gone to award dinners, and sometimes we both drink too much and say or do silly things, but I can't recall anyone dancing with her all night or what you might call pestering or pawing her. We do most things together but when she's out on her own, she never comes home smelling of someone else's after-shave or looking like she's been dragged through a hedge backwards.'

Jones paused as if about to say something profound. 'How well do you and your wife get on, Mr Langton? The reason I ask, is many of your wife's friends that I met at Williamson College were of the opinion the two of you were considering divorce.'

'What?' he shouted, and banged a fist on the table. 'The fucking gossips. Is nothing private?' He folded his arms as blood rose to his face, making him feel hot, as if his head was about to explode. 'We've experienced a few problems, I mean, who doesn't but we're working through them. We discussed divorce in a sort of casual way, you know, 'what if' but we never came close to taking it any further, no bloody way. She loves me and I love her and she would do nothing to hurt our boys.'

'You certainly cleared that up, thank you. How are the boys taking it?'

'How d'ya think?' he said, with a touch more aggression than intended. He was getting tired of these questions but he needed to be calm as it wasn't smart to sound angry and forceful in an interview, as he knew how badly it would read in the black and white print of a morning newspaper. He paused for a few moments until his breathing became steady and the heat drained from his face.

'They miss their mum, of course they do. The little one, who's only eight, cries himself to sleep every night.'

'Ah bless, it must be terrible for them. How are you managing on the domestic front?'

'Not too bad. A neighbour with a kid at the same school as ours picks them up in the morning and brings them home at night. Josh is thirteen and makes sure Ben doesn't get up to any nonsense until I get home around seven. He cooks tea for both of them, as long as it's something simple he can bung under the grill or pop in the microwave.'

'Good to hear, it must be a weight off your mind.'

He already dealt with all the household finances as even though his wife was a canny businesswoman and ran her business efficiently and profitably, she was hopeless when it came to managing her own money, unless spending the stuff in expensive boutiques in Brighton counted in such an equation.

'We have a cleaning lady and someone else comes in to do the washing and ironing, as I'm pretty useless in that department. To be frank, I need all the help I can get at the moment, as we're in the process of talking to all the big television companies as they are about to finalise spending plans for next year and trying to decide what they'll finance. It's important for me to be around.'

'I understand. How is your business doing?'

'Couldn't be better. *Prime Minister's Questions* is still the most popular political show of its type and we've also got *Newshunt*, and its sister show, *Newshound* will be available in the new year. In addition, in the last week we've finishing making a new documentary called *The Battle of the Somme: A Soldier's Lot*, which three channels are bidding for.'

'I'm glad to hear business is doing well, the last thing you need right now is money worries.'

'Money worries? I haven't had them since I was twenty years old.'

He said goodbye to Rachel Jones ten minutes later but rather than sit behind his computer and deal with emails and messages, as he intended, he stood at the window and stared out at the street scene below. Delivery drivers carried boxes into offices, locals headed back to their flats with their shopping, two guys stood on a street corner having an animated discussion over a fag, but his mind brooded over what he'd said or not said, and how it would appear in *The Argus* in the morning.

He knew all about the power of the press and if he sounded unsympathetic and aggressive, public opinion soon would turn against him and columnists would start baying for his arrest. He needed to be careful; this wasn't the time for faint hearts.

ELEVEN

DI Henderson's face was impassive as he sat in a meeting room listening to the reports of the teams responsible for interviewing the friends and relatives of Kelly Langton.

'I suppose it's something to do with the good start in life they had attending a posh school like Williamson College,' DC Sally Graham said, 'most of them seem to be in well-paid jobs all over the country, so not many have kept in touch with Kelly.'

'That's private school for you,' DS Walters said. 'A lot of the people I went to school with never moved more than a couple of streets from where they were born.'

'Most of the friends I spoke to didn't have a good word to say about her husband,' DC Bentley said, 'some suggesting she might have done better.'

'Of course, it might be snobbery,' Walters said, 'Kelly going to Williamson College and him only attending the local comp in Brighton.'

'Did no one else heard the rumour about Brian and his secretary?' Henderson asked

Lots of shaking heads.

'I'm disappointed as I would prefer a degree of corroboration, especially if we decide to come down heavier on Kelly's husband, because with only Liz's opinion to go by, he could dismiss it as wicked tittle-tattle, dreamed up by jealous or envious friends to drive a wedge between them.'

'I've seen it done,' Walters said, 'people are strange when it comes to money and other people's happiness.'

DS Walters had experienced at first-hand the effect of gossip on her own marriage when several of her neighbours in Portsmouth reported sightings of various women entering her house when she was out, on days when her husband worked from home.

Long and bitter recriminations between Walters and her husband followed before it could be ascertained the women in question were his sister, Miriam, who lived close by and a colleague from work who occasionally called in to deliver important documents, a woman old enough to be his mother. It didn't help that neighbours saw her from a distance or through net curtains, as she could easily be mistaken for a younger woman than her forty-eight years as she kept fit, wore tight and short skirts, and had her hair dyed and styled once a month.

'It's a mixed bag,' the DI said when everyone was finished. 'If they were my so-called friends, I wouldn't need any enemies as some of them sound downright nasty and jealous.'

Several laughed, not because it was all that funny but little in this case produced much to cheer them up.

He stood up and walked to the whiteboard. 'In cases like this, I like to establish a timeline but the only things we know are this: Kelly Langton left home at eight on the morning of 6ᵗʰ September to drive to Williamson College in Cowfold; she left Williamson to drive home, but she hasn't been seen since. We know she arrived at school because she also took the child of a neighbour...'

'Gina Jamieson,' volunteered DC Phil Bentley, an up and coming star if he kept his mind on the job and wasn't so distracted by office politics.

'Gina Jamieson, right. Gina said Kelly arrived at her house at five past eight and another couple of witnesses saw her at school so we know she got there ok, but we don't know anything after then. How are you doing with CCTV, Sally?'

DC Sally Graham put down the packet of wine gums she fiddled with and picked up a piece of paper. 'We didn't find her car on the A23, in Burgess Hill or Hayward Heath town centres.'

'Why didn't you examine Brighton?' Harry Wallop said. His hangdog face often gave the impression he was a crotchety old detective sergeant with years under his belt and retiring soon, but he was still in his late forties and his craggy features the result of too much sun from frequent forays to an apartment he owned in Tunisia.

'There's no need,' Sally said. 'The analysis of the A23 and A24 cameras would pick her up and we also checked the A273 in case she took any of the back roads to get there.'

'Good work,' Henderson said, resuming his seat. 'I take it none of the roads around the college are covered by cameras?'

'No sir, it's mainly country roads around there, and if she headed straight home after dropping the kids off and didn't go to someone's house for coffee or to work, no camera would track her.'

'Home is where we think she was going, as she doesn't go into work every day.'

'No, you're right she doesn't,' Walters said. 'When she was at work on Monday, she told Jacques Fournier her assistant manager, she wouldn't be coming in the next day as she intended to work on her book.'

'We know she got to school but we don't know if she left and if she did, if she was on her own or with someone. Carol we need to clear that one up. Take DC Agha and interview parents at Williamson College and get a handle on her state of mind that morning and if anyone saw her leave.'

'Ok.'

'If she did go home alone,' Henderson said, 'we can only assume something happened to her there, in which case we're looking at a crime committed at, or near her house. If a crime hasn't been committed then she voluntarily got into another car somewhere between school and home. Those, I believe are the only options we can surmise from the information we have at the moment.'

'In the first scenario,' Walters said, 'an abduction, happening near or in her house, someone must also have taken her car to the place where we found it at Pound Hill shops. In which case, I would expect to see it on CCTV cameras, in or around Crawley, but of course we can't be precise about the day.'

'We've only examined routes around Williamson College,' Sally Graham said, 'and between there and her home in Hurstpierpoint.'

'Widen the search to include Crawley,' Henderson said. 'If she or her kidnapper came though the town centre we will surely pick her up but if she came up the Balcombe Road which is rural, we're back where we started.'

'I'll get on to it sir,' Graham said with a degree of alacrity, surprising for someone who would be spending the next few days looking over grainy CCTV pictures.

'Seb,' Henderson said to DC Seb Young, a tall and skinny lad with boyish features, despite the rigours of a job which interfered with eating and sleeping patterns and exposed him to the darker side of human nature. 'Did you see any signs of a struggle at the house?'

'No sir, although my brief was only to find out what clothes and travel documents Mrs Langton took with her, which we know now was little more than she carried in her purse and handbag. But even with a cursory check, I couldn't see any indication of broken furniture, damage to walls, blood on the carpet, any of that sort of thing.'

'No new mounds of earth in the garden then, Seb?' Wallop asked.

'Not unless you count the mole hills but then it would make it too easy, wouldn't it?'

Henderson sighed and glanced down at his notes. 'I know it's not much to go on but the report by DS Walters and DC Agha after their interview with Kelly's closest friend, Liz Egger, hints at a motive which I'm finding hard to ignore, although to some it might sound like I'm grasping at straws. Carol, tell us more.'

'For those of you who don't know,' Walters said, 'or didn't read the interview DC Agha and I conducted with Liz Egger, Kelly Langton's best friend. She told us about strong rumours circulating around Brian Langton's production company that he is having an affair with his secretary, Melanie Knight. It's interesting to note Mrs Egger was alerted to this affair by Langton's Finance Director, Gemma Ferguson and so it's on a different level from malicious gossip, in my opinion.'

'What do we know about Melanie Knight,' Henderson asked, 'has anyone spoken to her?'

He glanced around at the faces in the room but no takers. He cleared his throat, it was conclusion time and many sat up, not only to hear his wise and considered counsel but because it was coming close to the end of the meeting and a long day and many were keen to go home or down the pub.

'First up, let's bring in Melanie Knight. It's a long shot, as she might not want to drop her boyfriend in the dirt since he also pays her wages, but whatever the outcome, I would like this rumour confirmed or denied. If she confirms it, an affair is not in itself prima facie evidence of Brian Langton's guilt, especially as Liz Egger says he's done this kind of thing before, but if we put it to him and he becomes evasive, drops the pretence or lets something slip, we can go after him with everything we've got.'

He returned to his office and after dumping the

Kelly Langton papers on the desk, picked up the Ricky Wood murder file before taking a seat around the small conference table. A few minutes later, DC Bentley, DS Walters and DS Hobbs all trooped in and sat down.

'Let's start with the P-M.'

'It was as much as we suspected,' Hobbs said without referring to his notes. 'Mr Wood was beaten extensively with fists and boots, breaking his nose, fingers on both hands, and two ribs before being stabbed five times. The killer blow was the second wound, as it went straight through the heart, slicing a major artery on its way.'

'Five times?' Henderson said. 'They wanted him dead, for sure.'

'That's how it looks. There was some alcohol in his system, consistent with a couple of pints at the match and some cannabis, likely a small toke before going out for the evening; not enough to slow down his reactions but maybe enough to make him unwary.'

'Not much he could do in any case,' Walters said, 'with four blokes laying into him.'

'It's interesting they broke his fingers, and him a journalist,' Bentley said. 'Sending a message perhaps?'

'What about DNA, prints?' Henderson said.

'Sorry boss, no DNA, no prints.'

'You're kidding me. Four guys with bloody knuckles, all frothing at the mouth, wheezing from the exertion and probably spitting on the poor sod as well?'

'Nope.'

'Any sign of the murder weapon?'

'It wasn't discarded at the Racecourse sir,' Bentley said, 'as most cars were gone by the time of the murder and so it's not likely it was pressed into the soil, making it hard to find as we covered an area of about two hundred yards around the murder scene. I think we must assume they took it with them.'

'Carol,' Henderson said. 'Where are we with our witnesses?'

'I've set up all the appeals at the ground and with *The Argus* and not only did they insert it into the news story on page 3, they also incorporated it into the football report on the back page.'

'Good. Many responses?'

'Yes loads, a team are wading through them as we speak.'

'Try and speed it up as we need something more positive. What about Mr Buckley's car? Is it fingerprinted yet?'

'Mr Hinckley.'

'Hinckley, Buckley, it sounds the same. Did you contact him? Tell me we've got the car.'

'I spoke to him before he flew off to Frankfurt on the day after the match and his car's been lying in an airport car park ever since.'

Henderson sighed. The lack of a straw to grasp was weighing him down. 'When is he due back?'

'Tomorrow.'

'Talking of Mr Hinckley,' Bentley said, 'what do we make of the, 'this is for Kerry or Kelly,' comment he said he overheard?'

'Are we settling on 'Kelly' rather than 'Kerry'? Walters asked.

'We'll keep an open mind,' Henderson said, 'but the 'Kelly' version seems too much of a coincidence to ignore.'

'The obvious conclusion,' Hobbs said without too much conviction, 'it's Brian Langton's pals getting their own back on Kelly's killer.'

'I thought the same,' Walters said, 'but Brian Langton's a television producer and he might be a rough diamond, but is he capable of rustling up four thugs to carry out a murder?'

'He met plenty in the old television programme he used to front,' Hobbs said.

'Yeah,' Walters said, 'but that was over ten years ago and any episodes I saw, they all wanted to break his neck, not to do him a big favour. Don't forget, we interviewed Ricky Wood, and even though I wouldn't trust any journalist as far as I could throw him, except Rachel Jones, of course, he didn't seem capable either.'

'This is the problem,' Henderson said, 'the theory lacks credibility. Ricky Wood doesn't look like Kelly's abductor and I don't think Brian Langton was Ricky's killer.'

He thought for a moment. 'We'll put the 'Kelly' comment on the back burner for now but all it leaves us with is the possible fingerprints on the Audi bodywork. Carol, we need to grab our witness as soon as he touches down and get his car in here and give it the full treatment, and I don't mean washing and valeting. If there's anything on it, find it. By the sound of it, it might be the only lead we've got.'

TWELVE

With a sigh, DS Carol Walters tidied up her papers and DC Khalid Agha did the same. They were sitting behind a desk in the main foyer of Williamson College the school on the outskirts of Cowfold that Ben and Josh Langton attended, and had just wasted the best part of the afternoon.

It was a long shot, interviewing parents, but those closer to Kelly such as friends, business associates, and relatives hadn't thrown any light on her disappearance and they'd been forced to cast the net wider. Too wide it seemed as most of the people they'd interviewed today claimed to know her by sight only.

The school building, once a sprawling country house set in two hundred acres of Sussex land that included orchards, grazing sheep, and cattle had been sold off in 1934 to pay the owner's mounting gambling debts. A few years later, it had been converted into a boys' school and nowadays it educated boys and girls from infants right up to A-level. It no longer boasted an orchard or kept animals but instead offered fantastic sporting facilities and a variety of after-school activities most inner-city kids could only dream about.

On a map, fifty miles lay between Williamson College and the high school in Portsmouth DS Walters had attended, but in all other respects it was a world away, as her school didn't have a swimming pool, tennis courts, climbing wall, or games room; but it did have two hockey pitches which flooded when it rained and gangs and cliques who would beat up anyone who didn't want to become a member.

Many of her fellow pupils were the sons and daughters of serving Royal Navy personnel who manned a fleet of aircraft carriers and frigates, regular visitors to Portsmouth Harbour at all times of the year. She didn't use pseudo-social theories and psychobabble to try and understand why some people were bad and others good, but in her experience, many of the kids who didn't see their fathers or mothers for months at a time were often the same people causing all the trouble.

The two officers had spent the last two hours interviewing parents and even though the DC called ahead and informed the school secretary of their impending arrival and requested a message to be posted on the notice board, several went straight home after picking up their kids. This attitude, people making their own decisions about what information would or would not be useful to the police, annoyed her more than anything else about her job, as it could damage what could turn out to be a key part of this investigation, and she could wring every one of their well-moisturised necks.

The interviews they did manage to conduct were pointless as no one claimed to have seen or heard anything unusual in Kelly's behaviour on the day she went missing, or in her relationships with other parents or staff, and even those parents who knew her well and spoke to her often were unable to add anything new. It had been a normal day and the more she heard this, the more she became convinced Kelly Langton had been taken by a kidnapper either on her journey between the school and home, or something had happened at her house when she got there.

Before saying goodbye to the admin staff, who went out of their way to be helpful, perhaps to atone for their earlier gaff of not putting up a notice, Agha decided he would go out for 'some fresh air,' the boy's euphemism for a sly fag. He came back into the building five minutes later with a face like a half-chewed toffee and not reeking like yesterday's ashtray.

'What's wrong with you?' she said, warming her back at a roaring log fire burning in the huge fireplace in the oak-lined main hallway. 'Somebody stolen your pencil?'

'This place is a fuc...it's a no smoking estate,' he said, his face angry but mellowing, as his eyes followed a young tight-skirted teacher walking past. 'If you can believe it, I was told off by a Sixth-Former who was way taller than me. What do they feed them on here?'

'Ha, you'll learn. Listen to someone who's been there. Give up, it's a hell of a lot easier what with all those no smoking restaurants, pubs, shops and now schools, you got nowhere to go, mate.'

'Humph, that's what I get for living in a bloody nanny state. Oh, I forgot to say, I spotted some cameras outside.'

'What, in the school grounds?'

'Yeah. It seems a bit of overkill in a place like this. It's hardly inner-city Birmingham, is it?'

'Where are they?'

'Over in the car park, where we drove in, and a place they call the Quadrangle.'

'Grab your stuff. We're going to the school office to take a look. Maybe this crap day can be rescued after all.'

The Bursar, Miss Brocket was an unsmiling, lumpy woman aged between forty and sixty whose true age proved difficult to ascertain as her clothes and hair were 'classic', meaning neither had changed since her early twenties. She did have a beautiful view of the school grounds from her office, through tall sash windows and out to a large expanse of grass and trees stretching into the distance with football and rugby pitches, a play park, and an elaborate climbing frame.

'The cameras?' she said, a sour look on her face and her hands clasped in front of her, as if considering the next Latin verb in the list or waiting for someone to tell her the capital of Lithuania.

'There are eight dotted around the building focussed on the playground and busy traffic areas such as the Quadrangle and outside the sports hall where bunching and jostling can often lead to disagreements.'

Oh, the poor things, DS Walters was tempted to say. 'What about the car park?'

'Yes, there's one there.'

'And the access roads?'

'Yes, there's one as you enter the school on the East Gate and one as you exit on the West Gate.'

'Excellent. Can we take a look at the tapes for 6th September, please?'

Miss Brocket creaked upright, crossed the room and opened a long glass cabinet with a key.

Walters tried to keep hold of her enthusiasm, as she was confident they would show Kelly entering and leaving the school. If there was nothing odd about the time interval between the two and if she travelled alone, they were no further forward, but at least the school could be eliminated from their enquiries. But what if she wasn't?

'6th September you said?'

'Yes.' Kelly had disappeared ten days ago but she didn't expect a school like this to recycle their tapes on a weekly basis as they did in a busy filling station or a supermarket.

Miss Brocket pulled a tape out from a neat row and popped it into the slot of a video recorder, the bottom unit in a small array of AV kit, tucked away in a corner of her office. At first the picture was black, then interspersed with white wavy lines and while she hoped it would soon start with something recognisable as a recording, it didn't, even when the Bursar pressed the fast-forward button. She gave up after a few minutes. She tried another from the following day, and another from the day after that, but they were all the same.

'Oh dear, there seems to be a little problem.'

Ten minutes later, they drove out the school gates. 'What a bloody waste of time,' Agha said, guiding the car onto the main road and pointing it south in the direction of Brighton.

'Yes, and no,' she said, trying to put a positive spin on things as she opened a window to let out the strong smell of garlic seeping out of his pores like cheap after-shave. 'I think we succeeded in reassuring parents we are working on the case and taking it seriously, as a few demanded to know what the hell we were doing about it.'

'Ha, I know what you mean. These people talked to us like bloody colonialists and we were their manservants or natives on a South-Sea island. What a bunch of toffee-nosed gits.'

'Easy boy, you'll blow a gasket.'

He shrugged. 'I know I'm stereotyping about posh schools and all that but the message I heard was loud and clear. It was uncharacteristic of her to go off like she did and we should take a closer look at her husband.'

She sat back and closed her eyes, thankful it was near the end and not the start of a long and frustrating day. 'Yeah, I heard it too. She seemed popular but nobody said a good word about him. I wonder why?'

They arrived back at Sussex House at six. She dumped the fattening Langton file on her desk and was preparing to head home, when DI Henderson barged in and plonked himself down in the spare chair, demanding an update. Her mind was already on a warm shower and a cool glass of Pinot Grigio to wash away the irritations of a crappy day but she recovered and summarised the parent interviews and the concern expressed by many of Kelly's friends.

'Bloody annoying about the CCTV,' he said. 'There's no point having the thing if it's not properly maintained.'

'I quite agree, but as the pupils are in the main, well-behaved and with only a few accidents in the car park each year, they don't look at it very often.'

'You sound like you're reading from their marketing brochure. What sort of fault was it?'

'There had been a leaky gutter with water coming down the walls inside her office and when it was fixed, they got a decorator in to re-paint. They think he must have disconnected the AV unit when he shifted the cabinet and forgot to plug it back in.'

'So simple, eh? I hope he received two weeks detention and a hundred lines.'

'I wouldn't put it past Miss Brocket, she's a tough old boot.'

'So where do we go from here?'

'Well, we drew a blank with her friends, ditto the gym, and now the school. The only place left to go, in my opinion, is either the husband or an unknown abductor. It's time to choose a card, partner. You play cards, do we stick or twist?'

'That's blackjack, not poker. Where are we on the Audi Q7 paw print?'

'Mr Hinckley's Audi Q7 from the racecourse?'

'Aye, the very one.'

'When did you last receive an update?'

'I know he came back from Dubai on Sunday and he told us we couldn't have his car as he needed it on

Monday but we could have it Monday night.'

'Forensics gave it priority and before I left for Williamson College they sent an email to say they found a number of fingerprints on an offside body panel. They also said the car is dirty and hadn't been washed since the match.'

'Good. Where are they?'

'Phil Bentley's doing the necessary.'

'Let's go see him.'

It was after six and like a good trooper, DC Bentley was still at his computer and waiting for the database to return matches of the fingerprints he'd entered.

'How's it going Phil?' Walters said.

'Oh, hi sarg, evening sir.'

'Forensics found a whole load of fingerprints on the offside of the car,' Bentley said, 'and I'm working through them. Of the ones processed so far, a couple belong to kids and I'm assuming they're Mr Hinckley's, and another is an adult belonging to a security guard at Heathrow who's got a record for stealing valuables from cars.'

'Keep him back,' Henderson said, 'as we might need him to boost our stats as I don't think this case or the Langton disappearance will be doing it soon.'

'Since when did you get so concerned about stats?'

'It's everyone's responsibility, Carol. The public and our paymasters the Government need to be reassured we are doing a good job.'

'You're sounding more like a CI every day. Are the exams coming up any time soon?'

'Might be. What's running now, Phil?' he asked, his eyes on a flickering, changing screen, as it picked its way through thousands of fingerprints, looking for a match.

'Two handprints lifted from the car. You can see from the photograph, they're clear.'

Henderson picked it up with Walters looking over his shoulder. It was enhanced by fingerprint powder and ultraviolet light and stood out clear and clean, highlighting the shape of spread-out fingers, someone pushing against the car to regain their balance. If someone fell against the car in the airport, she would expect to see the fingers slightly closer together or even to create a palm smudge.

'Looks like you were right about the criminals leaving their mark,' Walters said.

'Yes, or we'll find it was made by a holidaymaker when he tripped over his suitcase.'

She averted her eyes as the flickering screen was playing tricks with her vision and focussed instead on the untidy desks, cluttered whiteboards and deep piles of paper lying around the Murder Suite.

A few minutes later, the flickering stopped. 'Right, here's the first,' Bentley said, staring at the screen. 'It belongs to Jason Roberts, 58, sentenced to five years for armed robbery in '79, three for affray in '88, eight for culpable homicide in 2001.'

'He sounds just like the sort of person we're looking for,' Henderson said.

THIRTEEN

'Dragons Bar' in Ship Street is a cavernous sort of a place, wide and long with a beer garden out the back, its size unusual for a city centre pub. This and places like it, catered for the hundreds of tourists who flocked to Brighton in the summertime, looking for a good time and an opportunity to meet members of the opposite sex, but as blue skies and warm nights were but a fleeting memory on this cold Saturday in September, DI Angus Henderson could order drinks from the bar without resorting to sign language or being in danger of having his ribs bruised.

In Brighton there is a pub for every day of the year and so plenty of choice if he wanted to avoid a large commercial operation like this one, but as he didn't drink any of their huge range of 'throwing lagers,' the ale wasn't bad and the pub was located close to the restaurants around the Lanes and Duke Street and where he and Rachel had decided to eat tonight.

She looked sexy as she walked back to her seat after powdering her nose, or whatever the reason modern women gave for taking so long in the toilet. She wore a tight, pale red dress accentuating her pert breasts and slim physique but he sensed the eyes of many men in the pub ogling her generous bottom as she bent over the low table to give him a kiss, his reward for spending the best part of ten quid on two drinks, while they got their show for free.

When they started going out together, he was wary of talking to her about criminal cases, as she was a journalist and they liked nothing better than some titbit of information they couldn't find anywhere else, and even if she didn't walk the crime beat, she could let something slip to those who did and land him in a whole heap of trouble. So as they said in poker, he played his cards close to his chest.

He took a sip of his beer, it tasted bright and fizzy with a tang of something metallic but not unduly unpleasant. 'I haven't seen you these last few days as I've been so busy with press conferences and fending off your colleagues who waylay me every time I step out of the building. I never realised a late-thirties, ex-model could still have this amount of pull.'

'If it's any consolation to you dear detective, it's a mystery to us scribblers as well. It might be due to the large number of magazines that seem to be growing like fungus in WH Smith and gossiping web sites, as they all need something interesting to talk about every day and Kelly's prettier and easier to write about than most.'

'You could be right.'

'Would you like to know what I've been doing?'

'It would be very ungallant and let's face it, stupid of me to say 'no', so instead I will say, tell me my darling, what have you been up to?'

She gave him a quizzical look. 'Is this what it sounds like when a Scotsman's being romantic? You'll need to try a little harder next time. Now, let me tell you my tale. Speaking of former models who are still famous, take a look at this.'

She handed him a copy of *The Argus*. The headline screamed 'Foul' in large black letters, a story about angry householders dumping rubbish in the street as the refuse collectors were out on strike again, over what he didn't know; pay, pensions, working conditions or the length of their tea break? Pick one, every week it seemed to be something else.

'Which page am I supposed to be looking at, or have I died and gone to heaven as you're about to tell me you've joined the Sports Team and penned your first article about the Albion?'

'Don't be silly, you know I can't stand football. Turn to page two.'

He opened the paper and came face-to-face with a full page article headed, 'Former Brighton Model's Mystery Disappearance.'

'Oh no, not another story about Kelly Langton. Do you know—'

'Angus, read the name, the name of the reporter.'

He looked down at the newspaper again and read aloud, 'by Rachel Jones. You did this?'

She nodded. 'There's only one Rachel Jones in our office.'

'Well done you.' He leaned over and gave her a kiss.

'Good isn't it?'

'Excellent. Mind you, if my memory serves me well this isn't your first venture away from the safe and secure world of Rural Affairs and the Environment, is it?'

'Don't remind me but this time it's different.'

'For your sake, I hope so as the Brighton councillor you wrote about who raised all the money for charity, only for the story to fall flat the week when we arrested him for fraud, is still in jail.'

'Yeah, yeah.'

'However, I do believe this is your first time at anything so topical. I should think every paper in the land will want a piece.'

'I know and my editor's thrilled. Brian wouldn't do interviews with any of the nationals but chose *The Argus* as he's a Brighton boy and over the years, we've always reported what Kelly was up to, so I think he likes us.'

'How did you get it? I mean there must be–'

'What? Better qualified reporters than me?'

'Something along those lines.'

'Thanks for your vote of confidence, Mr H but I suppose you're right. Sarah Pendleton, who normally does this stuff, is off on maternity leave and Barry said he liked my writing style and sympathetic approach so much he chose me to do the interview in her place.'

'So what does–'

'No more questions, Angus, read.'

Former Brighton Model's Mystery Disappearance - Husband Speaks to The Argus

A week ago, former Brighton model Kelly Langton drove her two boys, Josh 13 and Ben 8, to school at Williamson College, an independent day and boarding school near Cowfold in West Sussex; but on the way home to work on the book she was writing, she mysteriously disappeared. Despite an extensive search by the police and her family, she has not been seen since. Kelly, who used to be on the books of Brighton glamour agency Models Inc and frequently appeared in the pages of Vogue and Elle magazines, was a devoted mother who left without saying goodbye to the two children she adored, and significantly, without her passport and any more clothes than those she was wearing.

Argus reporter Rachel Jones met Kelly's husband Brian at the offices of his television production company in London, Camino House Productions, and he is as perplexed as everyone else.
'She had no reason to run off,' he said. 'We have a nice home and she was a major part of it. We had no problems to speak of and she positively adored our two boys.'
Kelly's two sons_____'

'Great work Rachel,' he said, after he finished reading the article, 'it's really good.'

'What, for a woman or a stand-in?'

'Very funny. I mean as a piece of journalism. It'll make a name for you, I'm sure.'

'Thank you, kind sir.'

'It has to be more interesting than the Cranleigh flower show or the South of England Show or any of these agricultural events you drag me to. Before you know it, you'll be working for one of the nationals and running up to Hove Station in the morning with some of your heavily mortgaged neighbours.'

'No chance, and I can't run in these shoes.'

'How are the other papers treating the story? I presume most of their lines of enquiry are exhausted by now, because if we don't have much to go on, they must have even less.'

'Dead right, and you can see from the current editions, they're repeating stuff from earlier in the week, hence my editor thinks they'll bite off our hands to get this interview with her husband.'

He looked at the article again. It was a mystery, even to long-serving police officers, how a particular murder, rape or kidnap made it on to the front page of national newspapers and mainstream TV news broadcasts when other, more deserving cases, did not. He believed newspaper editors were attracted by victims who were young, female, and good looking and shied away from the ugly, male, or the plain uninteresting.

The victim's family could keep the story alive if they were active and vocal, by passing to newspapers and TV fresh information and different photographs, especially when the one displayed on every newsstand and news report was beginning to tire. In Kelly's case, this wasn't a problem as there seemed to be a limitless number of images and most of them seemed to be in the hands of newspapers and magazines already.

Looking at the photograph, he could see what the newspaper editor's attraction might be. She was thirty-eight and he had seen pictures of her in demure business suits with her hair tied back and wearing sensible shoes, but the scantily clad picture here of a cracking, sexy young woman with a flawless body and gleaming white teeth was taken in her mid-twenties. In addition, smaller pictures of the big house, smart cars, and a husband who was a millionaire, contained all the ingredients of a perfect story, as there was nothing the British public wanted more than to see a rich bod hauled off their high pedestal and given a big dose of crap being handed out to everyone else; or was he just being cynical?

'How was Brian Langton when you met him?'

'He didn't break down in tears and start crying on my shoulder, if this is what you're thinking, but he's worried as she's never done this sort of thing before.'

'So what do you think has happened to her? You don't speculate in your article.'

'It wasn't part of the brief but if you would like me to do your job for you, I'll give it a go.'

She held up her left hand and counted on her fingers. 'One, she might run away to be with a lover or into the wild blue yonder to get away from him, if he abused her or something. Two, she might be abducted by a kidnapper or a serial killer and taken to who knows where. Three, she might be buried at the bottom of the garden or a field behind the house, as she's been murdered by Brian or someone else who came to the house. Four? I can't think of any more. How did I do?'

'Not bad for a civilian.'

'What do you think?'

'We use three classifications for missing persons: lost, voluntary missing, and under the influence of a third party. For example, she may be 'lost' in the sense of being involved in a car accident and ending up in hospital with no ID and no memory.'

'I suppose so, but it's a bit of a long shot. It sounds more applicable to hill walkers and sailors like you.'

He drew a reproachful face. 'With GPS and basic navigational skills, only fools get lost. So, what do you make of the passport and clothes she left behind? A woman who decides to scarper would always take them with her, wouldn't you agree? I mean you can't hire a car, book into a hotel or buy an airline ticket without a passport nowadays.'

'True. If I decided to run away, I would take some clothes and my passport, although I would leave the car behind as I know how easily it can be traced and it wouldn't be a loss with the thing I'm driving at the moment.' She thought for a moment, a puzzled expression on her face. 'Maybe number four is, she did it to implicate her husband, you know, to make you guys think he's done her in, so you'll put him away.'

'Why?'

'I don't know but Brian's a big guy and maybe he beats her up or she wants to get her hands on his business. What do Sussex's finest think?'

'This is off the record, nothing quotable or attributable, ok?'

She nodded. 'Ok.'

'She'll have been missing for two weeks this Tuesday and with no contact and no definite sightings, sometime soon we will have to assume foul play, either by the husband, one of her friends, or an acquaintance.'

112

'It isn't Brian, I'm sure,' she said. 'He is a bit rough and brusque for sure, but he's grieving. I think he misses her and wants her back.'

'The truth is, I don't know what's happened to her and I suspect few other people do either, but we'll find her if she's there to be found.'

'We've talked enough about work for one night,' she said, rubbing his arm. 'What's the plan for this evening?'

'I haven't given it much thought beyond a nice candlelight meal at Luigi's, good food, great company and a fine bottle of vino rosso.'

'Sounds excellent for starters. To celebrate the publication of my big story, I've got a little something planned. At home, there is a chilled bottle of champagne and lucky you, I bought some of your favourite whisky for later. After we've been to the restaurant we can go back to my place and celebrate in style.'

He reached over and kissed her. 'I'm up for it.'

'Mmm,' she said, pulling away. 'Carry on like this, and we'll skip the Italian and head straight back to my place for dessert.'

FOURTEEN

He sat back in the chair as the waiter served his starter and picked up the wine bottle. 'There's not many in tonight, Antonio,' he said.

'No, it's been a quiet week Mr Green,' the waiter replied as he re-filled the giant wine glass with an inch of Valpolicello Amarone. 'I can't really complain as the last few weeks have been *bellisimo*.' If he hadn't been holding the bottle, Dominic Green was convinced Antonio's exclamation would have been two-handed, but instead he made do with one.

Antonio returned to the kitchen leaving him to savour the wine, his favourite. He didn't go in for all the highfalutin crap spun out on the airwaves and magazines by over-paid wine presenters who liked to compare the aroma of a wine with the air on a mountain top in Austria, their grandpa's tobacco pouch or the smell from the stall or arse of a sweaty horse, because to him, it was more simple.

If it reeked of too much of alcohol or nothing much at all, it was too young or plain rubbish, churned out by the vat-load by unscrupulous suppliers, intent on making a quick buck. If the aroma was floral and pleasant on the nose, he would drink it. In fact, the Amarone had floral in abundance with the odd hint of wood, a taste he loved as it slipped down his throat with the greatest of ease and deposited little taste memories on his tongue.

He spread the napkin over his clean, hand-stitched shirt and set to work attacking the carbonara. It was supposed to be a starter but like all the food served in this place there was enough in three courses to feed half a dozen homeless people, who were often to be found camping in doorways nearby. He wasn't a 'fill your boots' merchant, never had been, and skipped lunch to make sure he made a decent job of each dish, but he loved Italian food and this place served some of the best. It also helped that it was located in Ship Street, in the middle of Brighton and close to two of his busiest bars.

The bars were a side-line as at heart Dominic Green was a property developer and this had turned him into a millionaire many times over. His expertise was in buying run-down properties and eyesores only environmental nutcases ever cared about and turning them into swanky apartments for young executives to live in or up-market shopping centres for them to spend lots of their hard-earned cash.

He didn't spend much time visiting his bars as his managers had their heads screwed on and if they didn't, his minder John Lester would knock them off. He sometimes popped in for a minute or two on the way to somewhere else, as he could tell a lot about a bar by a quick visit, the noise, the age and styles of the clientele, and how well the staff were coping.

He also owned a number of cash-based businesses, casinos and bookmakers, handy at generating the readies and with everything electronic nowadays, who didn't want a pile of the folding stuff in their back pocket? They were also good for laundering money, the money he made in the drugs business and gambling dens, because the banks were in cahoots with cops, and people like him needed to be one step ahead to outfox them.

The remains of the carbonara were taken away and replaced by a steak, seared on both sides, pink in the centre and coated in a lovely tomato, oregano, and garlic sauce chef Luigi made especially for him. He was halfway through when he spotted John Lester entering the restaurant. There was no need for Lester to crane his neck or pace up and down the tables to find him, as it was quiet with few other diners and Green sat at the same table at the back as he usually did. With a curt nod to the waiter who opened the door, Lester walked towards him.

Green watched him approach, cupping the bulbous wine glass with both hands to warm it and bring out the heady aroma. It cheered him to see John had changed out of the suit he wore earlier and into something more casual, indicating he was set for a night of action.

'Good evening, John.'

'Evening Mr Green,' he said, sitting down.

'Would you like a glass of this stuff? It's very good.'

'No thanks, not when I'm working.'

'Fair enough. What news?'

'Our mutual friend is with us.'

'Where?'

'Picked him up in the middle of Brighton as he

walked back to his flat, piece of cake.'

'No little old ladies sitting at the window with their notebooks and telephones at the ready just in case something interesting happens in their little part of the world, perhaps?'

'Nah. Nothing. We picked him up down a side street near the seafront with a few dark spots due to a couple of dud lights, so even if anybody saw us, it would be hard to tell us from a couple of pissheads having a barney.'

'Good man. So what, he's down at Shoreham with Spike taking care of his every need?'

Lester nodded. 'Yep, the little man's looking after him.'

He finished the last of the Amarone in his glass with an undignified gulp, so unbefitting for such a fine wine, and after dabbing his mouth with the serviette, told Antonio he could drink the rest. The effusive Torinese looked impressed, as well he might, as it would make a welcome change from wine-lake rosso, his usual accompaniment to a late meal when all the customers were gone.

'Right,' Green said, 'we better get moving.'

It came as no surprise to see the car parked outside, as Lester hated walking, a fact at odds with the fit and toned individual in front of him, now reaching for door handle of the Roller. Green liked to walk, but as a recognisable figure around the town it didn't matter if he was sitting in a restaurant or out with his wife, celebrity-obsessed oiks would approach and ask him for the secrets of his success or to pose for a selfie. If the wife was out of sight, the offending twerp might get their arms twisted or their phone trampled but if she wasn't, he would impart one pearl of wisdom which usually went along the lines of, 'by trampling over little weeds like you'.

Within sight of the perimeter fence of Shoreham airport stood a building everyone in his team called the warehouse. Inside, they stored drugs brought in from the continent by light plane and distributed by a small group of trusted dealers. Also, alcohol and cigarettes from Eastern Europe, smuggled aboard grain ships which docked at Shoreham Harbour and merged with the kosher stuff within his entertainment businesses, but without paying the government a cent in tax; sweet.

The warehouse was flanked by the Shoreham Airport runway on one side and a number of empty industrial units on the other, ideal for bringing in contraband, as it wasn't overlooked by nosy neighbours, and when interrogating a suspect, only the seagulls could hear them scream.

Lester unlocked the door and pushed it open. Green walked inside to be greeted by the familiar sight of Spike sitting on a chair looking at his smartphone and giggling about some shit or other, while their guest for the evening, Wayne Garrett, swung from a rope attached to his outstretched wrists, his feet a couple of inches off the ground.

'Evening Spike.'

'Evening Mr Green.'

'How's Garrett?'

'In the mood for talking, I would say.'

'Good.'

John went off to make the tea while Green pulled over a couple of chairs. There was no time to waste so he didn't wait for a brew to arrive.

'Spin him round a bit Spike, I want to speak to his face, not his arse.'

'Right-oh, Mr Green.'

Job done, he took a good look at him. As usual, Spike hadn't bashed his face in, not yet, as he still required the power of speech, but he would bet he'd given his guts a sound pummelling.

'Garrett,' Green said, 'if you take a look around this place you find yourself in, what do you notice?'

'Eh? You guys–'

'No, no, you dickhead. Look at the merchandise, the shelves, what's on the floor.'

'Boxes and cartons and packages–'

'You don't get it do you? There's a hole, there's spaces, gaps where our recent shipment from Pakistan should now be sitting. Capish?'

'Ah, yeah.'

'To refresh: my boys went over to Shoreham Harbour to pick up said shipment on Thursday night and do you know what they found?'

'No.'

'Are you sure?'

'Yeah.'

'The whole place was swarming with fucking cops,' Green said, raising his voice.

'Too fucking bad.'

Green nodded to Spike.

The little dynamo, who probably ate spinach for breakfast, like Popeye, pummelled his midriff with a succession of punches, so quick they were a blur. A keen lifter of weights, a punch from him came not from the wrist or the fist, but from his powerful shoulders, giving the same impact as the kick from a mule, going by the mess it made of those on the receiving end. Spike stopped the beating and returned to his chair and his smartphone. He might be thick but he knew an incapacitated prisoner would tell them nothing.

There would be a lull now, as Garrett nursed his wounds, not easy with his hands tied up, and probably calculating his chances. John appeared at his side with a steaming mug of the good stuff. Green took it from him and placed it on the floor at the side of the chair to cool.

'Now Garrett, I know somebody down at the docks tipped the cops the wink about this shipment and you know what?'

'What?'

'I think it was you.'

'Bloody hell. No, no, Mr Green. It wasn't me.'

'There's no point in denying it. There's only you and one other guy down there on my payroll. You're the only people who knew about it.'

'It must be the other guy, has to be.'

'No way. He's a straight shooter. Listen up, Garrett, here's the big question. Did you tell your copper contact about me?'

'No, no I didn't. I swear I didn't.'

'So, you did talk to a copper?'

'No, no...'

Spike got up and pulled out a small stiletto knife.

He walked over to Garrett and with a practised movement, stuck the blade into his thigh, all the way up to the handle.

If any pigeons or seagulls were sitting on the roof, trying to sleep or resting after a hard day stealing peoples chips or shitting on their cars, they would all be halfway to France by now after the fright they received from Garrett's high-pitched screech.

Green gave him a few minutes to recover before he said, 'who's your cop contact?'

'He stabbed me, I'm fucking bleeding man, help me.'

'You need to help yourself, Garrett by telling me what I want to know. Who's your cop contact? What's his name?'

'Keep that fucking maniac away from me, y'hear? Henderson.'

'Speak up man, I can't hear you.'

'Detective Inspector Angus Henderson.'

He stared hard at Lester. 'Isn't he the tall Scottish bloke?'

'Yep, that's him.'

'Didn't we try to get him on the payroll?'

He shook his head. 'Nope, Jackie advised us not to bother. He said we'd both end up in jail.'

'Phah. Principles? Not worth a bag of beans where I come from. Everyone's got a price, you just need to find it.'

He turned back to Garrett. 'How much did Henderson pay you?'

'A grand.'

'A grand? The miserable Scottish bastard. You get

more than that from me every month, you wanker. What do you need more money for? Are you in debt? Are you a gambler or a drinker?'

'I gamble, horses.'

'Pah, gambling's a mug's game, and that's from a guy who owns a couple of bookies. Did you tell Henderson about me?'

'Nothing,' he said, between sobs incongruous in such a large, rough man. 'I swear I told him nothing.'

'You're lying.'

'I'm not fucking lying, I'm telling you straight up. I didn't say anything about you. I need help, Mr Green my leg, my leg's bleeding.'

Spike acknowledged Green's nod, put down his phone and walked over to the prisoner. He pulled out the stiletto and in the same practiced move, stuck it into the other leg. This time, it was obvious the sadistic little bastard hadn't heard enough screaming or seen enough blood, as he twisted the knife before pulling it out. Garrett screamed louder this time, probably frightening the sleeping birds on the roofs of neighbouring warehouses.

'This is your last chance Garrett,' Green said taking a slurp of tea. 'I'm in no mood to fuck about. Does Henderson know the shipment belonged to me?'

'No,' he said in a meek voice.

Green glanced over at John, who shook his head. 'I think he's lying.'

'Me too,' Green said.

'You want me to take Henderson out?'

'Hmm it's tempting, but no, not yet. Let's see how this thing plays out.'

'Fine. What about him?' he said, nodding towards the prisoner.

'Talking to cops is one thing, but having snitches in my organisation is something I can do without. Take him out on Danny's boat. You know where he leaves the keys?'

'Yep, in a plastic bag beside the wheelhouse.'

'Good man. Take Garrett out for a nice night time sail, just make sure he doesn't come back.'

FIFTEEN

After a twenty-minute delay the train pulled away from Stoke-on-Trent station.

'Thank the lord,' DS Gerry Hobbs said, 'I thought we'd be there all day.'

'I could never commute,' Henderson said. 'If I worked for the Met, I would need to move up there as I couldn't sit on a train every day and put up with all these delays.'

'You'd miss Brighton, you would but I couldn't do it either. As much as I hate traffic and putting my car in for its MOT and seeing a mechanic with a sour face who says you need new big ends or the gearbox doesn't sound right, I would miss driving into work every day.'

'What are you reading?'

Hobbs put down the can of Pepsi in his hand on the table between them and picked up the magazine in front of him. 'It's an article about this red-headed American actress, Jessica Chastain who's appearing in a new sci-fi film by Brighton's own Graham Dynes, *Interstellar Wars*. Have you heard of it?'

'Nope.'

'I don't usually go in for much sci-fi stuff but this one sounds good, I might go and see it when it comes out, if we can get babysitters. What about you? How's your book, mind I heard a lot of huffing and puffing and a lot of gazing out of the window.'

'Is it so obvious? I'm at chapter four and I still don't have a clue what it's about.'

'I hate it when—'

Henderson's phone was ringing.

'Hello Angus, it's Lisa,' Chief Inspector Lisa Edwards said.

'Morning ma'am.'

'We can ditch the ma'am bit, Angus. We'll be working together on many cases in future so let's pass on the added formality. Call me Lisa, ok?'

'Fine by me.'

'I'm going into a meeting about the Langton case with the ACC and his coterie this afternoon and to be honest, I would rather you were with me but I do understand why you needed to go to Manchester. Option two is for you to give me an update on everything you know and what you're planning to do and I'll pass it on to the ACC. How does it sound to you?'

'No problem but remember, I'm sitting on a train.'

'Got it. Now, we're what, three weeks into this investigation?'

'Four, this coming Tuesday.'

'God almighty,' she exploded, making Henderson pull the phone away from his ear in surprise. *'It's a long time to be missing in anybody's book.'* The phone went quiet for a couple of beats. *'Ok,'* she said in more measured tones. *'The evidence against Brian Langton is firstly that we believe he is having an*

affair with his secretary, Melanie Knight.'

'Allegedly, but while we received a statement to this effect from her best friend, we are yet to find anyone else to substantiate it.'

'Including Ms Knight.'

'Especially Ms Knight, as she kept her mouth shut throughout the interview and left us with the impression she and her boss are no more than colleagues.'

'She knows where her bread is buttered, that girl. Next on the list is a report by a neighbour of Langton, Charles Vincent, who claims he saw a mini digger in their garden.'

'Neighbour in the loosest sense of the word, as his cottage is about a quarter of a mile away, but he pops into Manor House Farm now and again to undertake bits of maintenance work.'

'I see. The digger came from where?'

'Builders fixing the pot-holed driveway, the poor condition of which was reported by several attendees of the Saturday night dinner party, the one held the weekend before Kelly disappeared. Langton asked them to leave it behind.'

'Why?'

'He said he wanted to level part of the back garden where it was uneven.'

'Hmmn, or maybe something else. Now, last and most compelling in my mind is that he took out a large insurance policy on his wife's life, three months before she disappeared.'

'Yes. Langton said he did it because his business was doing so well, and as a way of reducing his tax

126

bill.'

'Does he need the money?'

'I don't think so, as I understand it his business is successful, but he says it's a way of reducing tax.'

'Yes, but there's a big difference in being successful and being cash-rich, as many growing businesses find to their cost. Get someone working on the financial analysis, Angus.'

'Will do.'

'In addition,' she said, *'we've seen no activity on Mrs Langton's mobile phone, credit or debit cards or her bank account since she disappeared.'*

'Right, and we know she has her phone and credit cards with her as she always carried them in her purse.'

'It's all very strange.'

'Many of her friends and business associates told us she texted and updated Facebook and Twitter more than most people, and again there's been nothing since 6th September.'

'Plus, she didn't take her passport?'

'No, Brian found it at home, in a drawer in the kitchen.'

'That's the clincher for me. If she'd planned to scarper, she would have taken it with her as it provides essential ID for hiring a car, going abroad or booking a hotel room. Even if she possessed an ID card, it's not always acceptable in every situation.'

'In which case, her travel movements would be restricted to the UK,' Henderson said, 'so why haven't there been any sightings from other police forces, railway stations or newspaper appeals, as her picture has been plastered all over the media for the last three weeks?'

'I agree. Thanks for doing this, Angus there's plenty I can tell the ACC. Now in terms of what we are planning to do, I want you to get over to Manor House Farm and turn over the house and the garden and search ever inch. I'll get a warrant and it'll be here on your return but remember he's a high profile figure and you need to be on your best behaviour. However, if you find a blood stain, a broken piece of crockery or obtain a positive reading from ground radar in the garden, big-shot or not, he'll be spending his foreseeable holidays with us.'

The train hissed, belched and creaked as it crept along the platform at Manchester Piccadilly, moving like an asthmatic panther but with the weight and momentum to destroy all before it like a mythical beast if the driver released the brake too soon. Henderson stretched and pushed the debris littering the table to one side and eased himself out from the confines of an uncomfortable seat and restrictive table, and retrieved their bags from the storage area.

The throng on the station concourse appeared similar to London Victoria with the same type of shops, the same harassed travellers gazing at departure boards, and the same cups of coffee clutched in nearly everyone's hands. However, accents were harder and louder and despite the gentrification of many areas and the development of new industries requiring knowledge instead of brawn, names like Wigan, Warrington, and Macclesfield could still conjure a cold, industrial image.

A car picked them up outside the station and drove them through damp, busy streets towards the ring road. Henderson didn't say much as he mulled over the call from Edwards and the increasing suspicion surrounding Brian Langton, and his boss's warning to be on his best behaviour. He had dealt with celebrities before, a visiting rap star who was assaulted in the centre of Brighton as he tried to buy drugs, and an American actress whose jewellery was nicked from her bedroom in the Grand Hotel, but none had generated the same level of interest as Kelly Langton.

The car pulled up outside Pendleton Police Station and Jason Roberts was seated in the interview room by the time they passed through security and picked up a Manchester detective as their escort. Roberts was fifty-eight going on sixty-eight with a lined pale face, narrow eyes, bald head and tattoos all over powerful-looking arms, a poor imitation of a Premiership footballer. His nose was bulbous with the thin blue lines of a serious drinker and misshapen from being smacked too many times by a hard fist. He sat opposite and assumed the classic tough, villain pose, arms folded across his chest, a sneer on his face, and an expression saying, 'don't fuck with me, I'm telling you nothing.'

When Hobbs called Manchester CID and told them about the fingerprint gleaned from the car at Brighton Racecourse, they happily picked up Roberts as he was a career criminal with connections to various gangs, and with several unsolved crimes on their books they hoped a little lubrication from Henderson might encourage him to open up his ugly gob about their cases.

'Mr Roberts, I am Detective Inspector Henderson of Sussex Police and this is my colleague Detective Sergeant Hobbs.'

'You're a long way from home, Inspector. Up here for the sunshine are ye? Ha Ha.' The accent sounded pure Manchester, straight out of the Stretford End at Old Trafford.

'I'm investigating the murder of a journalist, Ricky Wood, at Brighton racecourse on Tuesday 13th September, and hoping you could tell me something about it.'

'I've been to New Brighton but never Brighton in your neck of the woods.' He smiled, a gold tooth sparkling among the coffee, curry and cigarette stains.

'So you know nothing about the murder of Ricky Wood?'

He shook his head. 'Nope. Sorry mate, you've got the wrong fella.'

'Sergeant Hobbs, please show Mr Roberts the photographs.'

Hobbs opened a file, removed several photographs and put the first one in front of Roberts.

'This is you boarding a Virgin Train service at Manchester Piccadilly,' Hobbs said. He put down another photograph. 'This is you exiting the railway station at Brighton some six hours later. To be clear, this is Brighton in East Sussex. The date, you'll notice, is Monday 12th September, the day before Ricky Wood was killed.'

His brief, Phil Slade leaned over and whispered something in his client's ear. Strangely for a con, he said nothing and listened. Had to be a first.

'Yeah,' he said, after a minute or two. 'Slip of the memory, I forgot.'

'How could you forget being in Brighton?' Henderson said, his face mock incredulous, a politician facing his opposite number across the floor of the House of Commons.

'I'd...I'd been drinking and taking medication for a back problem. I shouldn't, as it always fucks with my head.'

'You're damn right I does,' Henderson said, 'it must have been a helleva shock to the system to wake up in Kemptown or wherever the hell you were, looking for your local boozer and your mates, and finding out the pub wasn't where you left it and everybody's speaking in funny accents.'

'Yeah, too true, mate. Fucking weird it was. Did my head in. I came back to Manchester right away, on Wednesday morning.'

'We know, we've seen the pictures. What did you do in Brighton in Sussex?'

'I told you.'

'No, you didn't.'

'My client is cooperating with this investigation Inspector,' Slade said.

'If you believe that, you went to a different law college than any lawyer I've ever met. Let me try again. Did you go anywhere, Mr Roberts? Did you meet anyone?'

'I didn't do much. Stayed at a boarding house–'

'Which one?'

'Can't remember. I went out to a local pub a couple

of times then I came back here.'

'Which pub?'

'I never forget a pub, a place called the Temple Bar.'

Henderson knew a pub on Western Road called the Temple Bar, but with so many inns and pubs to choose from in Brighton, there was a fair chance another would have the same name. If they could narrow it down, they could maybe identify his guesthouse, providing it was as close to the pub as he said it was.

'While you were there, did you go to football on Tuesday night and see Brighton and Hove Albion beat the league leaders Sheffield United? If you did, you saw a great game.'

'I don't like football.'

'You say that, but aren't they football tattoos on your arms? What's this one,' Henderson said, pointing to the Manchester United logo on his forearm, 'City?'

Whoa, he'd touched a nerve as Roberts's face went bright red; how appropriate.

'Go fuck yourself, mate. I've been a Reds season ticket holder for over twenty years. I'll kill any fucker who says different.'

Henderson paused a few moments, to let the suspect's temper calm.

'Mr Roberts, we've established you do like football. Now, after the match did you and three other men go to Brighton Racecourse?'

'Don't like horse racing.'

'Oh, but I think you do.'

'Fuck off.'

'Mr Roberts, your blatant obstruction and lying is serving no purpose and I must say, it's becoming tedious.'

'I object to your tone, Inspector,' the brief said, looking indignant, as if his client was guilty of nothing more than a traffic violation or shoplifting.

'Sergeant Hobbs, show him the rest of our photograph collection.'

Hobbs placed four photographs in front of him: the Audi Q7, a close-up of the car's off-side door panel, and two pictures of fingerprints, clear as a bell.

They took a few minutes to explain the source of the photographs to the satisfaction of the brief, but not to his client's satisfaction as his thunderous expression could wilt fresh flowers. There were other fingerprints on the last photograph and the colour drained from Roberts's face when he heard they belonged to his brother and two of his mates. After a hurried and frantic huddle, the brief called for a recess.

They resumed the interview ten minutes later and for once, Henderson didn't feel confident of a satisfactory conclusion. He knew there was enough to convict Roberts of conspiracy to murder Ricky Wood, although he would prefer the full murder charge. If Roberts wouldn't admit it, his fall-back position was to put pressure on his mates when they finally caught up with them, but he wasn't hopeful of getting to the bottom of the, 'this is for Kelly' comment.

'My client,' the brief said opening the second stage of the interview, 'realises he is in a bit of a fix. He hasn't been entirely honest with you Detective

Inspector Henderson, but he says he did what he did to protect his friends.'

'Very noble, I'm sure.'

'He will admit being present at the attack on Mr Wood but he didn't hit him or kill him and he will not tell you who did or who else was there, as he fears for his safety.'

'You're trying to make my job harder but we'll find out soon enough when we conduct further analysis of CCTV, now we know who we're looking for. But listen to me Roberts, I don't care if you were the one who used the knife or not, you and your brother and your other two mates, when I get hold of them, were all present at the murder of Ricky Wood and as such, you all, repeat *all*, will be charged with his murder.'

They went into a huddle again and this time he knew what was coming.

'My client wishes to help the police in any way he can.' *Blah, blah, blah*. He'd heard it so often he found it hard to concentrate on the actual words.

In summary, they would tell the trial judge what a good and helpful man Jason Roberts had been, and ask them to go easy on the lying toad. If he received a murder conviction, it would be difficult for any judge to go easy on a mandatory life sentence, but he said, 'fine' and let the charade continue.

'First question, what's Ricky Wood to you?'

'He's a fucking journo isn't he? They're all scum, the lot of them. Nobody gives a shit about them.'

'Why him?'

'He wrote something about a friend of mine.'

'Did he?' Henderson asked, mentally sitting up

straight. This was getting interesting. 'What did he write?'

'He's an investigative journo, right?'

Henderson nodded.

'He spent months looking into Manc drugs gangs but he came too close to one for his own good, didn't he? I'm not saying I killed him like, but that's the reason I think someone else topped him.'

'Which one? Which gang or gang leader did he get too close to?'

Roberts shrugged.

'C'mon Jason this could be a big help. In any case, this sort of stuff is all public domain. Ten minutes on the web and we'll read the article and find out the name for ourselves.'

'Ah fuck, I suppose so. John Kelly.'

Henderson's mouth opened as if he was about to ask him to repeat it but there was no need, the penny dropped in an instant.

SIXTEEN

Three former footballers who didn't make enough money playing the beautiful game, or maybe they did, but didn't know what to do with themselves at the weekend, were pontificating on the Sunday afternoon football round-up programme. They rubbished Brighton's mid-week victory over Derby County saying it was drab, but Brian Langton had watched the match on television and the 'experts' were talking crap, as it had been a good contest with plenty of goalmouth action. It must have been, it had prevented him falling asleep despite the anaesthetising effect of a bottle of wine.

He stopped listening and concentrated on preparing lunch. He never thought of himself as being any good in the kitchen, as Kelly was such a good cook. He didn't come in here often except to eat, but ever since taking over the domestic duties he realised he could do more than he thought. He might have left Varndean School with not enough 'O' Levels to start a fire, but he could read and everything he needed to know was on the side of a packet or inside one of Kelly's vast library of cookery books.

With today's culinary treat ready, he called the boys down from upstairs and laid their fish fingers, potato waffles and baked beans on their plates and placed them on the table.

'Oh great fish fingers,' Ben said with feeling, as the little trooper possessed the appetite of a Victorian slum dweller and ate everything put in front of him, while the initial silence emanating from his older brother Josh signified disapproval.

He sat down at the table five minutes after the boys started, but neither was close to finishing, as they were too busy yakking. 'What were you guys doing upstairs?' he said, trying to spark a conversation.

'I was playing MOH on the PlayStation,' Josh said.

'What's MOH?'

'*Medal of Honour.*'

'And I played *Mario Kart* on the Wii.'

'Did you both win?'

'You don't win on MOH Dad, well not for months and not until all the Japs are zapped.'

'You can win on *Mario Kart* dad, but I came fourth in my last race and I didn't qualify for the next one.'

'You must drive like your mother.'

The doorbell sounded, causing one of the dogs to bark but neither moved from comfortable positions in their baskets, the lazy hounds.

'Who's there?' Josh asked.

Langton rose to answer the door shaking his head in puzzlement. Both boys received a high quality education, something denied to him and yet they still came out with this crap; but he managed to refrain from his usual riposte which went something along the lines of, 'how the fuck do I know until I open it?'

He opened the door, expecting it to be another reporter who would be sent away with a flea in his ear, or a concerned neighbour/friend/council official, who would get less aggro but still be sent away. It wasn't Mormons or double glazing salesmen, as he could tell by the way they stood, their poor standard of dress, and the gaggle of blue uniforms and white coats behind them, busy unloading equipment from a large, grey van parked at the front of the house. This unexpected flurry of activity encouraged movement from the throng of photographers and reporters camped at the bottom of the drive and they shuffled closer to the house and started snapping away at this new and interesting development.

'Good afternoon, Mr Langton. I don't know if you remember me, but I'm Detective Inspector Angus Henderson and this is Detective Constable Khalid Agha of Sussex CID. I have in my hand a warrant to search your house and garden.'

'What? What the fuck's this?' He snatched the proffered document from the copper's hand and like opening a novelty birthday card, a chorus of little voices rose out from the kitchen behind him and chimed together, 'Dad swore, Dad swore, we're telling Mu-um.'

'Can we come in, sir?'

'Do I have any choice? Am I under arrest?'

'No, you're not under arrest. The purpose of this detailed search is to try and locate any information, which will give us some idea about your wife's whereabouts. So if you'll please stand out of the way.'

He turned and with a wave of the arm, ushered his white-suited and booted colleagues inside.

Langton walked back into the kitchen in a daze. 'What's going on Dad?' Josh said. 'Who are those people in the hall?'

The boy looked frightened and no bloody wonder with half a dozen people piling into the house, all dressed up as if there had been an outbreak of bird flu or Ebola and making them feel they were about to be quarantined in Porton Down. Thank God there were no near neighbours as after this, they would be pariahs, everybody convinced he'd brought shame on their tranquil piece of Sussex or added something sinister to their water supply.

'They're...they're conducting a search,' he said, his head in a spin.

'What for?' Ben asked.

He shrugged. What could he say, as he didn't know?

'For Mum,' Josh said. 'They think dad killed her.'

'You didn't Dad, did you?' Ben wore his heart on his sleeve and now his face was a mass of puzzlement lines.

'Don't be daft son, of course I didn't. They're not going to find anything. It's a complete waste of time and money.'

After stacking the dishwasher and leaving the kitchen tidy enough to start cooking another meal in three hours time, he closed the front door that had been left open by the white coats as they didn't pay the cost of filling up the oil tank, nor did he want a scribe or a snapper sneaking into the house, before heading upstairs to see what his taxes were paying for.

Most of the activity appeared to be taking place in the master bedroom, and he stood at the door his anger rising as they rifled through Kelly's drawers with rubber-gloved hands, searching inside the wardrobes and peering under the bed. He was about to open his mouth and ask them what the fuck they thought they were looking for, when a hand was placed on his chest.

'I think it would be better if we went downstairs,' Henderson said, 'and had a little talk.'

Henderson was taller than him by a good half head but he was bulkier and not all of it fat, compared to some of the fat bastards in the media business, his partner Emilio included, who dined like pigs in a trough. He still managed to get to the gym a couple of times a week with Mel and ignored the aerobic machines, except to warm up, to focus on lifting weights.

The copper guided him downstairs and Langton directed him and his young colleague into his study, a place where the boys didn't barge in if they didn't want a thick ear, unlike the lounge and the master bedroom, which at times resembled a public thoroughfare.

He'd hired an architect to design and re-model what used to be a 16th century farmhouse into a modern country house and this room, once a laundry room, had been converted at huge expense into a study, with a big oak desk, bookcase, leather settee, large LCD television and variable lighting to suit his mood.

It was comfortable enough for a workaholic businessman to use while toiling at home, or a mature student studying for an Open University degree, but it wasn't designed for either of these purposes as all the studying he did was on Albion's league form and watching the programmes his competitors were broadcasting on television.

He closed the door and sat down, turning his chair to face his two interrogators, seated together on the two-seat settee. It was all the home comforts they would get, as he wasn't feeling charitable today, so no cup of tea and biscuits. On the other hand, if he could remember where Kelly kept her laxatives, he might change his mind.

'I'm sorry to be barging in like this, Mr Langton,' Henderson said, 'as I'm sure you've got better things to do.'

The cop spoke with a Scottish accent, but softer than Graham at work who came from the South side of Glasgow, and at times sounded more like a docker than a graphic designer. The lad with him was Asian and even though his skin was brown, he was green through and through like Brighton Rock, and seemed overawed to find himself on a job like this so soon after joining the police.

'The process we are going through here,' Henderson continued, 'is something unavoidable in cases like this and shouldn't take long.'

'Yeah, cases which have been splashed all over every bloody newspaper in the land, putting oh so much pressure on your Chief Constable to do something about it.'

'It can't be helped, sir. The activities of yourself and Mrs Langton are of interest to all sections of the media.'

He grunted. He didn't need a lecture from a cop about the rights and wrongs of media coverage. In fact he didn't need lectures from anybody.

'What we are doing is looking for anything to give us some indication of what happened to Mrs Langton.'

'Don't you think I haven't looked and know this house better than you lot? Don't make me laugh, you're not here to find anything to tell you what happened to my wife, you're here to find evidence to incriminate me, so you can get me into court and say to the jury, he fucking murdered her and buried her in the back garden. But for your information matey, you'll find nothing, because I didn't do it.'

'Calm down sir, there is no need to take this attitude.'

'What attitude? Bloody Nora, it's not your fucking house you and your spacemen pals are pulling to bits.'

'We'll be as tidy as we can sir, but consider this. If we do find evidence of a struggle, a hidden letter, a scrap of paper with a telephone number written on it, or God-forbid, a body, our automatic conclusion won't be in assuming you are responsible. Who knows, it might be a delivery driver, a friend from school or a man she was seeing, and if so, he will be the person we'll be out looking for.'

He was about to say the chances of her shagging another man were about as likely as being hit by an asteroid, but sense prevailed and he was struck dumb. The copper was right. It was not as cut and dried as it first appeared. He needed to listen more.

'Now Mr Langton, can you tell me when you last saw your wife, and describe what her mood was like.'

'I've told this to your people so many times. On the day before she disappeared, Monday 5th September I came home about eight–'

'Is this your usual home coming time?'

'No, a bit later than normal as I needed to finish off some stuff in the office.'

He couldn't tell him could he? The 'stuff' included banging young Melanie on the sofa in his office as they were both gagging for it and she'd stayed late on purpose: paid overtime and sex with the boss, don't knock it unless you've tried it.

'What happened when you got home?'

The sanitised version or the actual version? Kelly nagged him for being late, accused him of seeing someone as she swore she could smell perfume on his shirt and they fought like a couple of alley cats. As a result, he ate alone. She still wouldn't let it drop and a rowdy argument developed and it was all he could do to hold back from smacking her one, so inevitably he spent the night in the spare room. He was lucky, her choice would've been the garage.

'Nothing out of the ordinary. I came home, we ate tea and I helped clear up. Afterwards, I sat watching telly while she talked to her mother on the phone, and then we went to bed.'

'Her mother mentioned the phone call. She said your wife sounded a little agitated. Do you think she was worried or anxious about something?'

He shook his head and threw his arms up in frustration. 'She lives in a big house, she's got two lovely kids who are getting the best education money can buy, and she spends all day swanning around her businesses and spending like there's no tomorrow on her flexible friend. What the hell has she got to be worried about?'

'Some people want and need different things, and women, in my experience can be quirkier in this department than men.'

What the fuck did he know about women? Tall and slim with untidy fair hair and a face shaved by a blunt razor, as he could see one or two nicks, he would bet he still counted himself lucky to be living with his first love from school. In Langton's case, he'd been with dozens of women over the years and there wasn't a man he knew who could tell him anything new about them.

'I wouldn't know,' he said, 'I defer to your richer experience.'

'I'm sure you've asked yourself the same question many times sir, but is there anybody you can think of, man or woman, who might want to harm your wife, or who's shown more than an average amount of interest in her?'

'I can't think of anyone and believe me matey, I've tried. She doesn't have any enemies, there's no one she talks to all the time, no silent phone calls, saucy birthday cards, blank valentine cards, nothing. I know it might sound strange for a former glamour model who once had thousands of admirers, but it's true. '

'Let's talk about specific situations, as I think it helps focus the mind. We'll start with the school your boys attend, Williamson College. Any problems there with, for example, teachers, the headmaster, other parents?'

He thought for a moment. 'Yeah, once she had an argument with a woman who said Kelly cut her up in the car park and nearly ran over her daughter.'

'When did this happen?'

'About two months ago.'

'The woman's name?'

'Angela something, I don't remember as I don't go there very often but it was nothing, mild car park rage I call it. She got over it.'

'We can find out the details from the school secretary. Follow it up for me Khalid, ok?'

'Yes sir.'

'Anything else?'

He shook his head. He could mention the ten or so of Kelly's friends who are always bad-mouthing him behind his back, but no, there was no point in landing himself in another pile of shit.

'What about her business interests?'

'There are four businesses, clothes, swimwear, jewellery and fragrances and they're all managed from the place she's got in Burgess Hill.'

'Any problems with staff or customers?'

'Now you mention it, she did say she sacked her Accountant for stealing and he blew a gasket, threatened her, she said. Yeah, what about him? It might be him.'

'We've interviewed Mr Hardacre and he regrets his outburst, saying he went out drinking at lunchtime and lost control.'

'I'd go and see him again if I were you, Kelly got really upset about it.'

'We'll bear it in mind. This is perhaps a difficult subject to broach with you, Mr Langton, but there are strong rumours circulating among some of Kelly's friends about you having an affair with your secretary, Melanie Knight and Kelly threatening divorce if she found any evidence to suggest they might be true.'

Good try copper but you won't catch me out. Melanie went through all this with them and the press and without much coaching from him she denied any involvement. As he always said, if they couldn't produce a picture or a video with his bare arse on view, primed and ready to make merry, they had bugger all.

'I hear a lot of this stuff all the time but it doesn't bother me anymore. These people are jealous and want to spoil what she's got, and pissed off because someone like me, without a fancy education or a leg-up from Daddy, is making loads more money than any of the idiots they're married to.'

There was a knock on the door and another copper appeared; shame, as he was enjoying his little game with Henderson. It was a woman, one too attractive to be a cop, perhaps they employed civilians to do this sort of work. She was younger than Melanie with a pretty face, blond hair, and a nice pair of legs on display.

'We're about to finish up, sir. The SOCOs are packing away their stuff.'

'Right-oh Sally, we're just about finished here too.'

She ducked back out and closed the door.

'You see, Mr Langton. I told you it wouldn't take long and you had nothing to worry about. I can tell by the look on her face, they didn't find anything.'

SEVENTEEN

The car bumped up the uneven drive. He couldn't be bothered getting the road surface fixed as it was almost a quarter of a mile long and it would cost loads of money and there were other things he would rather spend his cash on. At least it prevented casual visitors and the jolt it gave woke him up from the light meditation he always enjoyed whenever behind the wheel of a car.

He stopped at the top of the rise, switched off the engine and stepped out of the car. He waited a full minute to allow his eyes to become accustomed to the darkness and for his hearing to get used to the ambient noise. It was dark with no moonlight or stars as thick dark clouds were obscuring the new moon, but even though it would stop temperatures from dropping too much, it would still be a cold night.

He'd checked night time temperatures these last few days and they didn't vary much between four to six degrees, and this evening appeared no different. Any lower and the ground would be like iron, making the job nigh on impossible.

Hearing nothing unusual, he strode across the courtyard to the barn and unlocked it. Inside, he walked to the far end, sat behind the desk and switched on the video monitor.

The bitch was sleeping like a baby. He'd given her a larger dose than normal, secreted in a Sainsbury's cottage pie, with a sharp, tangy sauce redolent of the rolling green hills of Tuscany, or so it said on the side of the carton. If the clean eating utensils were anything to go by, she'd scoffed the lot, unless of course a portion was shoved under the bed or had been flushed down the toilet, but Kelly Langton was too dumb to think of doing something like that.

He watched the motionless picture a little longer, his hand involuntary rubbing the front of his trousers, before unlocking the door and walking in. He stood looking at her body for several minutes. She'd lost a little weight since they'd been together and it suited her, as too many business lunches and coffee mornings were making her chubby.

She wore the jeans and jumper from the wardrobe, a 'gift' from her predecessor and even though she looked good in anything she wore, after all she once was a bloody model for Christ sakes, he preferred her in a dress or nothing at all.

He walked to the bed and removed a ligature from his pocket, a fine strip of twisted, coloured leather, his constant companion for many years, and in his experience unbreakable. He'd taken it from the neck of an Iraqi insurgent after beating him to death with his rifle butt, as the ignorant bastard had called him an infidel dog. The religion bit didn't bother him as he was an atheist, but he hated being called a dog.

He lifted her head and wrapped the ligature around her throat. In less than a minute she was dead.

No little prayers were said, no doves were released into the heavens, and he didn't regret her passing. She had served her purpose and it was time to move on.

He removed her clothes and rolled her up in the piece of carpet. With the aid of a steel wheelbarrow, he shifted her to the front door of the barn before switching off the lights and locking the door. Pausing to listen and look around, he walked over to the car and reversed it towards the front door.

With the package safely loaded, he closed the car door and started the engine, the metallic thud of the big diesel loud and intrusive amidst the still and quiet of the surrounding countryside; but comforting to him as it reminded him of the sound taxis made when they came to collect him and take him to a new foster home.

A mile or two later, he turned off the main road into a side road leading into a village. Beyond the cricket pitch, the clubhouse, the community hall, and houses around its perimeter, buildings became sparser and the houses grander, the homes of rich folk who wanted to experience village life but didn't want their privately educated kids mixing with the local oiks and picking up any of their bad habits.

The road narrowed and the car bounced over potholes and puddles, ones he couldn't see for overhanging trees and the dark shadows they cast. Ten minutes later, he slowed and with the headlights on full beam, spotted the track. He eased the car into the turn, the road surface changing instantly from smooth tarmac to a rutted farm track.

Tractors belonging to a farm about two miles

distant used it but they never came here after dark. The track came to a halt at a five-bar gate. He stopped the car and got out to open it. The air felt cold and sharp like a smack in the face after the sanitised, air-conditioned heat of the car's interior, but he gulped it down like a drowning man and stood for a moment, marvelling at the dark, moonless conditions, perfect for the job and better than he dared hope.

He guided the car inside the gate and rather than head straight across the field to his goal, a small knot of trees about half a mile distant, he drove along the perimeter of the field in the shadow of a dense canopy of trees and bushes. He didn't do it out of caution as nothing in the surrounding area bothered him or made him suspicious, but years of experience taught him never to take the same route twice in a row.

He reached the point of the shortest distance to his goal, marked by a tall and broad oak tree which had probably stood there for the past five hundred years, and stopped the car and rolled down the window. He listened for the sound of a car or the rustle of footsteps close by, the smell of a man's cigarette or the perfume and lust of a couple of midnight lovers, but there was nothing except owls and their strange, haunting hooting, as they repeatedly marked out their territories like a stuck record. He turned the car and headed straight across the open ground, towards the copse of trees.

He knew the territory and halfway across killed the lights and drove on instinct as the dark held no fears. He welcomed it as a shield for his activities and to offer an advantage over those more wary. A 'gentleman farmer' owned the land and lived with his wife and three children in a sprawling farmhouse, out of sight and over a ridge to the north. There were a few other farm buildings in the area and over time he'd reconnoitred them all, watching them for hours on end, learning their routines.

He stopped the car and got out. Using a night sight he scanned all around. Twelve-thirty on a sharp, cold Tuesday night in a remote part of the county, it was unlikely anyone would be around but it never ceased to surprise him what people got up to in their spare time. In the past he'd seen lovers looking for a quiet place to vent their lust, insomniacs walking their dogs, and lampers hunting foxes and badgers with bright lights and designer Army gear. Wankers the lot of them.

He opened the rear door and pulled the roll of carpet towards him. In a practiced movement, he took a deep breath, lifted the bundle and hoisted it over his left shoulder. He picked up the rifle and shovel and headed into the trees. A few minutes later he selected a spot beside a large bramble and after dumping everything close by, began to dig.

Sheltered by trees, the ground was soft and emitting a strong smell of rotting vegetation and leaves. Half an hour later, a hole two metres long and a metre and a half deep, lay in front of him. He positioned the carpet at the side of the hole and like a conjurer exhibiting his latest trick to a rapt audience, gripped the edge of the carpet with both hands and in a single movement hoisted it high, and Kelly Langton tumbled into her new bed.

He stood with the lazy, insouciance of a graveyard digger, leaning on the spade to catch his breath, waiting while the excess heat escaped into the night from under his clothing. For a moment, he reached for his cigarettes to spark up but gave his face a slap for thinking such stupid thoughts. The light from a cigarette would act like a beacon to anyone within a two hundred yard radius, with or without a night sight, and the smell would carry even further. He didn't want to shoot a couple of lampers if they dropped by to see what he was up to, but he would.

He picked up the spade and shovelled dirt into the hole. When it was filled, he covered it with twigs and leaves, a job he enjoyed. A few minutes later, he stood back and admired his work, knowing if he returned in two weeks' time he wouldn't have a clue where it was. He headed back to the car.

He put the rifle, shovel and carpet into the boot and closed the door. With the satisfaction of a mission completed on time and according to plan, he drove away, a fresh cigarette gripped between his fingers and wondering, who would be next?

EIGHTEEN

Henderson yawned while waiting for traffic to clear at a roundabout. It was nearing the end of the day and it felt like it, not helped by a boozy session the previous night when he joined Gerry Hobbs and the rest of the Ricky Wood murder squad in a celebration after the arrest of all the suspects. In the end, the refusal of Jason Roberts's mates to speak, and when they did to deny any responsibility, were all for nothing as a search of one of their houses uncovered the murder weapon, and following a bout of 'let's accuse the other guy' by each of the four suspects, Hobbs charged them all with Ricky Wood's murder.

The squad started out at the Pump House, and after a few beers, moved to the Royal Pavilion in North Street before decamping to a Mexican restaurant close to the Theatre Royal. Henderson stuck to beer in the restaurant, rather than switch to the Margaritas and High Balls, as some of the others did, and this morning his head was very grateful, but he couldn't say the same for many of his fellow imbibers, as some of the faces he saw first thing this morning were not pretty sights.

'Where did Gerry say they caught the last guy?' Henderson said.

'Holland.'

'Yeah, Holland I remember now. Did he go there on holiday or did he find out which way the wind was blowing and scarpered?'

'Like Jason Roberts, he's an old hand at this stuff and as soon as he does a heist or in this case, a murder, he hops on the first ferry out of Hull.'

A song Walters liked came on the radio and, against his better judgement, he let her turn up the volume. It soon became irritating with endless repeated lines of, 'I miss you, I miss you, baby,' and he was about to turn it down and no doubt start an argument about free speech and women's rights, when his phone rang and the car's internal phone unit did the job for him and muted the awful noise.

'Evening sir. Sally Graham here.'

'Hi Sally.'

DC Sally Graham was normally a placid lass and a keen animal lover and bird fancier, but when excited, she made up for all the silences she suffered at work and in the pursuit of her hobbies by talking fast, he couldn't get a word in.

'Dominic Green arrested, well I never,' he said, when the phone call ended and the radio returned to playing music, albeit at a lower volume than before. They were approaching the roundabout at Waterhall and after completing the manoeuvre, he accelerated hard as the slow progress of the bunched-up traffic now behind him was getting on his wick. He glanced over at Walters in the passenger seat.

'You don't seemed so stunned.'

'I am, but don't get me wrong, he's a scumbag in

my book, the worst kind as he masquerades as a respectable businessman, but he'll wriggle out of it. He always does.'

'Not this time, not with video evidence.'

'What did Sally say, a woman waiting for her daughter to finish work, saw what was going on and videoed it on her phone?'

'Yep, great isn't it? I imagine she was a distance away from the guy he and Lester were beating up so I don't think there will be any audio but Sally seems to think there's enough there to convict him.'

'Yeah, but you know what he's like, either the woman and her daughter will disappear on a long Caribbean cruise or something dreadful will happen to her cat.'

'Well, a day which started out with me thinking I would never feel my tongue again or eat another Mexican meal, just got better.'

Henderson tried to keep Brian Langton's arrest warrant quiet with no talk about it in the office and no calling of friends and journalists or Henderson would have someone's head on a spit. When they arrived at Manor House Farm on the outskirts of Hurstpierpoint, it became obvious the story was leaked, as a large crowd of television people, reporters, and photographers were gathered around the entrance to the house. Henderson couldn't get anywhere near the place in the car, forcing him to park further down the lane but as soon as they stopped, a group of journalists lugging cameras, tripods, lenses, and digital recorders lurched towards them like extras from a zombie movie.

It was after eight at night and with no street lights in this rural place, it should have been dark, but anyone wishing to look at the stars and galaxies on what looked like perfect viewing conditions would be disappointed because with temporary floodlights, cameras flashing, and the Langton house security lights ablaze, he could stand against the car and read the paper if he so wished. Providing, of course, he wasn't being surrounded by a large pack of baying dogs, often incongruously termed the 'gentlemen of the press.'

On opening the car door, a furry microphone, looking not unlike a long sleek animal or the sleeve of someone's fur coat, appeared in front of his face but he wasn't in the mood for talking or feeding furry animals.

'Can you confirm, detective, is Brian Langton about to be arrested for his wife's murder?' The voice was bossy and arrogant and emanated from a long-nosed, pasty-faced bloke with greasy hair, wielding the hairy microphone as a medieval lord would his sword.

'I can confirm if you don't get your bloody pet animal out of my face and let me get on with my work, I will ram it right up your arse and throw you and all your equipment into the boot of the nearest police car.'

Henderson stepped out, causing the journalist to step back but the guy didn't move far enough and a push from Henderson sent him sprawling against the fence. The others beside him tried to get out of the way but they weren't fast enough as they received a shove as well. He collected Walters and the two of them walked in tandem towards the Langton driveway.

Moving closer, he saw two patrol cars, the ones he requested and hopefully in the back of one was a Family Liaison Officer, ready to care for the children and their dogs. He now wondered if two cars would be enough, as the size of the media gathering was larger than he anticipated and even though four officers were doing their best, they were strained and looked as though they were undertaking the hardest work they'd done all week. If they thought they were coming here to control a small collection of placid protestors, they were mistaken as this lot were pushing, jostling for position and trying to edge in front and when they couldn't get there, reaching over the heads of anyone blocking their way and thrusting cameras, microphones and data recorders forward.

They reached the door after a scramble and picked up the FLO on the way. He knocked but before the door opened, a familiar face appeared at his shoulder.

'Hello, Detective Inspector Henderson,' Rob Tremain of *The Brighton Argus*, said, 'good to see you.'

'Hi Rob, it's good to see you too but this is not a good time or didn't you notice?'

'Fair enough, but is it true Mr Langton took out a million pound insurance policy on his wife's life, only a few months before she went missing?'

Henderson stared back at him in shock, as this information wasn't yet released to the media. He was about to demand where he got his information from when the door flew open. Flashing warrant cards, the officers were ushered inside by Brian Langton who, using his considerable bulk to keep the crowd back, succeeded in closing the door behind him.

'Bloody hell, it's worse than Victoria Tube Station in rush hour,' Langton said, wiping his brow.

They stood in the hall for a moment catching their breath, while listening to the shouting and banging going on outside. What Brian Langton made of it, he couldn't predict, as his face was impassive but maybe it was a common occurrence in this part of Hurstpierpoint at this time on a Friday night, or perhaps he was just getting used to all the media attention.

'You can probably guess why we're here Mr Langton,' Henderson said, 'especially with the amount of media interest going on out there.'

'No, not a bloody clue. What the hell's going on? Did you find her?'

'Brian Langton, I am arresting you for the murder of your wife Kelly. You do not have to say anything, but it may harm your defence if you fail to mention when questioned something which you later rely on in court. Anything you do say will be given in evidence. Do you understand?'

'Fucking hell,' he spluttered. 'I thought you were here to give me some good news or something, but I didn't expect this. You can't be serious. I didn't kill her, I swear.'

'Mr Langton,' Henderson said, his voice sounding cold and steely, conscious he needed to take control of the situation as even though Langton was smaller in height, he was heavier in build and appeared solid.

'We either do this the hard way, or my way. There are dozens of reporters and photographers out there who would love to get a picture of you in handcuffs and looking as guilty as hell, and believe me the picture will appear on the front pages of every morning newspaper and damage your defence no end. Alternatively, you can cooperate with me, put your coat on and we'll walk outside.'

For several seconds, even though it felt like minutes, Langton stood there deliberating, and for a moment Henderson knew what it felt like to be a member of the Scotland rugby squad, about to face his opposite number, a giant Samoan in the All Blacks pack.

Then, with a shrug of the shoulders, he picked up the leather jacket lying across a chair in the hall and walked to the door. 'Let's go,' he said.

NINETEEN

'He's innocent, I tell you, you've arrested the wrong man,' Rachel Jones said as she stood on the steps leading up from the galley. With only her head visible, she looked like one of those animated talking head figures at Disneyland.

Henderson tried to ignore her and nudged the rudder to port and brought 'Mingary' into the wind. A few minutes later with the boat almost at a standstill, he got up, slackened the mainsail and made his way to the bow and dropped the anchor. By the time he returned to his seat by the wheel, Rachel had disappeared below.

It was a fine October Sunday morning with a constant breeze, gusting occasionally. The variable conditions suited him but seemed to deter many other sailors from venturing out of Brighton Marina, either that or their boats were already shored-up for the winter. For many years, he'd sailed Loch Linnhe in Argyll, a long sea water loch with Fort William at one end and the Island of Mull at the other, and at times the weather could resemble the North Atlantic during a violent storm, while at other times it was calm and settled, suitable for a children's sailing school, but it got him used to whatever Mother Nature could throw at him.

He bought 'Mingary,' a thirty-one foot Moody yacht not long after moving to Sussex. It was a ten-year-old boat in need of a bit of TLC and after spending every free weekend re-varnishing all the wood, renewing old ropes and stripping and lubricating many of the winches and pumps, she was now in reasonable shape. While the old girl would never win any prizes for its pace, she was seaworthy and more than capable of undertaking trips to France and along the coast to Dorset and Cornwall, voyages he often made in the summer months.

Rachel climbed the steps up from the galley, taking great care not to spill either of the two mugs of steaming coffee she carried, as she once tipped a plate of chilli over herself when the boat was rocked by a passing speedboat. After placing the mugs down, she dropped down beside him, her waterproof jacket making a familiar crinkling sound.

'You're getting good at this,' he said.

'What?'

'Rustling up drinks and food on a moving boat.'

She shrugged. 'I told you before, I did some dinghy sailing as a teenager and liked it. I only stopped when I went to university.'

'Well, take it for the compliment it's meant to be, as a lot of people can't cook or sleep on a small boat because they find it too claustrophobic.'

'Oh I don't know, I like the cosiness of it all,' she said, rubbing his knee. 'When are you going to take me out for a long sail, when we can sleep on the boat overnight?'

'Are you up for it?'

'You bet. A chilled glass of Sauvignon Blanc on the deck on a balmy summer's evening, I can't wait.'

'If, and I mean if, there's nothing big going down in Serious Crimes and you're still in the same job and haven't moved to better things as a result of your big scoop, we could go over to France in May.'

'Great, I'll hold you to it. I'll stick it in my diary.'

He took a drink from the mug. It was piping hot when Rachel put it down but in the chilly, damp air it cooled quickly.

'Did you hear what I said a few minutes ago, Angus? I think Brian Langton is innocent.'

'I heard what you said, but I'm trying my best to ignore it. It's what I do and think about all day and I don't want to do it on my Sunday off.'

There was nowhere to go and no rope-tying or sail maintenance tasks to perform, she gave him no choice and he turned to face her. She had been bombarding him with information about the Langton case for the last few weeks and now she was incensed about Brian Langton's arrest. Despite telling her time and again about all the evidence against him, he was having to justify his actions all over again.

'But it's important.'

'I know it's important.' He paused, trying to keep cool. 'Right. What makes you think he's innocent? Your newspaper, along with all the others out there, has been baying for his blood right from the start.'

'I know we did but we're simply reflecting the views of our readership. Andy and I believe he's innocent.'

163

'Who's Andy?'

'The Features sub-editor, the guy I work with when I'm involved in doing all this profile stuff, like the interview I did with Brian Langton.'

'I hold the Langton interview personally responsible for interfering with my Sunday sail.'

'What? Are you suggesting I can't be objective because I've met the guy?'

'Something along those lines.'

He liked to sail with an empty head and all thoughts of the office with its endless piles of paperwork and the repulsive criminals who inhabited many of the pages, forgotten for a few hours. This became the time he allowed his body to absorb an overdose of fresh air instead of the sweaty fug of an interview room, and for his hands and arms to be doing something physical, a welcome change from having his arse glued to a chair and his fingers cemented to a computer keyboard.

They had sailed east along the coast from Brighton and stopped in a quiet bay, overshadowed by the magnificent Seven Sisters, the tall chalk cliffs near Eastbourne, a comforting sight for many a homesick sailor returning home. Rachel was promised more high profile interviews, as the Langton interview had been received so favourably, a sub-text for her newspaper selling loads of re-publication rights to other newspapers, and they wanted more. He could now see his Sundays changing to this, the peace shattered as they argued about the ins and outs of a case they both were involved in.

'The evidence you've got against him is

circumstantial at best. I mean having a digger in the driveway doesn't imply he killed his wife and buried her in the back garden, does it? Maybe he used it to build a rockery. Did you and your colleagues even think of that?'

'Don't criticise my colleagues. In fact, our job would be much easier if your colleagues didn't hang on to our coattails and dissect everything we do and say in the pages of every newspaper in the land.'

'Don't try to side-step the issue.'

'I'm not trying to side-step anything. We have evidence. We found out that Brian–'

'Evidence my eye,' she shouted. 'It's weak and incidental. It's got miscarriage of justice written all over it.'

'Hold on Rachel, you're out of order.'

'Am I hell. Look at the facts.'

'Look at the facts? Look at your face.' It was as stormy as anything he'd ever experienced in the Channel. 'I think you're getting a bit too close to this story. It's hard to maintain perspective when you know one of the main characters so well.'

'Don't patronise me, Angus Henderson. Are you telling me I can't come to my own conclusions because I'm too weak and emotionally involved? Just because I'm a woman doesn't mean I'm naive and innocent, and I can't see all the evil and nastiness in the world like you men. You're talking bullshit and you know it.'

'I didn't say anything about you being weak but I do think you're too emotionally involved.' It was his turn to raise his voice. 'You're a journalist for God's

165

sake, not a cop.'

A small boat in the middle of a calm sea was no place to have an argument as there was nowhere to go, its lightweight doors refused to slam, and with crockery that didn't break on a stormy night, never mind being thrown against a wooden galley floor. In addition, with nothing to impede its flight and no howling wind to reduce its venom, the shouting and screeching emanating from 'Mingary' travelled effortlessly across the water, much to the delight of a couple of boats nearby who were no doubt listening to every word and taking bets who would end up in the water first.

Point made, Rachel disappeared below and bashed and banged while he weighed anchor and headed for home. The wind had changed to a soft breeze so it didn't require the captain to trouble himself too much about the boat's trim or to hold on to the wheel with a steely grip, and at times like this, he would think about the week ahead. It usually sorted out in his mind the priorities his team needed to focus on and the various places along the way where his input would be most effective, but try as he might, their argument got in the way.

What he couldn't say to her was that another piece of evidence had surfaced. It didn't arise as a result of searching Langton's house and garden, which didn't tell them anything new, but from the trip Walters and Agha made to Williamson College. One of the women they talked to on the day called back and told them that on the night before Kelly disappeared, she and her husband had a ding-dong argument.

The argument was about his alleged affair with Melanie Knight, and Cathy Holden, the good friend of Kelly's who called in, told them Kelly said to her on the morning of her disappearance as she dropped her kids off at school, she was making plans to leave him.

It crossed his mind, as much as it crossed Rachel's that much of the evidence against Brian Langton could be considered supposition, and if one piece was taken out and analysed on its own, as Rachel did with the digger, it could appear innocent but when everything was added together, it was incriminating. Many criminals were convicted on much less.

It also crossed his mind that his boss, DI Lisa Edwards, was new to the job and eager to lay down an early marker, hence her enthusiasm for Langton's arrest. In fact, the case was tailor-made for someone with her media background, as she couldn't make a presentation at a meeting of the Women's Guild or conduct a road safety seminar for pensioners without thinking through how it would be treated in the media.

With Langton in custody, his car could now be forensically analysed, the forest near his house examined for recent excavations and they were also taking a closer look at his business financials.

Even without a body, there was enough evidence on the charge sheet to convict him, but he needed to be one hundred per cent sure in his own mind if he was to follow it through. Despite his stonewall defence of the work done by his colleagues with Rachel, he didn't think he was there yet.

TWENTY

Whenever Amy Sandford drove, she thought about her 'To Do' list. Today looked like being a busy day with two viewings, a meeting with a difficult client, a mortgage discussion with–

'Bloody hell!' She pulled out to overtake a slow-moving car but failed to see the low-slung sports car behind, which decided to do the same thing to her. If she hadn't heard the rasping horn of the Mercedes SLK or whatever it was, accompanied by an angry middle-fingered gesture from the driver, who knows how it might have ended?

'God, did you see what happened there, Jen,' Phillip said from the back, 'we nearly crashed.'

'Yeah, truly amazing. We could have been killed.'

'Yeah, and Mum would spend the rest of her life in jail on bread and water.'

'Great, loads of TV and no more homework.'

'How could you watch TV if you were dead, you dopey munchkin?'

'Oh yeah.'

'Shut up you two. We all make mistakes now and again, even Dad.'

'Yeah, but he doesn't drive as fast as you do,'

'You're too impatient Mum, you need to calm

down. Take a chill pill.' This from Jennifer, the seasoned and worldly-wise eight-year-old she could see in the rear view mirror, smiling stupidly from the comfort of her booster seat. She had preferred it when they were both in car seats and couldn't string whole sentences together.

The last few miles were driven by an exemplary driver who stuck to the speed limits and kept to her side of the road and as the car glided through the open wrought iron gates of Leapark School in Cuckfield; she vowed to slow down whenever the children were in the car and save all the fast stuff for the times when she was alone.

She liked driving fast and many of the rural roads around this part of West Sussex were ideal for showing off the car's capabilities, as it was lightning quick for short straits and with excellent brakes for the sharp, steep corners where she would bring it round hard, her right foot dabbing the brake but ready to roar off again at any moment.

To Phillip and Jennifer, she was nothing but a taxi driver, as they didn't talk much to her in the car, except to criticise her driving. She walked with them to their classrooms before they both ran off to start another rich and fulfilling day and she wouldn't see them again until pick-up time.

She walked back to the car park in thoughtful mood, the 'To Do' list coming to the fore once again. She was surprised to see so few cars around, but the reason she drove so fast this morning was due to being late.

She approached her car when her phone beeped.

She pulled it out and read the message, her shoulders slumping as she did so.

'Ru coming in today, as if.

Ha Ha, only kidding. Hope Jen and Phil r ok

Rem i'm in meeting from 11

Love you C xxx'

It was a poor attempt by her husband, Chris, at making amends for last night when he told her he would take the children to school but when he woke up, he realised he'd arranged to meet a client first thing and couldn't afford to miss it. She was annoyed, as this was the third or fourth time in recent weeks he'd cried off, and the mother of the Cotter twins was pestering her to borrow one of her cocktail dresses after she saw a picture of it on Facebook. The woman was notorious for borrowing and not returning and with a dress costing over six hundred pounds, no way would she take the risk. This morning she was late and missed her but it didn't excuse Chris for letting her down.

She stood at the car door, considering what to do, reply or ignore? She decided to reply but should she be nasty, neutral or nice? He didn't deserve nice. She wrote:

You'll see me when I decide to come in.

Amy'

No 'love', no little 'xxx's and no smiley face.

'Excuse me,' a deep voice said behind her.

She jumped at the unexpected sound and turned. A man was standing there, close to the back of her car. He was tall, well-built with a tangle of light-brown hair and while his face was handsome, the skin looked rough and weather-beaten. When Kelly Langton disappeared, she read every scrap she could about her, not because she knew the woman, as she didn't, but some of the other mums at school did. She and her friends and much of the chat on Facebook and Twitter believed Kelly had been abducted by some evil killer and vowed to be on their guard. With her husband arrested, the shrieking and panicking tone of the messages abated but many still advised taking care.

There were many suggestions on ways to protect themselves including carrying rape alarms, Mace sprays or something heavy like a small hammer or a spanner. Now, faced with the very situation many feared, she froze in terror.

Her phone was still in her hand but what use would it be if he decided to grab her? Hit him with it? It was made of plastic and glass and would most likely shatter into a thousand pieces on impact. Call the police? There wasn't time and her fingers were shaking too much to press the buttons.

He edged closer, causing her to step back between the car and a hedge, and behind her a tall wall. She felt boxed-in, like a rat in a trap. It took her a few moments to realise he'd moved to avoid standing in a puddle from last night's rain.

'Sorry to startle you. Even wearing industrial boots I still seem to walk quiet.'

'No...no, my fault.' Gone was the confident, assertive estate agent, replaced by a squeaky, nervous character from one of Jennifer's Disney films. 'I get too engrossed in this,' she said, holding up the phone, like an ancient charm to ward off evil spirits.

'I know the feeling. Is this your car?'

'Yes it is.'

'Are you likely to be moving it soon?'

'Yes.' If you'll let me, she wanted to say. 'I'm going... now. Why?'

'My company are contracted to refurbish the tennis courts over there,' he said, jerking a thumb behind him, 'and we're expecting the delivery of the new surface, nets, posts and the rest of the gear in about ten minutes. Our supplier couldn't find a smaller truck so a forty tonner will soon be trying to negotiate its way around this small car park. I would hate for your nice new motor to get damaged.'

Sandford Properties in Haywards Heath was on South Road, sandwiched between a bank and a cycle shop, a prominent position near the entrance to the Orchards Shopping Centre. It brought in many browsers and regular customers, but nowadays much of their business was now done on the web and they were considering moving to a cheaper location.

Amy breezed in through the open shop doorway at nine-thirty, daring anyone, most of all her husband to say a critical word. It was her business after all, well half of it and it wasn't as if she'd been out shopping. She had been dealing with the children, *his* children. She sat down at her desk, put her bag on the floor and glanced at the telephone messages stuck on the mouse mat.

Her desk, situated in the outer office, overlooked the road through floor-to-ceiling plate glass windows. There, she and five other agents fielded telephone calls and dealt with any members of the public who wandered in. Her husband, on the other hand, worked in a plush office at the back with a sign on the door marked, 'Managing Director.' It was now closed while he talked to a client. Good, not for the client but the closed door, as she didn't want to face him just yet.

The desk in front of her was occupied by Nick Morgan, now shaking hands with a departing customer and making promises to call him. Seconds later, Morgan swivelled his chair around to face her, as he always did whenever she arrived in the morning. Despite being married, and being married to his employer, it did not stop the cocky Mr Morgan coming on to her, and if she was being honest, she rather liked it, especially today.

They worked together most of the time as she ran the letting side of the business and he was part of a team of two with responsibility for finding tenants. Lettings had grown fast in recent years as buy-to-let investments became ever more popular, giving them a good supply of properties which were snapped up by divorced couples, unable to afford to buy two separate houses, large international companies shipping-in senior executives for six and twelve-month assignments, and young couples and singles who couldn't afford to buy a house of their own.

'Good morning, Amy. How are you on this damp and dismal morning?' he said smiling, as he straightened his tie. He was a fastidious dresser, higher than his pay grade but he proved popular with tenants and prospective clients and as a result, he also earned large commission payments.

His hair was gelled into a spiky peak which might be trendy amongst the whacky hair stylists in Brighton where he lived, but back-lit with strong light from the front window, his silhouette made him look like a Mohican Indian, which for a few moments brought a wicked smile to her face, which she hoped would not be misinterpreted.

'I'm fine Nick, all set for another hard day at the coalface. Did I miss anything while I was out?'

'Well, I hope you missed me because I missed you.'

'I meant phone calls and messages, you know the sort of thing.'

'Ah yes. Mr Haynes called to confirm his three o'clock with you, the lucky man.'

'Oh God, he would. I hoped he'd cancel after being run over by a bus or contracting a dose of gastric flu.'

'And you've got a message from Martin Swift.'

'Who's he?'

He pointed in the general direction of the yellow Post-it note, using it as an excuse to sneak a peak at her breasts, where one button was undone more than usual to spite the occupant of the MD's office.

In Nick's spidery hand it said, 'Urgent' across the top in red ink.

'He insisted on speaking to you, which is why I thought you knew him. He asked if you could call back before eleven thirty this morning as he's going up to London in the afternoon for a meeting and can't be contacted for the rest of the week.'

'Fine, I'll do it. Anything else?'

'No, but can I say how lovely you look today. The skirt and top you're wearing really suit you.' He smiled and returned to his desk, the cheeky scamp. If Chris didn't show some more remorse, who knows, she might take up one of Mr Morgan's lunch invitations and make him jealous. She picked up the note with the scribbled telephone number and little heart with an arrow running through it like a homemade valentine, and dialled.

'Hello, Mr Swift?'

'Yes.'

'Good morning. This is Amy Sandford from Sandford Properties in Hayward's Heath. You left a message asking me to call you.'

'Yes, I did and thanks for calling back. I own a flat in Horsham but I'm finding I don't use it much so I'd like to rent it out. Also, as I'm not around the area all that often as I go abroad on business quite a lot, I would like your company to manage it.'

The word 'manage' brought a smile to her face. Placing an advert on their web site or in one of a host of local papers and free-sheets to find a tenant was small beer in comparison to the fee received for a managed service with her company responsible for rent collection, organising maintenance and repairs, paying utility bills, and dealing with any other problems arising.

'When would be a good time for me to see the property and make our assessment of its letting potential?'

'This morning, if at all possible. As I said to your colleague earlier today, I am out all afternoon and it will be difficult for you to make contact with me for the rest of the week.'

TWENTY-ONE

In frustration, Henderson pushed back in the swivel chair but it collided with the low bookcase, knocking several books and magazines on the floor. Instead of staring at the ceiling for a few moments as an aid to inspiration, he found himself facing the floor as he stooped to pick up the fallen items.

Since the arrest of Brian Langton, DI Henderson had conducted two interviews with him and despite the weight of evidence, he still denied murdering his wife.

'Yeah, but you've been around the block as long as me mate and you know his denials don't mean a damn thing. The trial's the only game in town. If the evidence works there, nothing else matters.'

DS Gerry Hobbs only came into his office to talk about one of his cases but somehow the conversation kept coming back to Brian Langton.

'Do you remember the Billie-Jo Jenkins case?' Henderson said, edging his seat towards the desk and away from the spiteful bookcase that threatened to fall on top of him one day.

'Vaguely. Before my time, of course and yours as well.'

'Aye it was but if you read any of the stories about

176

Langton in the papers, it usually crops up in there somewhere.'

'I remember some of it,' Hobbs said. 'Her step-father got done for her murder, but he was freed on a re-trial, something like that?'

'Aye, that's right. The prosecution case focussed on traces of the girl's blood discovered on his clothes. He said they got there when he bent down to help her after he found her injured, while the CPS claimed it happened when he killed her. Plus a load of other circumstantial stuff that in the end, seemed to colour the jury's picture of him.'

'I don't remember the exact details...oh I get it. You think because he got convicted on what they said at the time was circumstantial evidence, there's parallels between it and the Langton case?'

'Yes and no. In the Billie-Jo case they had a body and a suspect with traces of her blood on his clothing, and we don't, but the process we're going through is much the same. When we arrest someone we believe to be the culprit, we take our foot off the gas and stop looking for anybody else.'

'I see what you're getting at,' Hobbs said scratching his cheek, the result of not shaving for three days or perhaps the start of a beard. 'Yeah, sure we do, but there's still all the evidence to be collated and the CPS–'

'I don't mean that. What I mean is we don't chase down the last few leads we've got and maybe don't bother tying up all the loose ends because there's no point in looking for a suspect when we've got one locked up in the cells.'

'And you think we should?'

'I'm beginning to think so.'

'But why?'

'The evidence hangs together as a whole,' Henderson said, 'but individually it doesn't, which means if we don't find something else irrefutable, an iron-clad accusation, a good barrister will tear the evidence apart, item by item. Plus, Langton is so sure of his innocence, I'm starting to believe him, even though we know he lied about the argument with his wife on what became her last night and his relationship with Melanie Knight.'

'Yeah, but there's no other lead to go on and why bother, Edwards will never wear it. Anyway mate, I can't sit around here gassing all day.' Hobbs stood up and stretched. 'Ahh, that's bloody painful.'

'Done something to your back or are you relegated to the spare room again?'

'No, not the spare room, if you can believe it. She's been in a good mood for weeks, the sun shines out of my armpits as far as she's concerned. No, it's the gym. My first time back for three years.'

'Well, you better take it easy the next time, you're not an indestructible teenager any more.'

'Thanks for reminding me but it still hurts.'

'If you see Carol out there, send her in.'

'Right-oh, boss. Catch you later.'

Hobbs was right, he didn't have anything else to go on, but a few days ago, in an effort to exorcise the demons nagging at his brain, he'd instructed DS Walters to review the missing persons database and see if any other cases exhibited similarities with this one.

If nothing was found in the files, he would stop all the speculation and concentrate on finding that irrefutable piece of evidence against Langton. If they did find something, it would reveal an unpalatable truth - she had been taken by an unknown kidnapper. Considering the 'clean and professional' way that her abduction had been carried out; without a witness, without a phone call, and the car vanishing only to turn up days later, it made him think it couldn't be the work of a family friend or a business associate like Ed Hardacre, but someone who had done this before.

Walters arrived a few minutes later bearing a thick tatty folder in both arms. Henderson joined her at the small meeting table and waited while she sorted her papers into some sort of coherent order.

'Me, Phil Bentley, and Sally Graham worked all day Friday and a good few hours on Sunday on this, and I must tell you, at the start we all thought it was a complete waste of time, and I'm being polite.'

'Have you changed your mind?'

'I'm not sure, I've been looking at screens and churning numbers so long I can't see the big picture. Maybe once I've heard your opinion it will be clearer.'

She found the sheet she was searching for and placed it in front of her. 'As you know, mispers are a minefield, ranging from one woman who went off to Blackburn to visit her sister but forgot to ask anyone to look after her dog, and we started a major search for her when the stupid mutt began barking its head off every night, to the woman from Billingshurst who walked out on her husband while he watched television and left his dinner burning on the stove.'

'Aye, but didn't we set up a few filters to screen these sorts of people out?'

'Hold your horses, boss. I'm setting the scene. Now using the criteria we established of a woman missing for more than two weeks in the Sussex area, and limiting the search to the last six months, the computer spat out fifty-seven names.'

'Fifty-seven? That many?'

'I'm afraid so,' she said, 'but hang on, the news isn't all bad. We went through as much background information as we could on the system, looking for situations where subsequent contact was made, for example, a detective confirming she wasn't being held against her will but was unwilling to return home on account of some domestic strife, like our Billingshurst woman.'

'Thank God for small mercies. This is an exercise to clear my conscience, not to drive a tank through all our budgets.'

'We also took out another four, because of on-going criminal investigations, three for fraud and one for a serious assault.'

'Ok. How many does that leave us with?'

'Um, you won't like it.'

'Try me.'

'Twenty-eight.'

'You're right, I hate it.' He got up and paced the room. 'It'll take days, maybe weeks to look in detail at all these cases and interview the detectives involved. I hoped the number would be less than ten as we don't have the time and if I take it to Lisa Edwards, she would never sanction the manpower.'

'So what do you think we should do?'

He turned and stared at the whiteboard on the wall where he'd sketched a crude mind map of the major elements in the Langton case. He pointed at the board.

'We don't know the MO of our perp as we don't know what attracts him to Kelly and maybe to a few of these twenty-eight women, but we know the effect.'

'How do you mean?'

He turned to face her, held up his hand and counted on his fingers.

'One, a disappearing woman. Two, no passport. Three, few personal possessions and four, didn't take her car. In fact we can probably whittle the personal things down to only those items she carried in her handbag.'

'Ok, but how does it help us?'

'Apply them to your twenty-eight, see who left home with just their handbag and didn't take the car.'

'I could, but what if the same criteria are common to all twenty-eight women?'

'How could it be? How many left without their passport, ten or twelve, maybe? How many dumped their cars near a railway station, five or six? How many never used their credit cards, as many as fifteen, sixteen, perhaps? But how many did all of these things?'

A light seemed to go on in that pretty, stubborn head. 'Ah, I get it. We're not looking for one common factor but several together. I think I can see where you're going with this.'

'Good. All the studies say the same thing, kidnappers, murderers and rapists don't choose people at random. They select people using a specific set of factors. Some might make it up as they go along and if it works, they'll use it again, but others might have been thinking about it for years. So a guy raping nurses doesn't change and make a grab for middle-aged college professors or shop assistants. If he knows a hospital, a section of railway line, or a piece of waste ground, he'll use it again and again and again.'

'They stick to what they know,' she said. 'I mean there's been plenty of cases in the past about the railway rapist, the nurse molester, and the hitchhiker killer.'

'You're right, they do it to ensure success, protect their identity and facilitate their escape. It makes perfect sense because there's a greater chance of them making a mistake and getting caught if they use a different and unfamiliar MO every time they go out.'

'I'm convinced. The question is, how do we do it?'

'Let me see your piece of paper.'

She handed it to him and he walked to the whiteboard, cleared a space and began to write.

'She left her car,' he said, writing 'no car' at the head of the list followed by 'no credit cards,' 'no contact,' 'female,' 'age thirty-four...'

'Hold up. Her exact age isn't important. If our perp is trying to pick someone up, he's not likely to ask her for a birth certificate before he smacks her over the head.'

'You're right and it's the worst chat-up line I've ever heard.' He rubbed out 'thirty-four' and replaced it with '35-45.'

'Plus it will be easier for Sally and Phil to work with, as they think anyone over thirty is an old fogey.'

'What does that make me?' Henderson said in jest, but part of him wanted to know.

Walters bowed her head and looked at her papers, as if something there suddenly became interesting.

He finished, threw the pen down on the table and sat down. 'Take this list and measure it against each of your twenty-eight women and strike out any who don't meet all or nearly all the criteria. I like being right as much as the next man, but this is one case where I hope my theory is badly wrong.'

TWENTY-TWO

The sat nav directed Amy Sandford to Richmond Road in Horsham and Mr Swift's description of a 'Victorian gem sandwiched between two modern boxes' was spot on. She rang the top bell on a bank of three as instructed, and after a brief pause, heard the sound of footsteps coming down the internal staircase. A well-dressed man opened the door.

'Mr Swift? Hi, I'm Amy Sandford from Sandford Properties.' She stuck out her hand.

'Amy. Good to meet you, Martin Swift.' They shook hands. His grip felt firm and business like. 'Come on in.'

He held the door open and she walked inside. At first she thought she recognised him as one of the parents from school but she met so many people every day, it was easy to make an embarrassing mistake so her rule was to say nothing until sure of the facts.

'I bought the flat three years ago and had it redecorated a couple of months back but now I find I'm using it less and less.'

'It's a great location and the communal stairway is in good decorative order.'

'Well here it is,' he said, pushing the front door of the apartment open. 'Take a look around. There's a few things I need to finish.'

Some clients were quick to tell her about their property being decorated, meaning it saw a lick of paint in the last twelve months but this was recent, perhaps a month or two ago as it looked and smelled fresh, the paintwork clean and bright. It was a lovely flat and in combination with generous room proportions, large windows, and the railway station and town at short walking distance, it would be easy to let.

He was writing at the small table beside the window in the lounge while she set about measuring up, jotting down notes and taking photographs with the small digital camera she always carried in her handbag. She finished her assessment and sat down at the table opposite him and outlined the Sandford Properties letting management service. He listened and seemed to take it in at first pass, which impressed her as many clients asked dozens of questions and got irritated about the most innocuous details.

He was mid to late thirties with dusky features as if he or his parents came from a Mediterranean country and even though he'd probably shaved this morning, a dark shadow covered the lower section of his face. When he smiled, his blue eyes sparkled. If, at this moment, they were sitting in a taverna in Lindos, a trip she wouldn't refuse to make if he offered, she might say it reminded her of the gently lapping Mediterranean Sea behind her, but this being Horsham, the only thing sparkling this morning were the remains of last night's rain on the pavements.

At the end of the meeting, she lifted her folio case

from the floor and placed the signed documents inside. Another satisfied customer, she thought with a hint of smugness. She would dump the papers on her husband's desk and make him eat humble pie. He assumed he was the brains behind the business but she would show him she was no deadweight.

Mr Swift put his hands on the table and looked at her, causing her to stop what she was doing.

'You know, Amy, I'm really impressed with you and your company.'

'Thank you, Mr Swift. We like to think we try harder than the competition and that's the reason we've grown so fast over such a short period.'

'Good. Now this isn't my only property. I also own a large barn conversion near Billingshurst and without too much trouble, it could be altered to create a comfortable family house but I'm thinking of selling it, as like this flat, I don't really need it. Our family always used Hamptons but I think I would like to give your company a try. What do you think?'

'It's kind of you to consider us. Please tell me more.'

'Even better, would you like to come and take a look?'

'When?'

'Now would be a good time. It's more or less on the way back to your office in Haywards Heath and would save you waiting two or three weeks until I'm back in the country.'

Here was a chance to get one over Hamptons and Chris at the same time. It sounded too good to miss.

'No problem Mr Swift,' she replied, 'even though I

tend to concentrate on the lettings side, I also deal with sales.'

'Good. It's settled. Shall we go?'

They descended the stairs and went out the front door. Her ears were immediately assailed by the rumble of cars driving past, kids playing in a nearby park and the voices of people standing on a street corner, noises she didn't notice inside the apartment, either because of good soundproofing or she had been concentrating so hard.

'Your car or mine?' he asked.

'Mine, if you don't mind.'

'Not at all. Your car it is.'

If he hadn't agreed, she would have refused to go, as stories of estate agents being assaulted and raped by clients were perhaps not common, but crept into conversations at meetings and conventions and she believed if it happened, it was the agent's fault for not taking the right precautions. One doubt appeared in her mind: he was so good looking, her mouth might say something her brain would regret.

They drove past Horsham railway station, the Capitol Theatre, and Black Jug pub, heading towards Horsham town centre but before arriving there, took a left turn and joined the A281 heading south. She knew her way around Horsham and even though most of their business was based in the Haywards Heath area, she often went shopping there and liked the independent shops with a good range of restaurants for a leisurely lunch.

They chatted as she drove and while he was pleasant and answered her questions, there was perhaps something on his mind as he seemed distracted, but maybe she did witter on a bit and he couldn't squeeze in a word. When he said they were almost there, she started reworking her diary, and estimated she would be back at the office before one and could fit in one more viewing before meeting her annoying client at three, and still have time to pick up the boys at four-thirty.

At the village of Cowfold they headed west towards Billingshurst and a few miles later at Coneyhurst, turned into West Chiltington Lane. She had been to the area a couple of times before, mainly dropping the kids off at parties and yet again, it surprised her how rural and isolated the area felt with only a few houses and farms scattered between large fields planted with cereals in summer, and surrounded by thick woods, but not far from Gatwick Airport and Brighton.

A few minutes later, he instructed her to slow down and they turned into a small track, which she would have missed if driving alone. It was a tight turn and she concentrated hard to ensure she didn't clip the stone posts either side of the gate. She made it through without mishap and jabbed the accelerator to surge up the steep slope but lifted her foot off again as the car bounced and heaved over potholes and rutted parts of the track like a small yacht in a big storm.

At the top she turned into the courtyard in front of a barn and couldn't help but be impressed by her surroundings, as the barn appeared sympathetically restored and a neat fit into the surrounding landscape with new windows and new roof and the exterior woodwork treated with a matt black finish. It faced west and the view from the panoramic lounge window would be stunning over gently rolling fields with occasional copses of trees and not a neighbour for miles.

Sandford Properties didn't sell many farms or agricultural land as the business focussed on commercial and residential properties, but now Mr Swift's barn gave rise to an idea of a new agricultural and rural department, managed by you-know-who.

Her phone rang. She pulled it out of her handbag and looked at the screen. It was Mr Slimeball, her husband checking up. Well, it was none of his bloody business, she thought in a flash of anger. She diverted the call and put the phone on silent before returning it to her handbag.

Inside, the barn was sparsely furnished but that couldn't take away from the splendour of the panoramic windows and a huge vaulted roof above her head. What a wonderful blank canvas for an imaginative new owner who could, without too much effort, turn it into a stunning and comfortable home. He offered coffee and as this was her first rural property, she wanted to take her time and make a good job of it, so she accepted.

'I've owned the place for about three years,' he said, as he leaned against the table in the kitchen, waiting for the kettle to boil. 'I bought it with the intention of living here but too many other things are getting in the way and now I've decided to sell it.'

He walked to the kettle and filled two mugs. After giving them a good stir, he turned and handed one to her. It pleased her to note they had a matching blue

189

geometric pattern and were not a couple of freebies given to him by the company he used to empty the septic tank or his favourite football team.

She sat on a stool while he talked about the history of the site and later, how he wanted it to be marketed.

'I'll need to take your advice on whether I should sell it as a shell and perhaps be forced to accept a lower price, or let interior designers loose and make it look pretty.'

She put down her half-empty cup, it was delicious coffee, although she always thought the first of the day was always the best. 'I always find...find...find...'

Oops. That didn't come out right. Her brain wasn't connecting with her mouth. How could she be drunk, so early in the day? No, she hadn't touched a drop. Her companion appeared to be unfazed, perhaps nothing was wrong and it was her being silly.

'What I...I...I.'

She couldn't remember what came next. Her head felt like one of the jellies she made for the kids, random thoughts were floating around in there like pieces of fruit, none of them piercing through. She felt hot, with sweat forming on her brow.

The room started to move and sway and she found it hard to focus her eyes. His handsome head shifted in and out of focus, but he sat there smiling as if her strange behaviour was the most normal thing in world.

With fierce determination, she put her hands on the worktop and tried to stand up but as soon as she applied any weight to her legs, they wobbled and she collapsed on the floor. As she fell, it felt like she was floating, lying on a cloud. For a moment, she felt weightless and free and smiled at the beautiful sensation it created but when she looked around to see who else was lying on her cloud, the power disappeared and the barn was cloaked in blackness.

TWENTY-THREE

Mid-October, the sun shining from a clear blue sky, the sea twinkling with calm serenity, Brighton seafront looked bathed in summer sunshine to DI Henderson; but then he was sitting inside a warm car with the windows closed. Some hardy souls rollerbladed on the promenade, but the illusion would be shattered if he could see over the edge on to the beach; it would be deserted with no one resting on the pebbles to watch the waves or throwing a ball into the water for the dog.

'I hate doing stuff like this so early in the morning,' DS Walters said, hunched up in the passenger seat with the same grumpy face as a 16-year-old. 'Not until two large lattes are injected into my bloodstream and I receive the sugar burst from a thick Danish.'

'Do you realise that's the first thing you've said to me since I picked you up at your place, ten minutes ago?'

'I know. I don't do mornings.'

'Seven-fifteen is not what I would call early.'

'To you maybe, but I should still be in bed, and maybe not asleep but certainly not awake enough to start doing any work.'

At least he had control of the radio, as the said non-morning person couldn't be bothered to change it from Radio Four, as she did at other times of the day.

They drove towards Newhaven Harbour, where early this morning the police launch had brought ashore a dead body, found by the captain and crew of a new fifty-footer yacht. They'd been engaged in sea trials off Cuckmere Haven, a floodplain near Peacehaven where the River Cuckmere flows into the English Channel, and in some respects, the crew aboard 'Mistral' were lucky to have found it, as most of the time, they were travelling at great speed.

When they arrived at Newhaven Harbour, he half-expected to see a phalanx of reporters and photographers, a common occurrence on the Langton case, but he didn't see a single one, making this incident seem less worthwhile somehow. It was wrong to think like that, of course, as in many ways this new case deserved more attention, as it involved the death of another human being while the other remained a missing persons enquiry, albeit one becoming more suspicious as each day passed.

The body came ashore at a dock accessible from Riverside and close to The Ark pub, which thankfully closed at this hour of the morning; a gaggle of curious boozers and a dead body were not a good mix. The body lay on the dock, covered by a tent, and he could tell by the car parked there, a grey Austin Healy 3000 with the fabric top securely fastened, the pathologist was there.

Henderson stopped to put on his protective over-suit and boots and Walters did the same.

'Morning sir,' the officer standing at the entrance to the dock said to him. 'Morning DS Walters.'

'Morning Ed. I'm afraid it's too early to get much of a response out of Ms W yet. What time did you get the call?'

'Just after six.'

'Was it still dark?'

'Yeah but not pitch, I could see a bit of sun coming over the horizon.'

'Did 'Mistral' stay out all night, or did they go first thing this morning?'

'All night I believe, sir.'

'Where are the crew?'

'They're all sitting in the little hut over there, if you can believe it.'

'How many?'

'Eight. I kept them together as I reckoned you and Sergeant Walters would want to talk to them.'

'Good man. We'll speak to them after I see the body. I don't imagine the interviews will take long, so they'll soon be out of your hair.'

'Thank God, they're a painful bunch. Public schoolboys to a man.'

'The reason you're standing out here?'

'Got it in one.'

'Cheers Ed, catch you later.'

They walked towards the tent and ducked inside. The pathologist was so engrossed in his work, he didn't look up if he heard their footsteps, or maybe their approach was masked by the noisy hammering and sawing taking place in one of the apartments behind them.

'Morning doctor,' Henderson said, as he bent down beside him.

'Ah, morning Angus, how are you today?'

'Not best pleased to see this guy to add to all the other work we've got on, but we all have our crosses to bear.'

'I'm none too pleased either, the mortuary is full to bursting, what with the recent bout of 'flu and that bad smash on the A27 the other day.'

Boy Wonder, Grafton Rawlings, finished top of his class at death school and in Henderson's experience, after dealing with him for three months, was a top-notch pathologist; but he still looked like his sixteen-year-old self. His body frame was thin so any suit he owned hung loosely, as if bought by his mother at an oversize shop, while the glasses with thick black frames and long, floppy hair gave him the air of an Oxford don. In fact, if he didn't carry a medical bag and ID, coppers like Ed would think him a chancer and tell him to sling his hook.

Henderson inspected the body. It once was a heavily-built male with large hands, someone who perhaps did heavy manual work, but equally a man of such size and build would be a welcome member of many criminal gangs.

'How long has he been in the water?' Henderson asked.

'Going by the loss of skin on the lower torso and the deterioration of the facial skin which you can see is flaking off, I would say a couple of weeks.'

'You can see here,' Rawlings continued, indicating deep gouges on the arms, 'this is where I think his tormentors tied him with ropes, possibly to something heavy like a cement bag, and then dropped him into the water. Clearly they didn't go to Boy Scouts as I think the knots came undone.'

'You don't think it might have been a boating accident or a suicide from a cross-Channel ferry?' He said the words more in hope than belief, as the pathologist's manner indicated he believed they were now dealing with a murder. That was all he needed.

'It's not all guesswork, Angus, as I found this little clue trapped in his jacket,' he said, picking up a sealed bag with a length of rope inside.

This type of rope could be found on any yacht, grey nylon with red flecks, one that didn't lock-up when wet and very hard to snap.

'If you're still not convinced, maybe this will seal it for you.'

He turned the body over and Henderson was appalled to see a deep indentation to the side of his skull, gashes to the face, probably caused by a fist or boot, and knife punctures on both thighs.

'He's been tortured?' Henderson asked, his face aghast.

'I would say so.'

'Bloody hell.'

Henderson leaned closer to take a good look at the head wound, trying to imagine what sort of weapon had done the damage, maybe the round edge of a boating hook, baseball bat or iron bar. The face lacked any colour, as pale as a ghost in the vampire movies Rachel liked, even down to peeling flesh.

'Did you find any ID?'

Rawlings handed him another plastic evidence bag, this time the personal effects of water man. Using glove-covered hands while trying to move something inside a plastic bag was the stuff of party games or Saturday evening television, but he soon found what he was looking for among a soggy collection of wallet, keys, glasses, and phone: a credit card.

'It wasn't robbery, then,' Rawlings said as he watched him turn the card over inside the bag and hold it up to the light.

'No, it doesn't look like it.'

The signature strip was non-existent and the gold or silver tint, which credit card companies used to coat the embossed name, had been rubbed off, either through use or lying in the water, but the indentations were still there. Catching the light in a certain way, he could just about distinguish the name.

'I think I know this guy,' Henderson said.

TWENTY-FOUR

She starred in her own Cadbury's Flake advert, running barefoot through a field of high corn with the sun shining in her face, long blond hair flowing in waves behind her. The air felt warm and the flowers smelled fragrant as her white dress brushed past them, billowing in the breeze as she ran and ran, never short of breath.

In the distance, standing behind a wooden gate, she could see her husband and children. They were waving, beckoning her to come to them. She waved back but no matter how hard she ran she could not get any closer. Frustration built up inside as she tried to reach them. She had to get there. They needed her.

Amy Sandford woke with a start. She started to move, then against all instincts, lay still. By her estimation, it was mid-afternoon on the fourth day, around the time she picked up the kids from school. No sooner would they get into the car than Jennifer would be regaling her with descriptions of the lovely food she ate at lunch while Phillip would be desperate to tell her how he got on with his maths or history test but wouldn't be able to get a word in.

It didn't take her long to realise what was going on. Her memory of standing in the barn was clear, but anything afterwards was a complete blank, and then she woke up in this place. She hadn't drunk anything before meeting Martin Swift, so it had to be drugs, but what had happened next rocked her. While she was knocked out, she felt sure the bastard who had put her in here, had come in and raped her.

Her clothes were arranged in the same way as she dressed in the morning to go to work, but all three buttons around the waist of her skirt were done up and she knew with utter certainty, the top one had been left undone. The skirt had always been a little too tight and she left the top button undone whenever she wore it. Hoping against hope he'd simply been re-adjusting her clothes after carrying her through to this prison cell, or perhaps having a sly grope, a detailed examination between her legs, particularly along the inside of her thighs where she was prone to bruising, confirmed her worst fears.

She was on the point of losing it and letting out a scream to wake the dead when she saw the notice lying on the bed beside her, telling her she was a kidnap victim. Crap. Utter Crap. No kidnapper she ever read about in any of the crime novels she read at the rate of one or two a week ever raped their victims. It was a sure-fire way of getting caught. The kidnapper would leave traces of dental imprints, semen or skin cells on the victim, allowing the police to identify them and giving them cast-iron proof with which to convict.

The pressure built up inside and demanded a scream. She did so, but only into the bed covers as she did not want Martin Swift, or whatever he called himself, to know he'd been rumbled.

She now believed she had a good handle on his routine. At the start, she thought her falling asleep after meals might be because of boredom as there wasn't much to do in this poxy room, save for a few old magazines even her mother would have trouble finding interesting. She knew he was spiking her food or drink and came in afterwards when she was asleep to have sex with her. The pleasure he got from screwing a comatose woman she would never know, so he had to be a sick bastard, and yet he was a good looking guy who acted and sounded normal. AH! She couldn't get her head around how when she first met him, she'd actually found him attractive.

The day before, she'd ditched the blackcurrant juice and had drunk tap water instead, but to her disappointment, it didn't seem to make a difference as she'd still fallen asleep. She didn't want to get rid of the food as the rations were on the light side. In a way, he was being clever as it didn't serve his purposes to starve her to death, but it kept her on the edge of hunger so she would eat all the food, et voila, she would keep taking the drug.

The room, like the food, wasn't bad and about the standard of some of the two-star hotels she'd stayed in when she was single and had back-packed around Europe, with basic everything. A window high up in the vaulted ceiling provided light, and also gave her some indication of the time of day. The door appeared to be heavy and sealed with a couple of locks, and a CCTV camera was perched high up on the wall.

This afternoon she wore a dress, a bright floral

number selected from the wardrobe, and it drove her crazy, trying to work out how a fruit cake like him owned such a reasonable collection of clothes, all washed and ironed. As she lay there motionless on the bed, she checked the side zipper of her dress: it had only been fastened three-quarters of the way, and sure enough, it was now fully zipped. She felt disgusted at what this low-life bastard was doing to her. He was soiling her, degrading her. She turned her face into the pillow and sobbed and sobbed.

Ten minutes later, her pillow soaking wet, she sat up and scanned the room; at the bed, the wardrobe, the curtained-off toilet area, the hatch where her food came from, the bolted door, and then back to the bed. Nothing looked different or had been moved, everything was just as she remembered it. She walked to the toilet, splashed her face in the basin and returned to the bed and picked up a magazine.

An hour after it got dark, around nine or nine thirty, the hatch in the wall rattled and she wandered over and picked up the food tray. No way would she let him know she felt hungry. For the first day or two she'd run to the hatch as soon as it sounded, shouting, pleading, crying into a hole in the wall and demanding to know when she would be freed, but all in vain, as she still didn't know if he was there, standing on the other side of the wall, or sitting in a Horsham bar enjoying a drink with his mates.

This time, a calm Amy Sandford went back to the bed and fussed around with the duvet for several minutes before starting to eat. If he was there, still watching her on camera, he had a lower boredom threshold than anyone she knew, as this would look no more interesting than a bee trying to find the opening in a window, or a Party Political Broadcast during an election.

Today, chef's special at the Kidnap Cafe was fish and chips with a small carton of trifle for pudding and she relished the prospect of tucking in, although with the pangs of hunger emanating from her stomach, she was capable of eating anything.

To drink, the same diluted blackcurrant and apple juice she served to her kids, too sweet for her tastes and in any case, she wanted to test once again if she could avoid taking the drug by ditching the drink. She stood, hid the beaker in her hand and walked to the sink. With her back to the camera she poured the juice into the sink, refilled the cup with tap water, walked back to the bed and resumed eating.

Ten minutes later, she placed the tray on the floor and flicked through the magazine. To him, she was looking at a boring magazine full of knitting patterns and pastry recipes, but all the time her mind was buzzing with what she would do if the drug didn't put her to sleep.

She shifted to the middle of the bed as she usually did, otherwise she could roll off when the drug kicked and what would Swift do with her if she broke her arm? Take her to hospital? She didn't think so. She crawled over the covers and put her head down on the pillow and shut her eyes.

To her amazement, sleep didn't come. She felt wide awake, her mind going over the next stage of her escape plan. When she tried to move her arms, legs, head, or open her eyes, nothing happened. A silent scream went off in her head. *Stop it girl. Think positive and stop panicking.*

She realised he'd split the drug between the food and the drink, so if she ditched one she would get the other, very clever, but surely it meant she'd only received a partial dose? She couldn't move but perhaps the drug's debilitating grip would diminish faster, with luck while the cell door lay open and he was still doing up his trousers. There were so many questions racing around her head, none of which she could answer, but they stopped when she heard the door open.

The noise sounded indistinct even though the room was deathly quiet, as if her ears were stuffed with cotton wool or wax. The tray rattled and footsteps tapped across the wooden floor, as he picked up the tray and took it outside. It was the strangest sensation, like an out-of-body experience or living in someone else's body. She could hear and understand everything around her but couldn't move or speak.

Stories appeared in newspapers and magazines about hospital patients being given inadequate doses of anaesthetic and despite looking knocked out to the operating surgeons, the patients heard and sometimes saw and felt what was being done to them.

The door closed. Silence. Did he go out? In the distance she heard his voice, fading in and out, like someone fiddling with the tuner button of a radio.

'You're such a fucking beauty –ford. I can't believe it –all mine to do what the hell I like. You won't be– I'm sure.'

She felt a hand pulling at her shoulder and rolling her on to her back.

'What lovely legs you've got, and those– I think I'll– and see– wearing today.'

It sounded like a radio play when an actor filled a vase with water or drove to the park, the sound effects giving the listener the job of trying to visualise the action.

A hand ran up her leg. It was not a normal touch with all the nerves sensitive to the movement, and with an immediate awakening of hormones and an increase in blood flow, it was a faraway feeling, like a numb cheek after an injection of novocaine, or she imagined, the 'dead leg' Chris sometimes complained about after playing football.

He touched her thighs, squeezing and rubbing. She did not want this evil man touching her. She wanted to scream into his stupid face before sinking her teeth into his cheek and punching his nose into a pulp. *You bastard, bastard, bastard.* In her head she was sobbing, but her body failed to respond.

Five, ten minutes later, a loud scream filled her head, his face close to her ear, and then the rhythmic bouncing ceased. A dead weight slumped over her body, his rapid breath slowing as his hair tickled her skin. He rolled off, and listening as hard as she could, she heard him moving around the room, the clanking of his belt as he put on his clothes and the movement of the bed as he leaned over to sort her underwear and dress. He moved off the bed and moments later the door snapped shut.

She tried to move or open her eyes, but like a five-year-old child, she knew what she wanted to do but couldn't encourage her limbs to do it. Frustration and anger built up to boiling point not only for her incapacitated state and another rape, but because her chance had gone.

In time, she calmed and the boom-boom sensation in her chest slowed to a whimper and little by little, she relaxed. She felt tired, it was ten or eleven at night and sleep was often the best way to allow the drug to wear off, but before she did, she went over her plan of escape one more time. It had to be soon as she didn't want to be in here one minute longer than necessary, and as time moved on, the weaker the sparse rations would make her feel.

If she lost too much weight, would he still be interested in a nightly screw? If not, what would happen to her then?

TWENTY-FIVE

Henderson shifted awkwardly while seated in one of the modern seats in CI Edwards' office. They looked trendy and brightened up the drab, utilitarian decor but he would be more comfortable sitting on a slab of rock.

'You're sure it's him?'

'When I first saw Garrett's name on the credit card, I thought so, given the build of the man but I harboured a hope, vain as it turns out, that maybe this guy stole his wallet or something; but I've confirmed with a DNA sample and a call to the place where he worked, as he hasn't been there for a couple of weeks.'

DI Edwards leaned across the desk.

'Do you think his killers are trying to send you a message?' she asked.

'In a roundabout way.'

'How do you mean?'

'Well, perhaps not directly to me. I think Garrett got topped because somebody found out he's a grass, and they used it to send a message to anyone else still in his pocket, to toe the line or the same will happen to them.'

'Any idea who's behind it?'

'If I knew the name I'd be shaking his tree right

now but your guess is as good as mine.'

'This is where your priorities lie. Find him and lock him up, then you can sleep easy. Can you do this and Langton?'

'I'll need to, as he was my nark and I don't want anyone going down there and mucking up whatever's left.'

'I understand,' she said. 'Do you think your name got a mention?'

'That's the sixty-four thousand dollar question, but we know he was tortured, so we've got to ask, why else would they do it?'

'Might be because they're a bunch of sadistic bastards. I met my share of them when I worked in Birmingham.'

'Maybe, but I can't take the chance, I've got to assume they know.'

'I agree. Do you want protection?'

'From what or who, I wouldn't know, but no, and thanks for the offer. I wanted to flag it up just in case I went missing or I become the next floater to be lifted out of the water by Ed and the rest of the crew in the police launch. On the other hand, we might be lucky and Garrett's killing might be the end of it.'

'Why, because they think we've no longer got any intel on their drug shipments?'

'Aye.'

She regarded him with a soft stare. 'That may be so, but I won't let a bunch of hoods take out one of my officers, Angus, not while I'm in this chair.'

Henderson walked downstairs in solemn mood but picked up when he saw DS Walters standing outside his office, clutching the misper folders.

'Are you waiting to see me?' he said.

'My, you're good. You should be a detective. Of course I'm waiting to see you, hence the reason I'm standing outside your office.'

'Any more cheek and I'll stick you on checking overtime payments and time sheets for the next three weeks.'

'Do that,' she said, slapping the files down on the table, 'and I won't tell you what's in here.'

He slumped in the seat opposite and held up his hand.

'Truce. Let's hear it. Does your refined analysis tell us anything new?'

'It does, but there's been a slight change.'

'How come?'

'We are no longer looking at twenty-eight. It's now twenty-nine. But before you say anything, take a look at this.'

She handed him a computer printout with the nine key factors they agreed to be important in the Langton case listed down one side, starting with 'No Passport' and ending with 'Good Looking/Well-Dressed.'

Across the top were names he didn't recognise, but Walters confirmed these were the twenty-nine names of missing women she and the team culled from the missing persons' database.

'You'll see they're colour-coded. Where there's no colour at all, there's little or no commonality with the Langton case and that's true in fifteen cases. Of the rest, most tick one or two features but if you look at the ones highlighted in red, each one there has five or more.'

'Let me think about this for a sec. If there is no commonality, it means they took their passport and credit cards but maybe didn't own a car or took a taxi. Yep, I see how it changes things. So, why did you say the number is now twenty-nine, did you miss one before?'

'Another misper came in this morning,' she said, 'and would you believe, it's similar to the Langton case in just about every respect.'

'When did this happen?'

'She went missing Thursday, last week.'

'Let me see the details,' Henderson said, holding out his hand, his fingers snapping with impatience.

He looked at the report. 'Bloody hell. It's so like Langton it's uncanny.'

He sat back in the seat for a few moments staring at the page. 'So, we know of five cases where there is a strong resemblance to the Langton case as they tick most of the boxes, including this new one.'

'Yes.'

He felt a wave of mixed emotions. Positive, as it proved his theory and the time spent by Walters and two DCs on what they regarded as a wild goose chase had not been in vain; but negative as in all likelihood the wrong man was still sitting in a jail cell and whoever took Kelly Langton had done this before.

'Let's apply a little savvy here,' Henderson said. 'In two of the five cases, both women took their passports and took their cars but in all other respects, they were similar to Langton as they never contacted anyone, they are well-off and members of a gym, kept themselves in shape, etcetera.'

'True.'

'Taking a passport and the car makes them fundamentally different from Langton. With Langton, if we assume for a moment Kelly has been kidnapped, it looks like the kidnapper did it before she could pick up anything from home, which is why we found all these things in her bedroom that we did and why her car was abandoned in Pound Hill, because she didn't drive away in it.'

'With these two women here,' Henderson continued, 'they took passports and cars, which indicates to me their disappearances were planned and they buggered off for a reason, to get away from an unsavoury relationship or a situation they didn't like. They didn't call and left their old credit cards behind because they didn't want to be traced and probably took out new ones months ago.'

'Hang on a minute though,' she said, sitting upright, 'some people carry their passports around with them for ID purposes and others might take it out to do something specific, like open a new bank account.'

'I know. I needed to do something similar myself a few weeks back, but what about the car? Taking it indicates a strong intention to get away.'

'What you seem to be saying,' she said, 'are some of these factors are more important than others.'

'I'm starting to think that too and the only way to get to the bottom of it, is to examine the misper file in some level of detail and talk to everyone involved, but I believe if they've taken their passports and cars, it's because they intended to scarper. If I'm right, we should be able to eliminate these two cases from this enquiry and not divert our attention away from these three more relevant cases.'

'I'll sort it out.'

His face screwed up in concentration. 'We need to try and build up a picture of these women, who they are, where they lived, and how they disappeared. Fast. We'll need to meet the detectives in charge of the cases and focus our discussions, as discreetly as possible of course, on the list of key factors and how similar they are to Langton. I emphasise the word 'discreet' as I don't want to stir up a hornets' nest and encourage the press and Chief Inspector Edwards to come breathing down our necks.'

She nodded. 'The press would have a field day, criticising the police for arresting the wrong guy.'

'Don't I know it, and they were the very ones saying he was the one who did it. Now something you probably don't want to hear, all this needs to be done by Friday of this week.'

'Bloody hell, that's a lot of work. Why so soon, what's happening on Friday? Are you going away for sleazy weekend with Ms Jones?'

'I wish, but no I'm not. I've got a meeting with Lisa Edwards to finalise the case against Brian Langton, in preparation for handing the whole thing over to the CPS the following week. If we've got any chance of stopping his prosecution, or at least putting it on hold, we need to come up with some good evidence to put in front of her.'

'Well, if we've got what I think we've got, you'll

have plenty of ammunition because if Langton, Sandford, and the other two women were abducted by the same person, I don't want to be the one to say it, but I think we've got a serial killer out there.'

TWENTY-SIX

DS Terry Hibbert placed three mugs of coffee on the table before closing the conference room door. Hibbert took a seat beside his colleague, DC Holden, with barely a glance at the man sitting opposite. He lifted up a thin file, placed it in front of him but didn't open it.

'So, if I understand this right, Detective Inspector Henderson, you'd like to review our Amy Sandford misper case as you can see similarities between it and the Kelly Langton case that you're investigating.'

'That's about right.'

The meeting was taking place in Haywards Heath Station, a modern, purpose-built nick housing offices, a computer centre and detention cells, smack-bang next to the town's magistrates' court. The central Sussex town didn't experience the same level of serious crime that existed in larger towns in the region such as Brighton and Crawley, but with a young population, they caught their fair share of joy-riding, Friday night brawls, and knife crime.

Hibbert, a no-nonsense, straight-talking London detective, transferred to Haywards Heath from Bermondsey two years ago. The official line for the move was to provide a better environment for his girlfriend and her three daughters, but in reality he needed to get away from gangster Harry Lansdowne who had threatened to cut off his balls and feed them to a pet hawk he kept, for his part in nabbing and jailing his right-hand man, Billy Bonds.

Hibbert wore a mop of greasy, black hair over a dark face which he suspected was not sunburn but a throwback to his Southern European ancestry. The hands bore the numerous scars of fights, street brawls and difficult arrests as he always liked to be in the thick of the action, and he possessed a nasty, volatile temperament to match the rugged exterior.

'Why the hell are you investigating this case at all,' Hibbert said, looking up, 'with her old man banged-up?'

'It's a good question. There is a review of the Langton case taking place at the end of this week, the final one before we hand over to the CPS and I want to go into this meeting fully convinced Brian Langton killed his wife. At the moment I'm not. So let's just say I'm exploring other avenues.'

'Do me a favour. If there's a link between Langton and Sandford, it would mean there's a bloody serial killer and I never saw one of them before, not even in the darkest reaches of East London.'

Even with the difference in ranks, Hibbert's pugnacious nature shone through but despite the provocation, Henderson felt no desire to become his latest browbeaten opponent.

'It's too soon to draw any conclusions, Terry. The similarities I can see may be down to coincidence or suggest the two women have run away together. I don't know but it's what I'd like to find out. No bodies are in the mortuary, so technically no murder has taken place. I just want to take a look at this case and understand what happened, and for you to give me an idea of what you're doing with it.'

DI Henderson was in Haywards Heath discussing the disappearance of Amy Sandford, DS Walters in Eastbourne investigating the disappearance of Barbara Dean, and DS Wallop in Crawley reviewing the case of Denise Quinn. Walters' analysis of missing women revealed five cases but two were shown to be too dissimilar from the Langton case and eliminated from their investigation. Five was reduced to three, but three was still too many in Henderson's book.

Hibbert put his hand back over the folder. 'If I do this for you, maybe you can do something for me.'

'Like what?'

'Do you know anything about the Dennis King case?'

Henderson thought for a moment. 'Are you talking about the security guard who was murdered during an armed robbery in Streatham about a month ago?'

'Yep.'

'Not much, other than the basics. Why?'

'A group of villains strong-armed their way into a warehouse holding precious metals and Dennis the security guard is shot in the head for putting up too much resistance. He's a father of four children and elder of the local church, if you can believe it.'

'Have we caught them?'

'Not yet, but this is where you come in. An old mate of mine at the Met believes one of your narks was on the fringes of the heist and knows a couple of the main players.'

'Who's the nark?'

'He's called Wayne something. Lives on the South Coast.'

'There's only one nark I know called Wayne,' Henderson said. 'Wayne Garrett.'

'Yep, him. My mate wants to talk to him. Only talk mind, there's no question of him being in the frame unless he's closer to the gang than we think.'

Henderson shook his head. 'Sorry Terry, only last Friday we fished him out of the Channel. He had severe head wounds and knife punctures on his legs, leading us to believe he was tortured before he was murdered.'

'Aw for fuck's sake. It's the only fucking lead we've got.'

Henderson gave him a few moments to cool, then said, 'We think it was somebody local. Upset a Sussex drugs gang, most likely.'

'Fine, fine,' he said, as if to himself. 'I'll tell my mate.'

Hibbert opened the file in front of him with a resigned air, a man handing over the winnings of a bet but feeling somehow the other guy had cheated.

'Mrs Amy Sandford went missing Thursday last week after leaving the estate agents where she works, to meet a man at a property in Horsham which he said he wanted to rent out. The man, Martin Swift, called Sandford Properties earlier in the day and made the appointment.'

'She never returned to the office, doesn't answer

her mobile or respond to text messages and she hasn't been seen since. The car she drove, a white Audi A5 convertible, and the personal items she carried, haven't been found.'

'Who reported her missing?'

'Her husband Chris, about nine o'clock on Thursday night.'

'I take it you're looking for her car?'

Hibbert nudged the man next to him. 'Kenny, your shout,' he said.

'Ah right, boss. The registration number is on the national database and a description of it and Mrs Sandford has been sent to all UK police forces. Our patrol cars have been briefed to keep a look out for it by searching lanes and rural roads when they're out and about, but so far no luck.'

'I told you before Kenny,' Hibbert growled, 'where do you see the word 'luck' in police work?'

'Sorry boss.'

'We conducted a basic search of the family house in Crawley,' Hibbert continued, 'and at the offices of Sandford Properties in Haywards Heath, an estate agent business Mrs Sandford owns with her husband, Chris. Between these two places, we uncovered many of her personal belongings, other than what you would expect to find in her handbag.'

'What did you find?'

'Credit and store cards, make-up, cash, her passport, laptop; you name it. Everything except her purse, phone, address book and a couple of other bits and pieces.'

In his head, Henderson ticked off many of the

items on their MO list.

'This appointment with Mr Swift...'

'We've investigated it,' Hibbert said shaking his head, 'but drew a blank. A bloke called Davidson went into another estate agent in Horsham about four weeks ago and paid three months money up front and provided all the necessary references. The estate agent in question can't get hold of him on any of the telephone numbers he supplied and at this moment, our focus is on the references and finding out if they are genuine, but I have my doubts.'

'Did you get a description of Davidson or Swift?'

Hibbert shook his head. 'Davidson did the rental by email and Swift made the appointment with Mrs Sandford by phone.'

'What about her office? Did they keep a record of the call?'

'Nope. The guy who took the call from Swift wrote his number on a piece of paper and gave it to Mrs Sandford, which she took it away with her. We'll try to pick the number up from phone records when we get them, but I'm not betting my mortgage it'll connect with our man.'

'You think Davidson and Swift could be the same person?'

Hibbert shrugged. 'Could be, might be a lover, friend or a relative for all we know.'

'What about friends and family? Did she have plans to go away, or was she suffering from any sort of illness?'

'We've made a start,' Hibbert said. 'We've talked to her husband and parents at the school the kids attend.'

'Which school is it?'

Hibbert spoke wearily as if at the end of the day and not the start. 'On Wednesday morning last week, Mrs Sandford dropped her two boys, Phillip 11 and Jennifer 8, off at Leapark School before heading into work. She does it every morning and picks them up again in the evening at four-thirty or an hour or so later if they're at a school club or something. Her husband does it now and again, to give her a break.'

Bloody hell, Henderson thought, it mirrors Kelly Langton, but he kept his cool. 'Very noble of him, I'm sure.'

A hand slapped the file. 'That's all we've got, so if there's nothing else Detective Inspector...'

'One more thing. Where are you planning to go from here?'

Hibbert crossed his arms and creased his face in concentration. It would be an ugly face at the best of times but now it looked malevolent. Why a woman would trust him in the same house as her three daughters was anyone's guess.

'The next stage is to step up the public appeal and interview a wider network of her friends. Her old man, Chris Sandford, is doing his bit by sticking her picture up in the offices of estate agents all over the South East. He's head of some regional association or something, and like every bloody estate agent it's been my misfortune to meet, he's a mouthy bastard and them upstairs,' he said, pointing at the ceiling 'think he might cause us a whole load of grief.'

'Not so good.'

'Yeah, but if he thinks we're a bunch of small town cops who can't tell their arses from their elbows, he's got another think coming. I can play dirty too.'

'What's your sense,' Henderson said, 'what do you think's happened to her?'

Hibbert leaned over the table to face him. 'To us in the sticks, we don't assume every woman who runs off with her boyfriend falls into the clutches of an axe murderer, as you boys from Head Office seem to do.'

'Watch your tongue, DS Hibbert and don't make light of a serious enquiry.'

He smiled a devious little smile. 'Your so-called connections with the Langton case will mean nothing if we convict Sandford's husband.'

'What makes you think you can do that?'

'His alibi for the afternoon she disappeared is full of holes.'

'How?'

'He left the office half an hour after she did and stayed out for the rest of the day. I mean, he told us he went shopping before viewing a couple of properties but it doesn't stack up. Show me a man who likes shopping and I'll show you a bloody liar. He said he bought a take-away lunch but afterwards felt unwell and went home to lie down. Later, he called his secretary and told her he wouldn't be back in.'

Henderson walked back to the car, deep in thought. The Sandford case had many, if not all of the hallmarks of the Langton case, but as much as this exercise was trying to prove his reservations about Brian Langton had some foundation, he could not believe, or didn't want to believe, both women were taken by the same man.

He felt some sympathy for his Haywards Heath colleagues as Mr Sandford sounded like a man who might cause them a lot of trouble and would add to the pressure the detectives were under, but Hibbert was an unlikeable toad and he deserved much of the grief coming his way.

The police station was located close to the town centre and as a result, there were plenty of road signs directing him back to the A23. He decided to give his brain a rest from missing women and surly coppers and turned on the radio. It was still tuned to Radio 4 from earlier and he left it a few moments to see what came on.

It was Women's Hour with an interesting piece about the number of lesbians appearing in mainstream drama, a subject which stirred his interest as he'd watched something the other night when the heroine all of a sudden announced she was gay. The actors feigned surprise but it was genuine on his part as there was no sign of it before and he cursed lazy scriptwriters for trying to spice up a weak story. No wonder he didn't watch much television.

His phone rang and brought this small dose of R&R to a close.

'Angus, Lisa Edwards here. Where are you?'

'On my way back to the office. I was at Haywards Heath nick.'

'Do you know DCI James there?'

'I do, but I was talking to that poor specimen of a human being, DS Hibbert.'

'I don't know him but James called me

complaining in words of one syllable about you muscling in on one of their cases, and he's not too happy about it.'

Henderson knew James to be a perfect companion of Hibbert, taciturn, aggressive and a man who climbed the slippery slope with a record number of convictions and a reputation for clearing up low-level crime with a heavy hand.

'It takes a lot to make DCI James happy,' Henderson said.

'I realise there's a bit of bluster and chest thumping going on but what are you doing?'

He explained the purpose of his trip but steered clear of mentioning what Walters and Wallop were doing.

'What do you mean there's a connection between the two cases?'

'The similarities between the Langton and Sandford cases are uncanny, down to how the women look, their background, age.'

'Good God.'

'I'm not jumping to conclusions and suggesting there's a serial abductor or killer but...'

'I bloody hope not.'

'I'm not ruling it out either, although the connections between the two women might also suggest they did this together, or the person assisting them used the same method to help them disappear.'

'I understand. I won't ask how you found this out, you can save your explanation until we meet on Friday, but Angus, no word of this must reach our lords and masters and nothing, repeat nothing must appear in the press. Am I being clear?'

'As day.'

'The slightest word and it would generate scepticism and panic in equal measure, the fall-out of which would see your head rolling down the street a minute or so before mine.'

TWENTY-SEVEN

'So this nark of yours not only knew about the drug shipments coming into Shoreham,' DS Walters said, 'but he also knew something about an armed robbery in Streatham and the murder of a security guard. Where did you find him, Criminals Inc.?'

'I'm not at liberty to divulge my operating methods,' Henderson said, half in jest.

'Fair enough but he did involve himself with some heavy characters and any one of them might have been tempted to chuck him overboard in concrete underpants.'

'You have an interesting way with words.'

'Maybe I'm dyslectic, it's all the rage nowadays.'

'Not being able to spell doesn't make you dyslectic, thick maybe, but nothing medical.'

'Cheeky git,' she said, punching his arm, 'but the guys who dropped him in the drink must be bloody incompetent for the ropes to have come loose like they did.'

'If you want to get rid of somebody, the sea's a great place to do it as there's a hundred and one things that could happen.'

'Do I detect another sailing story?'

'No straight up, the body could be churned up in

the propellers of a passing ship, get nibbled by fishes, get battered by waves and if left undisturbed, it would float close to the surface for a couple of weeks until all the internal gasses dissipate and then sink forever. Not to mention it's a harsh environment and it would be more or less unrecognisable as a person in a few more weeks.'

'So we're looking for a couple of incompetent violent thugs with a good knowledge of the sea, who can sail a boat. In which case, the pubs around Shoreham Harbour would be a good starting point.'

'No, my cynical sidekick, we're looking for a couple of violent thugs who can't tie a knot and if this doesn't mark them out as non-sailing types, I don't know what does.'

Henderson turned off Kingsway into Wharf Road, and Shoreham Harbour lay out in front of them. Henderson felt quite at home among the sights and smells of the dockside, although most dockers would feel they were at the other end of the spectrum from those who inhabited the marinas and quays along the South Coast, from the amount of money they took home in their pay packet to the selection of their favourite tipple at the bar.

They found the offices and warehouses of the Landman Group and after parking the car, made their way inside. In common with many office buildings, there was the ubiquitous secretary sitting outside the manager's office, an abundance of tall filing cabinets, photocopiers, coffee machines and people tapping at computer terminals, but it felt different from a knowledge business like Jack Monaghan's software company.

This place was a little rough at the edges and lacked many finishing touches, with no art-deco pictures on the wall, thick-pile carpets, high-tech computers or flash suits, as Shoreham was a working dock. It would not be unusual for the manager to don his sou'wester and hard hat before making his way outside to solve another small problem, or for any of his people to walk in with muddy boots and wet jackets and bring another one for him to deal with.

Bill Hegarty had been site manager in Shoreham for twenty-seven years, he was married with one daughter studying History at Lancaster University, he was retiring in six months time and intended seeing out his final days in an apartment he owned in the Algarve. Henderson discovered this by not saying a word, the information volunteered by the garrulous site manager a few minutes after meeting him.

'What can you tell us about Wayne Garrett?' Henderson said, when he spotted a gap in another long story.

'Wayne?' He picked up a file from his desk and shouted, 'Claire.'

The phone outside slammed down with a heavy thump and the pleasant eighteen-year-old who earlier, greeted them with a smile and offered them coffee, stomped in, her face bearing the scowl of an angry cat.

'What?'

'Can you make a copy of Wayne's file for these two police officers here?'

She grabbed at the papers but he didn't let go. 'I

don't imagine it should take long, so don't be all day about it.'

She snatched the file and strutted out of his office before slamming the door hard, shaking the thin walls and making Hegarty flinch.

'Wayne, what can I tell you about Wayne? He started here about ten years ago as a general worker in the days when a lot of what we did involved manual labour, lifting planks of wood and bags of cement out of ships, hand to hand. Nowadays, there's so much machinery we can lift cargoes straight off a ship without any manual intervention and the cargoes themselves are better packaged. About six or seven years ago, Wayne started driving a fork-lift around the warehouse before moving up to driving one of our delivery trucks, the job he did before he disappeared.

'What you must realise Inspector, is a lot of what we do involves aggregates, rubble and materials for the building trade and it can be a rough place to be, so it's good if there are a few tough guys like Wayne around to keep things hunky dory. You see when you're dealing with building firms...'

Henderson tuned out for a minute or two until interrupted by the return of Claire. She slapped a copy of the file on the desk and then the original before turning and leaving the room without saying a word.

'She's my niece,' Hegarty said, after she slammed the door shut once again. 'I promised my sister I'd give her a job but I'm starting to regret it now. She's always been a difficult kid and it got worse when her father left home, but what can you do when it's family?' He handed the copy to Henderson and put the original into the out-tray. Best of luck getting Claire to file it.

'I'm sorry Wayne's gone, as he was a good worker and took no crap from anybody, but in some ways I'm not surprised.'

'Why do you say that?'

'Well, I'm told he mixed with some unsavoury characters. I mean many of them around here do, as they see themselves as Dirty Harry types, invulnerable to death and don't care who they upset. Every now and then a couple of hoods turn up looking for some guy or another but we get rid of them without any bother as we've got more tough guys than them.'

They left Hegarty's office ten minutes later and stepped outside, the early evening sunshine no longer in evidence and soon it would be dark.

'Carol, I want you to put together a small team and take statements from the list of Wayne's friends and associates that Hegarty gave us. It shouldn't take long as it's not a very long list.'

'It's not surprising as he didn't sound like a nice person and I'm not looking forward to meeting some of the people he used to hang around with.'

'Hey detectives.'

Henderson glanced to the left where a cigarette glowed in the shadow of a warehouse. He felt wary as Wayne Garrett could have been murdered by someone at Shoreham Harbour, perhaps a disgruntled colleague or the husband of one of the unfaithful wives Garrett was alleged to have bedded, and what better place to find a boat?

He walked towards the darkened doorway.

'Yeah?

'Are you cops here about Wayne Garrett's disappearance?'

'Who wants to know?'

'I'm his best mate, Des Raynor.'

'I'm sorry to tell you Des, but we're now investigating his murder.'

'He's been murdered? Aw fuck.'

The man bent double as if suffering stomach cramps. Henderson explained what little he knew.

'He's a mate of yours?' Henderson asked after a few minutes.

'Yeah,' he said, lighting another cigarette with shaking hands. 'We worked together, drank together, went stock car racing together.'

'He got involved in something illegal, didn't he?'

Through deep drags of the cigarette lighting up his face, Henderson knew Raynor was wrestling with some serious issues.

'He liked to think of himself as a gangster and hung around with some nasty types but they liked him and he did stuff for them, so why would they kill him?'

'What sorts of things did he get involved in?'

'He took money to let certain cargoes go, kinda under the radar.'

'What cargoes, drugs, guns, illegal immigrants?'

'Nah, never that. Drugs. Heroin and cocaine mainly.'

'And you think they killed him for something he did or what he knew? Did he deal?'

'Nah, nah he didn't like drugs. Do you remember a big shipment of stuff coming in from Pakistan a few weeks back that the cops nabbed? You're local cops, some of your people must have done it.'

'It was me. I planned the raid and by rights, I should have been on it but something else got in the way.'

'Wayne tipped the wink to one of your lot, that's what got him killed, I'm sure.'

'Tipped the wink to who?'

'One of your lot, DI Henderson, I think is his name.'

'You think he was killed for what? Telling Henderson about the shipment?'

'Got it in one.'

'Whoever missed out on their packages must have been pretty upset to kill him.'

'I'm thinking that too.'

'You know the next question. Who are we talking about?'

'I can't tell you or it'll be me you'll next find floating in the drink.'

Henderson couldn't argue with his logic although it was now looking like a toss between himself and Raynor as to who would be first.

'C'mon mate. The guy who did this will be as cagey as hell now and watching your every movement like a hawk. Is this the way you want to live your life? If you don't do it for yourself, do it for your friend.'

A long couple of minutes passed as he lit another fag and inhaled it deep into his lungs as if short of nicotine or he wanted to speed up the arrival of an early grave.

'If I tell you, is it enough to put this guy away?' he

said.

'I don't think so, we can let the next shipment go through and nab them with their dirty mitts all over it. There's no way anyone could wriggle out of that.'

He paused a few minutes more.

'His name is Dominic Green,' he said.

TWENTY-EIGHT

On Thursday morning at eight, Henderson met with DS Walters and DS Wallop in his office. His fourth coffee of the morning lay empty as did half of the bottle of water beside him. The hangover thumping inside his head had forced him to eat paracetamol instead of cereal for breakfast and left him with an unquenchable thirst.

Last night, he and several members of the Wayne Garrett murder team got together to plan the downfall of Dominic Green, armed with Henderson's report on what Garrett's friend, Des Raynor, agreed he would do. They'd arrested Green a couple of weeks ago on an assault charge and while he was subsequently freed on bail, awaiting a hearing that would leave him with a fine and another notch on his criminal record, what they were cooking up last night would give him some serious jail time.

Feeling buoyed at the prospect of locking Brighton's top criminal away for a long stretch, he called Rachel. Their disagreement aboard 'Mingary' had happened two weeks ago and despite calling her twice and leaving a conciliatory message on both occasions, she hadn't called back.

It was decision time, make or break. At forty-three

with one divorce under his belt and too many years in the police, he was becoming too selfish and cynical to be bothered with fragile, pouting women and if she didn't want to know, he was prepared to let her go and return to life on his own. To his surprise, she agreed they were both being silly and decided to get together for a drink and resolve their differences.

There came a point in the evening when he wanted to go home for a good night's kip but she dragged him back to her place and insisted on making love until the wee small hours. It became a raucous and exhausting affair and he couldn't be sure if his hoarse voice this morning was due to this, or trying to hold a conversation in Yates Bar earlier, as it was packed to the rafters and extremely noisy.

While downing a couple of pain relief tablets in the bathroom of her flat she said, from a provocative position on the bed, it was a shame it wasn't Viagra as she could call in sick and make a day of it. The face in the mirror stared back mortified, as if it wasn't haggard enough without adding any more lines and crevices and even now, it tired him out thinking about it.

Walters brought him back to reality as she kicked off the meeting by describing her visit to Eastbourne. Five months ago, Barbara Dean went for a walk along the seafront and had not been seen since, but unlike Langton and Sandford, her passport was never found. Walters placed a photograph of the woman in the middle of the table.

In a picture, obviously taken on holiday, she wore a light floral dress and was standing in front of a tree-fringed swimming pool, under an azure blue and cloudless sky. It couldn't be Eastbourne, as even though it was occasionally blessed in the summer with blue skies, he had been there plenty of times and had never seen any palm trees or bougainvillea.

In spite of the tan, the simple but elegant clothes, and graceful stance, she looked different from both Langton and Sandford. She was a big lady, six or seven stone overweight with a plain face and uneven teeth. He stayed silent and let Walters continue.

'There are many similarities with the Langton case such as no phone calls or emails and she recently joined a gym, but that's where it stops. The Eastbourne detectives believe she did a runner because of her husband's drinking, and with no close friends or relatives in the area, she could cut loose and start afresh without a problem, hence the missing passport. In any case,' she said, pointing at the picture, 'who would want to abduct someone like her?'

'Oh I don't know,' Henderson said, sounding more playful than he felt. 'I like a big woman. How about you Harry?'

'Now you mention it, she reminds me of some of the girls we used to have working on my dad's farm over at Fakenham in the summer. I liked a rumble in the hay, I did. The bigger the better, I always said.'

'Come off it guys, quit mucking about,' Walters said. 'You know what I mean, even from a logistical point of view, it would be difficult to bundle a woman as large as her into a getaway car.'

'I agree,' Henderson said. 'Taking her passport suggests to me she's done a runner.'

'There hasn't been any activity on her credit cards or phone,' Wallop said, 'surely that's significant?'

'Perhaps not,' Henderson said. 'She could have bought a new Pay-As-You-Go phone and if the disappearance was planned a few months in advance, she probably signed up for a couple of new credit cards as well.' He looked at Walters for confirmation and she nodded. 'Ok we agree, take her out. Harry, let's hear your report.'

'I was in Crawley investigating the disappearance of a woman called Denise Quinn,' Wallop said. 'She was a swimming instructor and life guard from Haywards Heath, who worked at The Triangle sports centre in Burgess Hill and the K2 sports centre in Crawley.'

He handed out copies of her photograph. It showed an elegant, good-looking woman with shoulder-length blond hair, much in the style of Langton and Sandford.

'In January this year, she finished work at K2 about two in the afternoon and hasn't been seen since, despite numerous appeals in the media and an active campaign by her banker husband John.'

'I remember hearing the story,' Henderson said. 'I assumed as I didn't hear anything more, there must have been a happy ending.'

'No, there wasn't. In terms of our MO list, she ticks nearly every box as she left her passport, there's been no activity on her phone or spending on her credit cards, and they found her car a week later.'

'You're right,' Walters said, 'so she does.'

'Not only the MO,' Henderson said, 'look at her

picture. You could take her for Kelly Langton's sister.'

'She and her husband got on well,' Wallop continued, 'and apart from one or two rumblings at the start of the investigation when they took him in for questioning, he's never been a suspect.'

'Excellent work Harry,' Henderson said. He pushed his chair back and paced the room, to help him think and try and shake off the nauseous feeling in his stomach.

'I don't think it's significant she and her husband seemed to get on well, while Kelly and Brian Langton argued and Amy had a minor disagreement with John...'

'Chris,' she said. 'Amy's husband is called Chris.'

'Ah right, Chris. You see, I think our man got lucky as Kelly's husband is such a bastard and Amy Sandford's husband thinks more of his work than his wife and children, so perhaps they were distracted when he approached. I mean, how could he know such a thing?'

'He could be a common friend,' she said, 'taking advantage of a time when the women felt undervalued or vulnerable.'

'True, but he or she would show up in the witness interviews.'

'You're right and they didn't.'

'I think the key items in his selection criteria are how they look, how he meets them and where he picks them up.'

'So you're convinced there is a serial abductor?' Walters said.

'Let me tell you about Amy Sandford first before

we talk about serial abductors.'

Henderson outlined his visit to Haywards Heath and handed out a summary of his discussion with DS Hibbert. When he finished speaking, he picked up his coffee cup to relieve a parched throat but found it empty. He reached for the water bottle instead.

'I'm now convinced,' Henderson said, 'we've got three similar disappearances or abductions, and there might be one or two more if we look further back in the records.'

'Bloody hell,' Wallop exploded, his face a mass of emotions. Never a man to keep his true feelings in check. 'How could this be happening on our patch without us knowing?'

'Yeah,' Walters said, 'and if we didn't see it, how come none of the papers spotted it either? Too busy covering bloody football and country shows, I'll bet.'

'Hold up a second,' Henderson said. 'Before we all lock our thinking into place, I think we should take a minute and make certain our methodology is sound.'

'Didn't we prove it by finding three similar cases?' Wallop asked.

'Humour me, Harry. I just want to go over the methodology one more time to make sure it's resting on secure foundations.'

'Do you still have some reservations?' she said.

'I do, because if this is true, not only are we saying we might have three abductions, as if that isn't bad enough, but we've arrested the wrong man. I don't have to remind you two about the media frenzy when we arrested him. They'll be calling for heads to roll if we turn around now and let him go.'

'Fair point boss,' Wallop said, 'but we're not going to shout this from the rooftops, are we? We can't say too much to anybody until we have more concrete evidence.'

'It starts with the methodology.'

'What did you have in mind?' Walters asked.

He paused a few moments to collect his thoughts. 'I think the way this guy works is to target good looking women from well-off backgrounds, which means they dress well and can afford to go to the gym or in Denise's case, are already fit because she works in one. He meets them down at the gym, on the way back from school or at the swimming pool and watches them until he sees an opportunity to snatch them or entice them into his car.'

'It must be a snatch,' she said, 'or he must know them. Why else would they get into his car?'

'It would explain,' Wallop said, 'why they left their passports and other personal stuff behind. Also, why there's been no traffic on their mobiles or credit cards, they were most likely dumped or trashed. It wouldn't happen if the motive was robbery or kidnap for ransom.'

'I think the MO is as good as we can make it,' Walters said. 'Even though they're not young women, they all seem to take care of themselves, not easy I imagine when looking after children.'

'Children,' Henderson exclaimed, his sudden outburst startling the other two. 'I meant to raise the topic earlier. Is it significant all the women have children? I mean Kelly and Amy both went missing after dropping their kids off at school.'

'They did,' Wallop said, 'but the Langton and Sandford kids are at different schools, and in Denise Quinn's case, her kids are grown up with two at sixth-form college and another at university.'

'Yeah, and Kelly Langton is the only one to disappear on her way back from school,' she said, 'Amy Sandford was visiting a property with a client when she went missing.'

'Two things,' Henderson said, determined not to lose his chain of thought, 'well three things. One, he may be meeting them at school. It's a bit unlikely I know, as he would need kids at two different schools.'

'Could be a maintenance or service man,' she said.

'Yes, that occurred to me as well, it's something we need to follow up.' He picked up a pen and jotted it down. 'Number two, he may be using the kids thing as an opening, to start a conversation with the women at a park or a swimming pool.'

'Speaking as a woman, I think it's got to be the crappiest chat-up line I've ever heard.'

'Number three, the kids thing might be a feature of the age and type of women he's targeting.'

'Kelly and Amy differ in age by about four years,' she said, 'but all three women *look* about the same age.'

'Following your chain of thought, boss there could be a number four,' Wallop said. 'All the kids might be attending the same club or go to the same horse riding lessons or swimming lessons.'

They batted around the questions and issues for the next fifteen minutes before Henderson called a halt.

'I think we've got enough to put in front of Edwards and request a full investigation but while we've done a good job outlining the problem, we need to think about the solution? How are we going to catch him?'

A silence descended over the little room, each detective aware that what they had achieved so far was in many ways the easy bit.

'I'll give you my take,' Henderson said, 'but bear in mind I'm thinking out loud so it might be utter rubbish. We need to look at how all the women were abducted by driving or walking over the route they took, and try and find the best spot for him to make his move. Put ourselves in his shoes if you will.'

'We should go back over all the evidence,' he continued, 'and have it forensically tested for prints and DNA. The three cases were initially treated as missing persons, so it's unlikely any of this has been done. The Amy Sandford case is the most recent and the one I think we should focus our efforts on. We need to get into the flat in Richmond Road as soon as possible and see if Mr Swift left anything behind.'

'We need to look at the interview statements for the two new women,' Walters said, 'and see if there are any anomalies and similarities with Langton we can explore. If the same guy pops up as a friend or acquaintance or if all the women are members of the same gym or casino or something, it will give us an opening.'

'Good idea, get it organised. Anything else?'

'Well, we mentioned schools earlier,' Wallop said, 'and talked about the maintenance people. We should talk to the schools and the sports centres and find out what companies they're using.'

'In terms of the maintenance people in schools, it might be hard for them to get to know the parents, but they'd have the advantage of a van or truck already on school grounds. Get it organised Harry.'

Henderson paused.

'Now, before we let the troops loose on all this, I've a difficult meeting with Edwards tomorrow to get through.'

'Do you think she'll buy it?' she said.

'Part of me says it's obvious, so why wouldn't she, but you know how senior management can see only what they want to see especially when faced with ever reducing budgets and the might of the press.'

'What then?' Wallop said, as his brow wrinkled in concentration or perhaps consternation. 'We wait until another woman gets snatched? No way.'

'Yeah, it's crazy boss,' Walters said. 'We can't let this guy take any more women. If she doesn't give us the green light, we'll do it on our own.'

TWENTY-NINE

On the top floor of the Regency Casino and Gaming Club in Worthing, Dominic Green was playing his favourite game. Sentimentality wasn't a word often heard in property development circles, but he had been accused of buying this place not because it was a great money-spinner, but because of its fantastic snooker facilities.

What bullshit, and if it hadn't been his friend John Lester saying it, he would have cut the speaker's tongue out a long time ago. He never bought anything unless it made money and in fact, after a few tweaks, the casino downstairs was now a better performer than the similar-sized one he owned in Hove.

What could not be doubted was his love of snooker and if anybody said he was born with a cue in his hand, they wouldn't be far wrong, although sometimes it was there to bash someone's head with. He was a natural at the game and rather than turn professional at the age of sixteen, as many thought he would, he instead used his skill to scam money from shysters who thought they could play, and raised enough, with the twenty grand he stole from an over-trusting uncle, to start his property business,

His opponent this evening wasn't aware how much

of Green's youth had been spent on the green baize, but the days of fleecing drunks and public schoolboys with their hand-made cues were over. The game tonight was business and so he didn't mind if Gerry Malone believed his skill and cunning were behind a score of 2-2 and a lead in the final frame, rather than anything to do with Green pulling his shots.

The reason for being so nice was because his rotund, balding and gold-decked opponent owned a small supermarket in Worthing, smack bang in the middle of a small parade of shops. Green owned the rest and with a little assistance from Mr Malone, would soon be the proud proprietor a plum site, ripe for development.

In the Dominic Green charm book, this was part one of a two-stage process. If Malone still refused to sell to him, and providing the sticking point wasn't just about money, he would find himself in the boot of an old car, ready to be pushed over Beachy Head or dangling from a rope in the warehouse with Spike standing close by, picking his nails with a sharp knife.

It was Green's turn and an automatic calculation told him all he needed to do to win, was pot the red, then black, pink, and the black again; easy-peasy. He lined up his cue. People always told him a steady cue was the key to winning a game, but not for him. He didn't know where it came from, but he could tell exactly how far the coloured ball lay from the cue ball with unerring accuracy and from there, determined how much pressure to apply to the cue.

He hit the cue ball dead centre instead of slightly to the left, as his instinct told him to do, and as expected, the red kissed the cushion and rolled back, right in front of the hole.

'Oh, bad luck Dominic,' Malone said, the Irish twang leaking out of his whisky-soaked mouth. Malone wasn't so oiled he couldn't see an easy pot when presented to him, and so a few minutes later, he cleared the table to win the game. Green shook his hand and passed over two hundred pounds to his companion and for once, he parted with money wearing a genuine smile.

At ten, and after refilling his guest's whisky glass, Green guided him downstairs and left him in the capable hands of gaming manager, Tony Morati with two hundred and fifty pounds worth of chips in his pocket to play the tables. After his success on the snooker table, he must have thought his luck was in, and would probably blow the lot on one spin of the roulette wheel.

Green headed back upstairs to the bar on the first floor and sat with the gaming club boss, Alan Steadman. He wanted to pick his brains on attracting more high rollers down to Worthing from London. Steadman's idea was to use the boutique hotel Green owned on the seafront, 'The Landseer,' to offer combined hotel and gambling weekends. He liked the suggestion and was on the point of hammering out the finer details when John Lester approached.

Ten minutes later, Green and Lester made the short journey to the warehouse at Shoreham. Once inside, John went off to make a brew while he waited for Des Raynor and Spike to stop nattering. No way was it a rumbustious debate between sabre-sharp intellects, as Raynor operated a fork-lift truck at Shoreham Harbour and thought ships and fish were interesting, while Spike liked to maim people and watch porn.

'Right gents,' he said, when boredom became too much and he was forced to interrupt. 'Where are the goods?'

'Over there,' Spike said, nodding towards the table at the back, 'we were waiting for you.'

Green got up and walked to the table and waited while Spike lifted up each of the two holdalls and dumped them on the table. John handed him a brew as Spike started unloading the bags of dope. The packages came tightly wrapped in thick, smelly greaseproof paper and inside, the goods were bagged in polythene, all ways of trying to disguise the smell from sniffer dogs, but as soon as Spike opened one, the pungent aroma of grade one Pakistani black made his head spin.

'I can't believe we got it all, after what happened last time.'

'What? You can't believe Shah could be bothered sending us another consignment,' Lester said, 'because he's a devious, money-grabbing bastard, and would rather smoke it himself, or that the cops didn't nab it like before.'

'I wouldn't trust Shah with your granny and I know she's dead, but the latter. No trouble at the docks, Des? No hint of the filth?'

'No, Mr Green. I did everything you said and more. You know, I checked the approach roads, listened on the short wave radio you gave me and I asked around, subtle like. Nope. No fucking sign, so I went back on the ship, met with the deck hand and he handed it over. Couldn't have been easier.'

'See what I mean John? We keep everyone's mouth zipped and it works like a dream. Now we've got rid of the blab in our organisation it works the way it should.'

The first holdall contained top-class marijuana, the product of choice for Brighton's middle class professionals, university lecturers and students at the city's numerous educational establishments. The second holdall was filled with bags of heroin. They would be cut up with something benign like flour or calcium carbonate, otherwise the purity of this stuff would kill many junkies whose scrawny bodies were used to a weaker solution.

Green glanced at Raynor while this was going on and something about his demeanour made him appear nervous. He was a tough man and afraid of nothing, one of the reasons Green liked him, but his highly tuned nose told him something didn't feel right.

Green led him away from the table and back to the chairs.

'Des,' he said, leaning towards him, 'how do we know this isn't a set up and the filth didn't plant a bug in our consignment, or follow you? I mean they nabbed it last time, I can't believe they didn't try something again.'

Raynor's face looked a picture, and wouldn't have been much different if he'd been slapped.

Spike could be a thick sod at times and wouldn't

know which channel Mastermind was on, never mind be able to answer any of the questions, but he possessed an uncanny sense of knowing when something wasn't right. He stopped dealing with the dope and hovered close to Green's little tete-a-tete with Raynor.

'What, what do you mean? The Pakistani guy sealed the packages, how could they get into them?'

'I don't know. Use the same tape, the same oily paper. You tell me.'

'I dunno either. I got them from this Korean bloke, the one I always deal with. He's straight as a ramrod and would tell me if somebody'd fiddled with it.'

'Ha. How can he be fucking straight, if he's bringing in dope and getting backhanders from us?'

'You know what I mean.'

'I know what I mean Des,' he said, raising his voice, 'and I think there's something dodgy going on here.'

Raynor's quick glance at the door told him everything.

'Spike, nab him.'

Spike grabbed him by the throat and punched him on the side of the head until he stopped struggling. He tied him to the chair.

'What's the problem Dominic?' Lester said, walking towards him.

'I think Henderson's behind this. I think there's a tracker on the dope, and he's hoping to catch us handling it or selling it.'

'Are you not being a bit paranoid? I didn't see anything odd in the packages or inside either of the holdalls. I'll take another look if you want.'

'Watch and learn.'

He faced the man in the chair, a rope securing his arms and legs.

'Now Raynor, I'm not in the mood for fucking about. Save yourself a lot of grief and tell me what's going on.'

'Nothing Mr Green, I swear. It's all cosha.'

The way Spike had tied him, his hands lay flat against his thighs. Green nodded to Spike and the little guy drove his knife straight into Raynor's hand.

'Aggggg. You fucking bastard,' Raynor screamed. 'Agggggg,'

Blood seeped under his hand, as the knife also went into his thigh. Double pain from a single blow; sweet.

Green took a drink of tea but it tasted cold now. He could ask John to make another but he wanted to get this sorted quick-style and get off home. He waited until Raynor quietened down before resuming.

'Listen mate,' Green said, 'your other hand is lying in the same position as the first. One word to Spike and he'll do the same again.'

He strained against the rope, trying to move his arms but they wouldn't budge. The tough guy wept tears of pain, frustration and fear and had probably crapped in his pants. No matter, the fishes didn't care what they ate.

'What the fuck's going on Raynor?'

'It's Henderson,' he said, sobbing.

'Henderson what?'

'Henderson what made me do this.'

'Do what?'

'Let you get the dope.'

'See, what did I tell you, John. Here's another fucking nark in my organisation. Right, I've had enough of this Scottish bastard, I've decided what I'm going to do.'

'What?' Lester said.

'We know Henderson's a principled fuck and wouldn't compromise his precious justice for any amount of the readies?'

'Yep.'

'We also know he's got a girlfriend who's a reporter for *The Argus*.'

'Yeah.'

'Christ, you wouldn't even need to grab her off the street, just tell her a juicy story and she'll come running to you.'

'Neat.'

'Lift her sometime over the weekend, bring her down here and we'll see how long Henderson sticks to his fucking principles.'

'No problem.'

'Right Raynor,' Green said, 'this is your starter for ten. What's Henderson up to?'

He didn't reply, either because he'd lapsed into unconsciousness and couldn't speak, or he was acting schtum to protect his precious jock cop. 'Spike, chuck water on his face and wake him up, I don't want to be here all night.'

The little man smiled a cunning smile, before the roof fell in. The roof didn't actually fall in, it just felt like it did.

First, he heard an almighty bang, and then a team

of heavily-kitted people ran into the warehouse. He thought for a moment they were the Stanislav brothers, making a last desperate attempt to muscle in on his territory, but when they shouted 'Stop Police! Stop what you're doing. Show us your hands,' he knew it wasn't them.

He stood with hands in the air, like a frightened customer in a Wild West saloon facing the wrath of a feared outlaw gang, led by who else? His nemesis, the Scottish-bastard, DI Angus Henderson.

In his peripheral vision, he saw Lester pull a gun out from the waistband of his trousers.

'No, John, no,' he bellowed.

But it came too late.

A volley of flame erupted from the coppers' weapons and Lester fell with red blotches peppering his white shirt, gun still in hand. His gun fired as he fell and the bullet narrowly missed embedding itself in Raynor's skull. Shame, it would have been one less witness for the filth to call, and the last selfless act by his dearest friend.

THIRTY

DCI Lisa Edwards was busy when DI Henderson arrived outside her office for their Friday morning meeting. With a regal wave of the hand she indicated he should wait.

He'd spent a large part of the previous night lying on the sofa and sipping a glass of whisky, trying to calm down after the raid on Dominic Green's premises. With all the paperwork, he hadn't got home until two in the morning, but it wouldn't end there. There would be internal enquiries, an IPCC investigation, the media to deal with, on top of the forensic and other police work required to make sure Dominic Green stayed in jail and for them to dismantle as much of his organisation as they could. Green was major scalp and everyone involved in the raid would go down in Sussex Police folklore as heroes, but he wished he felt better about it.

Five minutes later, the officer occupying the visitor's chair in the DCI's office departed, and she called him in.

'Morning Angus, how are you?'

'Tired, as you might expect. How's yourself?'

'You should be as high as a kite for arresting Dominic Green. He's before my time of course, but I do understand we've landed a big catch.'

'The worst sort, an out and out criminal posing as a respectable businessman, as he's feted by some and hated by others.'

'Was anybody injured from our side? I assume no as I didn't hear of anyone.'

'Nope. The only down-side is the fatality, Green's right-hand man, John Lester.'

She sighed. 'Another IPCC investigation and losing a good officer for six months or a year, what a stupid way to run a modern police force.'

'I couldn't agree more.'

'What do we know about Lester, and don't tell me he's got five children and half a dozen dependent relatives or newspapers will make him sound like Robin Hood.'

Henderson smiled. 'Nope, nothing like that. He's married but with no children.'

'That's a relief. I imagine when someone goes round there to tell her it won't come as a sudden shock.'

'If she knew anything about his employer, it won't.'

She tidied her desk, cleared a space in the middle, clasped her hands in front of her, and stared hard at the DI.

'The Kelly Langton case: can we let the dogs of the CPS loose?'

'I'm not sure we can.'

Carefully, as he didn't want to get bogged down in detail, he summarised the work he, DS Walters and DS Wallop had been doing over the last few days and laid a summary report in front of her. She started reading.

Lisa Edwards was aged 45, tall with short, blonde hair, a noble facial bone structure, and flawless skin, surprising for a woman of her age and considering the job she did, which at times could be highly stressful and made huge demands on her time, day or night, and could take her outside in all weathers. The view of the troops downstairs was of an attractive woman with a fiery temper but with a scowl to curdle milk and frighten small animals.

She finished reading and sat for a few moments considering the implications. He liked that about her, as many senior officers, including his old boss, DCI Steve Harris, would shoot from the hip in a display of macho bravado, emphasising their hunger for action and the need for a quick solution.

'I understand your argument Angus, but many of the factors you mention can be found in just about every misper case we investigate.'

'Yes, I know and I suspect it's the reason why no one spotted anything was going on. However, in all three cases, we have found the same list of factors, because the women disappeared only with whatever was in their handbags. No woman voluntarily making a break for it, or running away with a new boyfriend would leave home so light-handed.'

She nodded.

'Also, no one's heard a peep from any of them by phone, email, postcard, or letter and their credit cards have never been used. In every misper case I've ever heard about or worked on, at least one transaction shows up on their credit cards or someone receives a text, giving us the confidence they're still out there, even if they don't want to be found. With these three, we've heard nothing and both Kelly and Amy were regular Facebook and Twitter users, Kelly in particular had over two hundred thousand followers.'

'Yep, I see where you're coming from. The point you're making about the only items missing being the things they needed for the day ahead is a good one.'

Henderson nodded, thinking *She's getting it*.

'More importantly,' Edwards continued, 'no woman I know would run away from an abusive husband or try to start a new life in another town or another country without her children. When my sister ran away from her violent husband she spent most of the morning packing up an estate car. It isn't a case of just grabbing the kids and making a run for it, they need their favourite toys, clothes, food. Her daughter can't sleep unless it's with her battered teddy.'

This was the first time Edwards had ever mentioned her family, he hadn't known until now she even had a sister. He suspected this lack of personal information was behind an opinion held by some that she was aloof and not a team player.

'Do all three missing women have children?'

'Yes.'

'There you go, that does it for me. Let me think about this a second.' She pushed back the chair and rested her legs on an open drawer. The view of nylon-clad legs looked a prettier sight than Steve Harris with his smart suits and stylist-cut hair, but he knew it would be stupid to underestimate his replacement or attempt to get too friendly.

She sat up, her stare unwavering. 'You do know the folks in Malling House will hate me for telling them this. Not only will they say we've been incompetent in arresting Brian Langton, but we've been doubly incompetent for not spotting a serial abductor.'

'I know but–'

'The press will have a field day with headlines like, 'Serial Killer Stalks Streets' and 'Is No Woman Safe' plastered all over their front pages and we'll be under pressure every day until we make an arrest.'

'I agree and so we can't let this story out without stronger evidence.'

'No, Angus, we can't let this story out full stop. In any case, when you get stronger evidence you're only a couple of steps away from finding out who the perpetrator is.'

She chewed her lip. 'Put together a small team of officers and fully investigate all three cases, but we need to keep this under the radar until we're confident of our ground. Get out there and talk to the friends and relatives of the two new cases, much as you did with Kelly Langton, and see if you can find anything definite that links them together, such as a boyfriend or a personal fitness trainer.'

'Ok.'

'These women do look similar, they come from good homes, they're all married with kids, and they look after themselves and all the rest, so there must be something in this mix which is attracting this guy to them.'

'I agree.'

'Thinking outside the box, what if there isn't one?'

'What do you mean, one thing that's attracting him, or one guy?'

'What if he's picking his targets at random and the factors you've got here, are nothing but coincidence?'

'It's too much of a coincidence if you ask me, but statistically it's unlikely because–'

'I know the stats,' she said, with a dismissive wave of the hand. 'I did an FBI Profiling Course, but what if this guy is a genuine gold-star one-off? What if his only criteria on picking up these women is the opportunity when it presents itself?'

Henderson ran fingers through untidy hair. His hair always grew long during an intensive investigation, but far from discovering a new biological truth and something he could market to balding men, it was a case of personal grooming being ignored until a case had been resolved.

'It would give us a major problem,' he said, 'as random killers are, by definition, the hardest to catch. However,' he said, holding up a hand to silence the anticipated interruption, 'it's a risky strategy from his perspective, because it means he needs to invent an MO again and again and in doing so, sooner or later he's bound to make a mistake.'

'Whether he's using your MO or not, finding commonality among the three cases is key, but also, look for differences in approach, places where he might have made a mistake.'

Henderson left her office a few minutes later and headed downstairs. He walked into the Murder Suite and found Walters at her desk and told her about the decision taken by the Chief Inspector to set up a small team.

'Great news, but how come you don't look so pleased?'

He slumped into a seat. 'I wasn't thinking like a DCI and considering how the press and top brass are going to react. I'm only focussed on catching our kidnapper. If word gets out about this kidnapper, we'll see panic in schools and gyms and everywhere else where these women hung out. We'll be inundated with sightings and handed lists and lists of missing people by tearful relatives. We'll be involved in daily press briefings, top brass meetings and experts in psychology, sociology, and personality profiling will descend and occupy all the meeting rooms.'

'We'll just need to keep a lid on it,' Walters said, 'like the DCI says. It will be pointed out to everyone in the team every day, and we'll threaten them with the sack if they don't.'

'It's not as simple as that, Carol. In order to investigate this further, we'll need to talk to investigating officers at other cop shops, witnesses, friends of the victims, relatives, and all the rest. How do we keep a lid on all of them?'

THIRTY-ONE

Henderson trudged up the path, his legs feeling heavy. It was eight in the evening and this would be their seventh interview in two days, this time at a house in Maidenbower, Crawley. It was the least imposing property visited so far: a modest three or four-bedroom detached house built in close proximity to its neighbours in a large, modern housing estate on the edge of town.

The first task of his clandestine misper team was to interview teachers, parents, maintenance teams, administration staff, anyone with a connection to Williamson College and Leapark School, schools the Langton and Sandford kids attended. Leapark made the task a little easier, being a primary school any movement of pupils between schools was usually from there to Williamson and not the other way around.

He knocked on the door and a vivacious Hispanic-looking woman with waves of deep, jet-black hair and wearing bright red lipstick opened it.

'Detective Inspector Henderson and Sergeant Walters I presume,' she said. 'I am Leticia Richardson. How do you do?'

She proffered her hand, which Henderson shook. It felt light and soft and not really a handshake at all, more like a delicate touching of hands. Perhaps it passed for a handshake in the part of the world she came from. She invited them inside and the two detectives took a seat on the sofa. The television was on, but soon switched off by Leticia when she came back into the room.

'Can I get you something,' she asked, 'a cup of tea or coffee perhaps?'

'No, thank you Mrs Richardson, we've still got a few more calls to make. We don't want to keep you long.'

Their initial analysis of movement between schools threw out fifty-seven names, but reduced to a more manageable size following introductory phone calls as several families had moved from the area and a few lived abroad. They were put on a reserve list and would be visited later if the initial search proved fruitless.

The teams were instructed to cover ten points with the two items at the top being the most important. One: they were to meet every member of the family involved in taking children to school and assess their ability to stage a kidnap, along with their character, motivation, and knowledge of the victims. Two: determine if they have access to a place where a kidnap victim could be held, either at home or at their place of work.

'My husband will be down in a minute, Inspector. He is just putting the children to bed. It's his job in the evening as I deal with them all day.'

'Your garden looks neat and trim,' he said, standing up and walking towards the patio doors.

It looked small, a developer's idea of a garden and already crowded with only a few shrubs, a barbecue, and a shed, and through its dusty and rain streaked window he could see numerous garish-coloured children's toys.

'Thank you. I do it myself as Henry hates gardening.'

Henderson walked back to the sofa and a few minutes later, a short, slightly plump man with thinning salt and pepper hair entered the room.

'Sorry to keep you,' he said, shaking hands with the officers, 'the little one wanted to know who was at the door and so I made something up and incorporated it into the story I was telling.'

Henderson did a double take of the man in front of him and the wedding picture beside the fireplace, unsure if he was Leticia's uncle or father, as he seemed so much older and more dishevelled than his well turned-out partner. The picture matched the features on the face but with a lot more hair, less wrinkles and a great deal slimmer. If confirmation was required, he sat on the edge of her chair, put his arm around her shoulder and gave her a kiss.

'So what can we do for you?' he asked, turning to look at the police officers.

'As my sergeant said on the phone,' Henderson said, hoping his face did not betray his amusement, 'we are here in connection with the disappearance of Mrs Kelly Langton, a parent at the school your children attend–'

'We know Inspector,' she said, 'as it's all over the school. I thought you'd arrested her husband and charged him with her murder?'

'Yes, you're quite right, we did. What we are doing today is additional background checks to help strengthen the case.'

'I see. Well, I didn't know her personally as our children are in different year groups from her children, but I know of her because of her celebrity status.'

'What about you sir?' Walters asked.

'I work in London and leave early in the morning so it's always been my wife who takes the children to school. I only know Mrs Langton from what I read in the paper and seeing her occasionally at the school ball and sports day, nothing more. It's hard to miss them. Shrek and Beauty, I call them.'

His wife gave him a playful slap. 'Don't be cruel, Henry. She is a nice person, despite what is written in some newspapers.'

'Where do you work sir?' Henderson said.

'At AIG Insurance in the city, I'm a loss assessor.'

'Do you travel much, for example to see clients or visit sub-offices?'

'I don't do much travelling nowadays, not as much as I did six or seven years ago as I've got a team of twelve staff to do it for me. I'm a desk jockey now and up at head office in London every day, rain or shine.'

Over the next fifteen minutes they discussed the culpability of Brian Langton and Leticia told them how everyone at school looked forward to the trial and obtaining justice for poor Kelly, wherever she might be.

When they returned to the car, Walters drove while

Henderson completed an interview assessment form.

'I think they're a green, a definite green,' she said, as the car nudged though a narrow space between several parked cars and bounced over sleeping policemen, one after another.

'Don't joke about this, Carol, it's serious. Neither of them needed to open their mouths to tell me it isn't them.' He pulled out a red highlighter and made a broad stroke over the top corner of the form.

'Sorry boss.'

He picked up the interview list from the folder and ran his finger down the names. 'The Archers are next. Their two kids attend Williamson College but they used to go to Leapark. They live in Horsham at–'

'I'm on it boss,' Walters said, pointing to the in-built satellite navigation system in the dashboard of her most recent purchase, a three-year-old VW Golf. 'It says we'll be there in sixteen minutes.'

'Still enjoying the new car then?'

'Make the most of it, it'll soon wear off.'

'You need to use a sat-nav around Maidenbower, it's a warren. One wrong turning and we could be here all night.'

Driving slowly through the chicane on Billinton Drive, another experiment by urban planners to slow traffic, they approached the lights at Three Bridges Railway station. 'What did you think of the Richardsons, as a couple I mean?' Walters said.

'She must have bad eye sight or all the effort he's been putting in to satisfy his young wife is having a detrimental effect on his appearance.'

'I agree. It makes you wonder how such different

people get together. It's the same in my street where this handsome, young guy is living with a woman who looks twice his age. Bought him on eBay, if you ask me.'

Henderson opened his mouth to say something, but thought better of it. With only three serious girlfriends in his life and a marriage he'd mistakenly thought would last forever, he didn't feel qualified to philosophise on what might be the main ingredients for a happy relationship. In fact, far from philosophising, he realised after the previous interview that he knew less than he thought.

They drove past the Hawth Theatre where this week's offering was a romantic comedy called *Afternoon Delight* featuring several actors and actresses he didn't know, not much of a surprise there, as he rarely went to the theatre much and only occasionally watched TV. A few minutes later, a place more to his liking came into view, the home of Crawley Town Football Club. He still called it the 'Crawley Stadium,' refusing to acknowledge its dopey new name after a large company signed a lucrative sponsorship deal and re-christened it.

'Does visiting all those fancy houses and seeing those flash cars give you a hankering for a more expensive lifestyle?' he asked.

'Is this the part when you tell me I'm not getting a pay rise?' she said laughing. 'No, I'm not jealous of them. I mean, it's not like pop stars and footballers with money coming out of their ears for doing next to nothing. These people are lawyers, doctors and businessmen who work for their money. I respect that. Even Kelly Langton started at the bottom.'

'Don't you think with the good start in life many of them enjoyed, and no doubt their children will follow suit, you might have gone to university and became a lawyer or a doctor as well?'

'Life is what you make of it, my old gran always told me.'

'I think your old gran was right.'

The satnav directed them into Compton's Lane, a broad tree-lined street on the outskirts of Horsham. They soon found Rusper Lodge, a large and imposing double-fronted house with a wide front garden. It was planted with several mature trees and a variety of shrubs, the soil underneath friable and black, as if recently turned over and composted, ready for planting this autumn or next spring.

After knocking, a boy aged about eleven or twelve answered the door. 'Is your mother in?' Henderson asked. 'We're officers from Sussex Police.'

'Come in. She's in the kitchen. She's expecting you.'

They walked towards a strong cooking smell and as the boy pushed open the door leading to the kitchen, they could see the slight figure of someone he presumed to be Lidia Archer hunched over the stove.

'Mum, the police are here,' the boy said in loud voice, trying to make himself heard over the noise of an extractor fan. 'They're arresting you for feeding your children terrible food.'

She turned and wiped her hands on her Wines of Italy apron. 'If I had a cloth in my hand I'd throw it at your head.'

'You can get her for child abuse as well,' he said as

he ran off down the hall.

She had straw-coloured hair, cut in a short, layered style, highlighting the narrow features of her face and underneath the apron, a stylish red dress. Her make-up was subtle and unsmudged, despite this late hour on a damp Monday evening and working in a hot and clammy kitchen.

'Ah, Inspector Henderson and Sergeant Walters, pleased to meet you,' she said, walking towards them and shaking hands. 'Let's move into the lounge, we'll be more comfortable there.'

They declined the offer of coffee, even though this would be the last call of the night, as it was a long drive back to Brighton and there were few service stations on the way.

'Your constable said on the phone you wanted to talk about Kelly Langton's disappearance.'

'That's right. These are routine enquiries, we're talking to everybody who knew her and adding background to the case against her husband.'

'I see. So, which theory are you investigating, the one alleging he murdered his wife or one of the many suggested by *The Argus*?'

Henderson and Edwards shouldered the burden of press conferences between them and he knew most of the silly stories. Interest in the case peaked on three occasions, each time flooding the incident room with calls and sightings; firstly, when Kelly Langton disappeared, when they arrested her husband, and the third time with the disappearance of Amy Sandford.

Many papers tried running the serial killer story again but with no hard evidence and no rumours leaking out of Sussex House on threat of demotion to anyone who did so, it soon ran out of steam. Instead they printed whatever their editor fancied.

'We are sticking to facts as we know them, Mrs Archer, avoiding some of the more fanciful theories some papers are throwing about. How well did you know Kelly?'

'I spoke to her whenever I saw her. Sometimes just to say hello and at other times we would stop and enjoy a good natter. So, I would say I know her quite well.'

'Do you have any idea why she disappeared?'

She blew a long gasp of air between closed lips and shook her head. 'None whatsoever, not a clue. She was a happy girl in my opinion. Ok, her husband could be a bit of an arrogant pig when the mood took him, but she was sparky and tough and I believe could cope with anything he could throw at her without running away.'

'Do you take your children to school,' he asked, 'or does your partner do it?'

'It's primarily me but my ex-husband does it once or twice a week, especially when I've got an early morning meeting in town.'

'What do you do?'

'I run my own public relations company in central London. I work for train companies and the airlines.'

'What about your husband?'

'Ex-husband.'

'Sorry, ex-husband.'

'It's all right. I'm at the 'I don't give a shit about him' stage. His name is James. With the money I made from the sale of my first company, I set him up in a furniture making business as he said it was always something he wanted to do, that is, after completing his helicopter pilot licence, a journalist course, a couple of creative writing summer schools and God-knows what else. After the divorce, he kept the business and a flat in Horsham and I kept this,' she said, waving her arm to indicate the house, 'and my PR business. He called me a shrewd, conniving bitch among a lot of other things at the time, as he believed he got the sticky end of the pole, but what the hell, I can take it, I'm thick-skinned.'

'Does anyone else live here apart from you and your three children?'

'No.'

'How do we contact your husband?' Henderson asked.

'I'll get his details for you but first let me check on the meal, if you don't mind. The kids hate burnt food, as you can probably tell.'

For a divorcee with three kids at private school, Lidia Archer wasn't doing so badly, Henderson thought as he looked around the lounge. It was lightly furnished, minimalist even, but what furniture they had was expensive and high quality, from the floral-patterned sofa they were sitting on, the large Bang and Olufsen LCD television and sound system dominating one wall, to the antique-framed oil paintings hung all around the room, tastefully illuminated by gold picture lights.

Mrs Archer returned a few minutes later and handed Henderson a business card. 'This is his

267

business address and phone number and there's a map on the back. You're more likely to get him there than at his flat in Horsham. He's never at home when I call.'

'Why did you move your children from Leapark to Williamson College?' Walters asked.

'Charlie, my son, is good at maths and when his teacher left Leapark and went to Williamson, he made such a fuss we decided to follow. There's no way I can take three children to two different schools in the morning, although my husband could, but the unhelpful sod said he wouldn't do it, so they all moved.'

'Before you ask,' she continued, 'I know there are plenty of good schools in Horsham, including two within a half-mile of this house, so why don't I send my kids there? You see, I received a private education, and I don't see why my children shouldn't do so as well. I can afford it, so why not?'

On the pretence of stretching his legs, Henderson walked to the window where he could see an extensive garden of dense, mature shrubs at the back of the house but no outbuildings. He could think of no reason why Lidia Archer would kidnap Kelly Langton or Amy Sandford and he mentally crossed her from the list.

However, her husband sounded a more interesting prospect and joined a small but growing band of husbands and ex-husbands who owned separate business premises or other properties where kidnap victims could be held.

If this was the good news, the bad news was they

all needed to be checked out and assessment reports finished by Thursday morning, three days time, as Edwards was impatient for a result. His sleeping hadn't improved and with the work piling up, it was unlikely to do so any time soon.

THIRTY-TWO

Since the formulation of her escape plan earlier in the week, Amy Sandford made sure she stayed strong. She ate every scrap of food and drank every drop of juice irrespective of the hideous consequences and while the CCTV camera would record her lying on the bed reading a magazine, in reality her mind buzzed like a bluebottle as she went over the details of her plan, searching for flaws.

She tried and failed to recall much of the terrain around the workshop; when she first arrived she was driving and concentrating on not scratching the car's bodywork on the posts either side of the entrance and then negotiating the bumpy drive, and as a result, had seen little. The only bit she could remember was standing beside her car and looking at the view, a seemingly endless row of fields, dotted with the odd farmhouse and the occasional copse of trees, but she didn't have much of a clue what lay the other way.

Two questions remained. On her arrival here, Swift had taken her into a barn, the one he said he'd wanted to sell, but she didn't know if she was still there, or had he moved her somewhere else? The ceiling in her room suggested the high vaulted roofs often found in barns, but for the purposes of her plan, it would be an unsafe assumption to make.

The second question, another she couldn't answer, was, when she escaped from this room would the main door of the barn be locked? If so, she would be trapped and forced to confront Swift, who would be less than pleased by what she was planning to do to him.

Tonight, Amy put on two pairs of trousers and several layers of blouses and cardigans, all taken from the wardrobe, and she would fret about their origins in the safety of her bedroom when safe and at home. The additional layers were not there to make Swift's nightly rape more difficult, but to keep warm when she was outside.

The drug he put in her food to knock her out sometimes left her a little disorientated, but it soon wore off. There had been some sunshine over the last few days, but night time temperatures were cold with clear, crisp nights as she could see the stars through the upper window, and frost clinging to the glass in the mornings.

Ten minutes later, the hatch rattled with the evening meal. She took her time, waiting for Swift to get bored and bugger off, and so she did a bit of extra stretching before ambling over to remove the tray. She smiled when she saw bangers and mash with a banana for dessert. She didn't like sausages at the best of times and missing out on such a culinary delight wouldn't be a hardship, but she could eat the banana, an unanticipated bonus, as she hadn't expected to eat anything tonight.

She spent more time than usual getting

comfortable and looking for a magazine, all designed to waste time and to make sure he didn't see the next bit. Charade over, she put down the magazine, picked up her plate and walked to the wardrobe, opened the door and scraped all the food from the plate into the corner and covered it with clothes. She closed the door and walked to the sink and poured out the fruit juice, rinsed the cup out and filled it with tap water. The first stage of the plan complete, she sat down beside a clean plate and slowly ate the banana.

Her meal finished, she put the tray on the floor and read the magazine for five minutes before faking tiredness and sprawling over the bed. The kidnapper seemed to think of everything. The cutlery, cups and plates were all plastic, giving her no chance of using them against him, and all the furniture was bolted to the floor or wall so it offered nothing to hit him with or throw. Then, through a combination of drugs and a camera, he could do anything he wanted. That is, until he met Amy Sandford.

Five minutes later with nothing happening, she wondered if he was taking the night off or had fallen and injured himself. Negative thoughts raced through her head like wild birds trapped in a cage and it took all her willpower to muffle the scream of frustration forming in her throat.

Everything buzzing around her head came to a sudden halt when the door opened. She kept her eyes closed, listening hard for every movement and sniffing the air discreetly, trying to identify any new smell to give advanced warning of something new or different; as this could be the night he decided to kill her.

The items on the tray rattled when he picked it up and carried it outside. She'd considered attacking him at this point but decided against it as he was standing and she knew she would be no match for him. She could tell even from their brief encounter at the house in Richmond Road he looked strong and kept himself in shape.

In truth, she would like nothing better than to take him as he was about to slip his dick inside. With a quick flick of the wrist she would break the one-eyed trouser monster and damage his balls so irreparably, he would never be able to inflict such a degrading humiliation on anybody else. This plan did not make the final cut as she would be left half-dressed, if not naked, and in panic would run straight out of the room, as she didn't want to be in here a second longer than necessary and shuddered at the prospect of flagging down an unsuspecting motorist without at least her bra and knickers.

He came back inside the room and closed the door. 'You're not wearing a skirt or a dress this evening Amy? Tsk, tsk. What a pity, I only want a quick fuck before I bugger off home as I'm starving. No matter.'

His hand ran up her leg and he pushed it between her legs. He rubbed hard against the thick material of her trousers for several moments, a sharp nip almost forcing her to shout out, before turning her onto her back. He pulled her legs apart, and climbed on the bed and knelt between them.

'Fancy a fuck now Amy? I know I do. Let's see what nice knickers you've got on today, shall we?'

He fumbled for the catch on her jeans, his fingers

digging sharply into her skin. She could smell him now, a pungent mix of garlic and expensive aftershave. With the top clip undone, she half-opened an eye to see where he was positioned, before bringing up her knee and whacking him hard on the side of his face.

He fell to the side, more in surprise than from the force of the blow she suspected, but before he could react and attack her, she pushed him in the chest with both feet. His arms were flailing in the air as he struggled for balance, but lost it and disappeared over the side of the bed; she heard a loud crack. She leaned over. He was where she wanted him to be but to her surprise, he was out cold with a large red mark on his forehead, the result of a collision between him and the edge of the wardrobe.

She was caught in two minds, should she rush outside and find a piece of wood or a hammer to bash his brains in and make sure he never woke up again? But all her instincts were screaming, RUN GIRL, RUN!

She put on her shoes, fastened up her trousers and leapt from the bed and ran out of the room. She found herself in an open area, bright and warm, and realised she was inside the barn, the place Swift said he wanted to sell all those days ago. Great. Now she knew which way to go.

She reached the door and pulled the handle hoping against hope it wasn't locked. It wasn't. The fresh, cold air hit her like a wet towel and it took several moments for the giddy feeling in her head to disperse and her bearings to return. She had seen the place only once but as an estate agent, she had a good memory for property and knew which way was out. She took a deep breath and ran.

Away from the shadow of the barn, it was lighter and she could now see the access road leading down the hill, the wide-open space of a field to the right and the silvery thread of the road at the bottom of the hill. The track she remembered was rutted and uneven with long grass growing in the middle and she needed to be careful not to trip over some of the potholes and loose rocks lurking there.

Halfway down, she didn't feel too out of breath or tired, but concerned about the lack of food over the last few days which would leave her with not enough energy to run for long, but this was probably balanced out with her new, fitter shape, and overall she felt good.

The next stage of her plan was being formulated as she ran. At the road, she would turn left and head towards the first house not guarded by impenetrable gates and looking occupied, and start banging on the door. What they would make of a bedraggled and frightened looking woman at this time of night, she couldn't tell, but she was gifted with a persuasive tongue and she would persuade them to help her.

Just then, she heard the sound of a diesel engine firing up in the courtyard behind her. For a moment, she regretted not going back and bashing his head in with a stick, but was mystified as to how he'd recovered so quickly. She had a choice to make. She could either carry on running and hope to beat him to the door of the first house, or climb the fence into the field and hide in the bushes and long grass.

She glanced back and saw the lights of the car dancing over the tops of the trees as it moved across the courtyard, and felt a wave of panic course through her being, and the confidence to reach the road before him evaporated into the cold, night air like warm breath. She stopped running and climbed the fence. Thankfully there was no barbed wire and she got over easily and jumped into the damp field, before flattening herself in the long grass behind a small bush. Seconds later, the car raced past.

She waited a few moments before looking up. The car, a noisy, clattering Land Rover Defender, was now at the bottom of the driveway and about to turn in to the road. She desperately wanted to jump up and run, but a voice in her head told her to wait, there was still a chance he could see her in the rear view mirror. She lay there panting, her heart pounding against her chest, red cheeks warming her face despite the chill of the cold, damp air.

The car turned and disappeared from sight and without hesitation, Amy jumped to her feet and started running across the field in the opposite direction. It was a large, open field and she could make out a copse of trees about a half-mile distant and the twinkling lights of a farmhouse, the same distance on the other side.

She ran and ran, her pace slower than on the access road due to the uneven terrain, which seemed to be full of rabbit holes and thick divots. Five or six minutes after leaving the track, she heard a car.

She stopped to catch her breath and look. It was

travelling along the road in the same direction as she was, and for a moment she considered running down the hill to try and stop it, but it was too far away. When she looked closer, she realised it could only be him. She could hear the clatter of the diesel engine and could see in the moonlight the square, boxy shape of a Land Rover. Cars like this were popular in the country, used in the main by farmers, landowners, and rich people trying to look like farmers, and it was possible it belonged to a local, but in her heart she knew it was him.

She started running again. In a few minutes, she reached the shelter of the small copse of trees she'd seen from the track and stood in their shadow, gasping for breath. In truth, she only went to the gym to keep her weight down and admire the physiques of the young body builders who went there, so any improvements in her cardiovascular fitness and strength were accidental. She regretted it now, as over a week on light rations had sapped her energy levels and she knew it would take an enormous effort to get her legs moving again.

When her heavy breathing subsided, she stood there listening. To her right, and somewhere over the brow of the hill, the faint hum of cars moving on a main road and up above, the slow rumble of planes as they made their way in and out of Gatwick Airport. It was a cloudy night, the sliver of a crescent moon obscured by thick, cloud formations, which helped hide her presence and stopped temperatures falling too low, but with all the clothes she'd put on, she now felt hot and sweaty.

Her uphill vantage point offered a good view over a long section of road to the right and left, but in all the time she stood there, no other car came by. About five hundred yards up ahead, she spotted a gate. She couldn't be sure as it was indistinct, but she could just make out the shape of a car or a van parked beside it. Her spirits rose. She didn't know what country folk got up to at night, but if someone had parked there to walk the dog or if a couple of kids were having a snog, it would be easier reaching it than the farm.

She stepped out of the shadow of the trees and peered harder, aided by the moon when it appeared through a gap in clouds and could see the car clearer now. Her spirits sagged; it was a Land Rover, his Land Rover.

A wave of panic coursed through her, leaving her faint with trembling hands and her heart racing. She tried to channel the nervous energy into movement and seconds later, forced her tired legs to run again. She took a deep breath and started to jog across the open field. Realising her silhouette might be visible against the skyline even in the dark, she edged downhill and ran as fast as the surface would allow. The lights of the farmhouse looked closer now; one last heave would do it.

In the silence, only punctuated by her footsteps on the grass, her heavy breathing, and the pounding of her heart, she heard a sharp crack and without warning, her legs gave way and she fell to the ground. An excruciating pain shot up her leg and immediately she thought she had caught her foot in a divot and the noise was the sound of a bone breaking. She tentatively moved her hand to the area of pain and touched a sticky substance that felt like animal poo or thick dew. It was warm but with no smell and the way it coated her hands, she knew it was blood, her blood.

She felt around the area, trying to locate a protruding bone but instead found a hole. It was small on one side, but twice the size on the other with blood pumping out like an opened tap. She almost fainted when she realised she had been shot. It was him, had to be, but how the hell could he see her in the dark?

She needed to make a decision: stay and try and stop the bleeding, or run. Fear seized her in a vice-like grip and it made the decision for her, she needed to get away. She forced herself into a kneeling position and tried to stand when a boot hit her in the chest and sent her sprawling on her back in the grass.

'You thought you could get away from me you fucking bitch,' he sneered, 'but you can't. You can't run, 'cause you know I'll catch you.'

He stood there, towering above her. She could only see his shadow, but she knew it was him. The shape of the body and the cold, evil, malevolent voice.

'Let me go you bastard. I've got money, I can–'

'Shut up, you fucking slut. I don't want your money. You're no use to me now. We had a good thing going, but you've screwed it up, like every woman I've ever known.'

There was a metallic squeak and an intense flash of light.

THIRTY-THREE

He thumped a fist on the desk. 'What the hell is this? My wife said I work all bloody hours and I'm never at home, did she? Yeah, but did she also tell you, I do it so she can enjoy her spa and bloody pampering sessions and to keep her three kids at their friggin' private school?'

'She never said anything of the kind sir,' DI Henderson said, 'you weren't at home when we called and we needed to talk to both of you.'

Henderson sipped at the lukewarm brown liquid in the plastic cup. For an upmarket car dealership with gleaming posh cars and luxuriant sofas, the coffee tasted like something that came from the drip tray. For customers about to sign up for a brand new 4x4 or a big saloon, they would be served from the complicated coffee machine over in the corner, because if they ever received this crap, they would buy their new car elsewhere.

His small team of investigators had completed the first round of interviews last night and they were now dealing with the 'no-shows,' but without doubt, he and Walters had picked the short straw. Garage-owner Darren Kingston had been in a bad mood ever since they met him at nine this morning and nothing they said seemed to please him.

'So what's all this about? I don't have much time to give you as I've got lots to do today. I'm one salesman down and my secretary's on bloody maternity leave. She would go and have her bloody sprog just when we've hit a rich seam of sales, wouldn't she?'

'We won't keep you long sir,' Henderson said, sounding a bit more patient than he felt. *Does this guy think he is the only one with a busy schedule?* He might have sales targets to meet and grumpy mechanics to deal with, but he didn't have the top brass of Sussex Police and half of the nation's press breathing down his neck, waiting for him to slip up or fall on his face. 'We understand from your wife you regularly take your children to school at Williamson College.'

'Yeah, I do. I may as well spend some time at the place, as I'm paying so much for the bloody privilege. It's more or less on the way here which helps.'

He was about mid-fifties, with a round, tanned face and slicked-back hair, making him look like an archetypal East-End car spiv, willing to do a good deal on any motor as long it was settled with used readies. However, in the gleaming showroom behind him, they didn't sell anything costing less than thirty grand and would be suspicious of accepting something so grubby as cash. Kingston looked smart in a tailored shirt, silk tie, expensive suit and Rolex watch, all the trappings of a successful businessman who owned one of the most profitable car dealerships in the country, if he believed all the guff on their web site.

'How well do you know Kelly Langton, Mr

Kingston?'

'Kelly Langton? The lovely girl who buggered off into the wild blue yonder? I know her quite well, I would say. I always spoke to her whenever I bumped into her, which was about a couple of times a week. Damned attractive woman she is. Still got a model's looks, if you ask me.'

'What do you think happened to her, sir?' Walters asked.

'It's obvious init? She scooted off to get away from her big brute of a husband. I didn't know him so well, but I don't think he did her in. Sure, he didn't treat her right, messing about with other women and never at home, but why kill her? Get divorced, I say, and he can afford it. Divorce isn't about kids or houses or love, is it? It's about money. I should know, I've been married three times.'

'When your children attended Leapark,' Henderson said, 'did you also know Amy Sandford?'

'Amy Sandford? Of course I did. She bought a car from here. Nice woman she is too. Our kids only moved to Williamson College last year, after being at Leapark for six years, same as Amy's. She's one of the organisers of the summer ball and sports day and I always make a point of donating a prize for the raffle. Nothing cheap of course, maybe a weekend with one of these babies,' he said, jerking his thumb to the glittering line-up out in the showroom, 'or a weekend in a health spa. She'd phone me up and switch on the charm and twist my arm, trying to make the prize even better than the year before.'

'What do you think happened to her?'

'Now you mention it,' he said, curiosity writ large on his smug, tanned face, 'she's another one who buggered off into the sunset. Was it something I said? Ha, ha.' He leaned over the desk. 'You guys think there's a connection, don't you? Tell me, I can keep a secret.'

Henderson almost burst out laughing. Who was he kidding? Car dealers were worse than journalists and couldn't keep their mouths shut if they fell off a boat into the sea. 'There's no connection, sir. We are simply investigating the disappearance of two women.'

'Yeah, with kids at the same schools my lot attended,' he said.

'Can I ask for your whereabouts on a couple of dates?'

'Fire away.'

Henderson gave him the dates both women disappeared and questioned him on his movements. Kingston was confident members of his staff would confirm his alibi and Walters left the room to talk to them.

'I'd like to take a look around the garage if I may,' Henderson said.

'Yeah, be my guest,' Kingston said. 'Fancy a new car do you? I could do you a good deal. We already supply cars to the Hampshire force.'

'I'm thinking more about the servicing bays and workshops, the stuff out back.'

'What?' His face rapidly transformed from the calm, controlled salesman to an aggressive animal spotting an intruder muscling in on his territory. 'You think I'm a fucking suspect don't you? No, you can't go there. Why the fuck should I let you poke around in my business?'

Henderson was taken aback by the outburst but decided enough was enough. He walked around to Kingston's side of the desk and stood in front of him, his face close to the car dealer's.

'Listen mate, if you don't let me take a look, I'll get a search warrant and in an hour this business will come to a halt, as thirty heavy-handed coppers come down here and take this place apart, brick by brick. Now, if one of them accidentally scratches the bodywork of one of your nice, new cars in the process,' he said with a shrug, 'I'll tell them not to worry, your insurance will cover it.'

'You're bluffing Henderson. I've seen the movie too. You've got nothing on me.'

Maintaining his stance, Henderson pulled out his phone, pressed speed dial and called the office, asking for Sally Graham. 'DC Graham, it's DI Henderson. Can you prepare a search warrant for Kingston Motors in Shoreham, K-i-n-g...'

Kingston's hand pulled Henderson's phone away from his ear. 'That won't be necessary Detective Inspector, my mistake. Go right ahead.'

Twenty minutes later, Henderson edged the grubby Mondeo pool car out of the car park, its pale red paintwork dull and dirty beside a line of large and gleaming saloon cars and 4x4's.

'What a first-class prick,' Walters said. 'He's so used to getting his own way with all the young salesmen and mechanics, he doesn't know how to talk to the rest of us.'

'Where do you think he belongs on our suspects list?'

'At the top, no question, green.'

'I think so too. He knew both women, which is a first in all the interviews we've done, and he thought they were both attractive. Mind you, if he did kidnap them, why did he tell us he knew them so well?'

'We would find that out anyway from talking to other people, so perhaps he thought it better not to lie.'

'What? A car dealer?' Henderson said. 'They're born liars, it's in their DNA.'

'I suppose.'

'He owns his own business and maybe property we don't know about. He seems to work his own hours with nobody checking when he comes in and out. He's an aggressive bastard to boot. One to be watched and investigated further, I would say.' Henderson took out a green highlighter and marked the top of the page.

'If he did kidnap them,' Henderson continued, 'he wouldn't be holding them out the back as I didn't see any cubby holes or out-buildings and in any case, too many people work there.'

'But as you say, he might own other properties.'

'I've been thinking about that. If Kingston or one of the other suspects we add to our list owns another house, a storage unit, or a holiday cottage out in the sticks, and Amy and Kelly are being held there, how in the hell are we ever going to find it?'

THIRTY-FOUR

'So remind me,' Henderson said, as he accelerated away from yet another roundabout. 'Who are we seeing next?'

They were heading towards Billingshurst, away from the up-market garage owned by the downmarket Darren Kingston. Henderson felt perkier as there was now one entry in the suspects list, but he wanted more because as much as he didn't like Kingston, he wasn't yet convinced of his guilt.

Walters picked up the folder. 'On Monday, if you remember, we saw Lidia Archer. She was the well-dressed lady we met as she was cooking in the kitchen at her house in Compton's Lane.'

'I remember.'

'She told us her husband, sorry her ex-husband, owns a furniture making business and he took their boys to school now and again.'

'She set him up after the divorce when she sold her PR business. A bloody good deal if you ask me.'

'She's a shrewd lady and no mistake.' She looked down at her papers. 'There was nothing suspicious about her house or the garden but her husband's workshops are out in the sticks and you said you were keen to see them. Put your foot down boss, we've got another two to do after this.'

They found the lane leading to Archer's workshop at the second attempt, despite Henderson driving slowly down Adversane Lane for this very purpose. It consisted of two barns facing one another with a paved courtyard between. Sound was coming from the one on the right as the door lay open and the buzz of something like a sander leaked from its interior. They walked over and introduced themselves to James Archer.

Henderson liked the place almost as soon as he walked in, as he loved the smell, the look and feel of real wood and even though he didn't own much furniture, the bits he did have were made from solid wood with no chipboard, MDF, or plywood in sight.

His father had worked as a carpenter before retirement two years ago, and when he wasn't installing kitchens in houses around Fort William, working away in Inverness or Glasgow, or building stands for exhibitions and conferences, he made alterations to their house. He built bookcases, put up shelves, extended the patio, installed fitted wardrobes in all bedrooms, and converted the attic as a bedroom for seven-year-old Angus when the arrival of Archie left them short of space.

Archer spoke eloquently and looked relaxed in their presence, answering questions without drama or becoming flustered. He was of average height but solidly-built with collar-length straggly brown hair and a couple of days growth on his chin, suggesting he didn't take much pride in his appearance. They'd obviously interrupted him at work, as he wore dusty overalls with a multiplicity of pockets for tools and screws, and what at first looked like dandruff or a new style of hair colouring to mimic the George Clooney look, turned out to be sawdust.

After explaining the purpose of their visit and sounding like an old, scratched recording, as this was probably the tenth or eleventh time he'd said it, they took seats beside the workbench.

'Your wife told us you took your boys out of Leapark,' Henderson said, 'to follow a maths teacher who transferred to Williamson College.'

'That's only half-true,' Archer replied, 'some bullying went on.'

'It must have been serious to move your kids.'

He smiled. 'No, it was my kids doing the bullying. You see, they're both a bit big for their age and you know what kids are like. It didn't amount to anything bad, but I needed to do something to teach them a lesson. If she wants to gloss it by saying they were following a maths teacher, I don't care.'

'Can you tell us your movements on a couple of dates?' Walters said.

'Sure, when?'

Walters reeled them off and Archer walked to the bench at the back of the workshop, where numerous notes were stuck to a board on the wall and box files marked 'Invoices' and 'Statements' lined up on a shelf. He picked up a large desk diary. Pinned up on the wall Henderson could see pictures of Archer skydiving, at the controls of a helicopter, and coming out of a plane to do a solo parachute jump. He found it hard to square the sedate, easy going job he did now with the thrill seeker on the wall but Henderson had been doing the job long enough to understand not to pigeon-hole people.

By analysing CCTV pictures in and around Richmond Road in Horsham, the place Amy Sandford went before she disappeared, they spotted her car heading into Horsham with someone, presumably Mr Swift, sitting beside her in the passenger seat. The pictures were taken from a camera some distance away and all they could tell about the passenger was he had blond hair and he was tall and stocky.

In every visit, the two-man teams were instructed to compare the man they met with the artist's impression of the man captured by CCTV cameras and Henderson looked at it now. Archer was well-built with untidy, long hair, but it was brown not blond. The rest of the picture was too vague for the artist to get a real likeness and the teams were told to treat it with caution.

With most of the sawdust now shaken from his hair, he could see it was brown, but even in colour and a shade or two lighter than his eyebrows, suggesting the use of a hair colourant. It was possible for him to have been blond at Amy Sandford's abduction and to have dyed it back to its natural colour to throw everyone off the scent. He didn't think so, as his hair looked the same as the pictures on the wall and for many men in their early forties like him, the first signs of grey would have them reaching for the succour of *Just for Men*.

'I worked here both days,' Archer said, turning to face them, 'and as I said earlier, I work alone. On your first date, I made a delivery late afternoon to a customer in East Grinstead. I spent most of the morning finishing the piece off before preparing it for transport. On the other date, I worked here in the morning and went to see a wood supplier in Worthing in the afternoon. I can give you names and address of both sets of people if you like.'

'If you could sir,' Henderson said.

He wrote them down and handed a piece of paper to Walters.

'How do you find customers?' Henderson said. 'Is there a showroom or do you have a tie-in with a furniture shop?'

'No, it's all word of mouth. I started out doing some work for a few of my neighbours around here and they told other people and it's gone from there. Nowadays, I don't need to look for customers, they come to me.'

After fifteen minutes, both officers had exhausted all their questions, more or less the same ones asked of all the previous interviewees and he was tired of hearing the same answers, and glad when they reached the 'can we look around' stage. Far from objecting, as Darren Kingston did, he invited them to do so on their own, as he said he wanted to carry on working and handed them the keys to the barn opposite.

They started by looking around the barn they were in, but being a workshop and filled with woodworking equipment they completed the job in a few minutes and stepped outside and walked towards the other barn.

'Don't you love the smell of wood, Carol? It's a better aroma than many expensive wines and aftershaves in my opinion.'

'I'm just glad to get out into the fresh air for a few minutes, I couldn't breathe in there.'

'I agree it was a bit dusty, but there's no mistaking the smell, boy does it take me back.'

'A little less of the nostalgia, if you please sir and open the door. We've got a few more enquiries to make today.'

'Philistine.'

He put the key in the lock, turned it, and nosily rattled the bolt and padlock together as if experiencing a problem and when Walters made to walk in, he put a hand out to stop her and placed an upright finger to his lips. The only noises they could hear were blackbirds twittering in a nearby tree and the intermittent buzz of an electric sander, Archer once again working on the new wardrobe he was making for a customer.

He dropped his hand and walked inside. It didn't surprise him to find the barn full of wood, as Archer told them he used it for storage, and it took Henderson a few minutes to work out how it was organised and when he did, he felt confident Archer could find any piece he wanted in a few seconds. Attached to the wall at the back he could see a comprehensive racking system with hinges, bolts, screws, Rawlplugs, and all manner of fittings and accessories used in making bespoke furniture.

He edged past the wood piles taking care to avoid snagging his trousers or whacking his shins and made his way there. Standing in front of the racking system, he pulled out several coloured bins containing brass hinges and door handles.

'Look at these,' he said, weighing a pair of hinges in his hand. 'Solid brass, none of your brass plated steel for our Mr Archer.'

'Really?'

'My father would call it an extravagance.'

'Yeah but I bet he didn't own two barns in the country and a flat in Horsham.'

Henderson picked out a few more items before putting them all back and walking towards the door where Walters now stood.

'You're in the wrong job, Angus. You should be sawing planks and making dovetails.'

'There's no way I could do this. There's no money in it unless you're good,' he said, as he shut the door and locked it. 'In any case, I'm useless at most of the practical stuff. Anything I've ever tried to make is usually dotted with bloodstains where I cut myself.'

'I can see it now, in the John Lewis furniture catalogue, now in, the new Bloodspot Range.'

They returned to the workshop and found Archer sanding down a small filing cabinet. 'Is everything ok?' he asked after he switched off the machine and removed safety goggles and mask.

'Yes, no problem,' Henderson said.

'Can I have a drink of water, please? This dust is catching the back of my throat,' Walters asked.

'Sure.' She followed Archer into the small kitchen at the back.

With his back turned, Henderson searched around

for something marked with his DNA or fingerprints. Near the end of their meeting with Kingston earlier, he'd left a folder behind in his office on purpose and when Kingston started talking to a customer, he went back to retrieve it. He'd picked up the folder and Kingston's plastic coffee cup from the bin, the only one left uncrushed.

There were many small pieces of wood lying around which Archer had probably touched, but Henderson thought it unlikely they would yield traces of DNA or fingerprints. He gave up looking, but wasn't too disappointed as anyone making it onto the suspect shortlist would be invited to Sussex House for further questioning, and DNA samples and fingerprints would be taken then.

He couldn't make up his mind about James Archer, whether to classify him as 'red,' needing no additional investigation, or orange as a 'possible.' He claimed not to know any of the missing women and his name didn't crop up in the lists of the women's friends and acquaintances, not surprising as he only went to the school three or four times a month, but still there was this nagging doubt.

Yes, Archer gave them free rein to look in the barns and while both were full with not enough space to hide a cat, he couldn't get away from the notion that it was a fine place to hide a kidnap victim.

THIRTY-FIVE

Henderson stared out of the window. The sky looked dark and oppressive, mirroring his mood. The drizzly weather and the exasperated expressions of the harassed people queuing in their cars to get into the nearby retail park only added to the feeling of despair. He turned from the window and faced the four officers spaced out around the long table in Meeting Room 2.

'So what you're telling me is nobody did it?'

DC Sally Graham started to say something but a sharp look from Henderson stopped her.

'We've been here,' he said, looking at his watch, 'for over two hours and not one of these so-called suspects has the slightest bit of form, no possible motive we can think of, and only four have access to facilities where we think they could hide a kidnap victim.'

He paused.

'C'mon fellas, I need more or this investigation is about to come to a grinding halt.'

If the pressures on the team weren't enough, CI Edwards had instructed him to bring her concrete information about a serial abductor or the operation would close, put up or shut up she said, as new revelations about Brian Langton had surfaced the day before.

His name had popped up in a bribery case at the Old Bailey where three senior television executives were on trial, accused of making underhand payments to US producers in a bid to have their programmes aired on American television networks, and of procuring young women for their pleasure. Langton was alleged to have participated in many of the activities and several loud voices were calling for him to be charged with these new offences.

Many of the top brass at Sussex Police were congratulating themselves for having the foresight to arrest such a dangerous criminal, and were more confident than ever of gaining a conviction when he appeared at trial for Kelly's murder, sometime in the new year. Edwards in particular, came in for much praise and if Henderson had needed to climb a hill earlier to persuade her to investigate the kidnappings, he now had a mountain to climb if he wanted them to continue.

Lying in bed, wide awake at three in morning, he'd seen that their weakness and the killer's strength both stemmed from the police approach to missing persons. In perhaps an indictment of modern life, no one seemed to question why a grown woman would abandon her home and her children if the pressures became too great, and it took time before anyone realised something else might be wrong. During this time, the car, the house, the office, and everything else that might offer vital clues as to the woman's whereabouts, were likely to be cleaned, altered or destroyed.

If, as he now believed, the same man had abducted both Kelly Langton and Amy Sandford, he was confident at least one name would drop out of their analysis and interviews of friends, business contacts, relatives, acquaintances and people from each of the schools; but other than Darren Kingston and James Archer, neither of whom were entirely convincing, there was no one else.

Now, instead of Brian Langton walking free from jail and the investigation being scaled up to the level he believed it needed to be, Langton would stay in jail and his investigation would be wrapped up in the next few days. If this happened, Henderson was not sure he could continue banging his head against a brick wall every time the press or budget considerations raised their ugly heads. Perhaps it was time for him to do something else.

'We need more, we need more,' he said, to the deflated group. 'We seem to be at a dead end and out of ideas of where to go next.'

Silence greeted his comment. He was about to call a halt to the meeting and suggest they regroup later when everybody might have clearer heads, when Sally Graham said, 'I've just had an idea.'

'Let's hear it.'

'It might be a bit of a long shot sir, but why don't we do a search for any incident taking place close to the houses and premises where we know each of our suspects live and work and the four properties where we think a kidnap victim could be held.'

'Go on.'

'What I'm thinking is this. Let's say, the kidnapper

is holding them for some time and not killing them right away, but keeping them hidden for some sadistic or sexual purpose. He would need to feed them and look after them. What if, someone reported a woman screaming or a scuffle in the back garden or glass breaking? It would be filed as a domestic disturbance, but if it happened near any of these properties, it could indicate something else was going on inside the house, such as the woman trying to escape or him beating her up.'

'I like the sound of this,' Walters said. 'If he's been keeping Amy captive for any length of time, somebody might have reported hearing a shouting match or some unusual banging if she tried to attract somebody's attention.'

This went on a few more minutes, survivors of a sinking ship clutching at the remains of a broken lifeboat, before Henderson called a halt.

'We'll take a break from this for a few hours. Sally, there seems to be some consensus about your theory, and although I'm a bit sceptical, I'm going to let you run with it. Find yourself three or four officers and try to get it done before close of play today.'

'Right sir.'

At twelve-thirty, he walked out of the building and over to the Asda superstore nearby for lunch. He returned straight away, despite the empty fridge at home which needed to be topped up with a bigger shop than this, and ate the egg and bacon sandwich at his desk, no one daring to enter and risk the wrath of his grouchy mood. For the next two hours, he attended two meetings back to back. Both were unrelated to the kidnapping investigation and although each dealt with important administrative and procedural issues, neither received his undivided attention.

He arrived back at his office at five and was about to call Walters, Wallop and Graham back for another tedious update, when Sally Graham walked in. She was a pretty girl with blond hair tied back in a ponytail and big brown eyes, making some of the younger lads swoon, but several fell into the trap of assuming she was all style and no substance, fur coat and nae knickers, as an old desk sergeant in Glasgow used to say. She was smart with her heart set on progressing through the ranks.

'Sorry to interrupt sir, but I think I found something you should see.'

The paper she put in front of him was an Incident Report, written by a police constable at Billingshurst police station. It concerned two lampers who reported the discharge of a gun in a field near the place where they were hunting.

'A lamper?' Henderson said looking up. 'Aren't they those wannabe army types who gear up with night-sights and bright lights and go out shooting deer and badgers in the middle of the night?'

'I think so. Why are they called 'lampers' and not shooters or hunters?'

'They carry these extremely bright lights and once they find their prey, they shine the light into its eyes. For a few vital seconds, the animal is mesmerised, giving them enough them time to raise their weapons and take the shot.'

'Ah, the poor deer.'

'Latest reports say there are over a million deer in Britain and to many farmers they're nothing but a damn nuisance as they eat saplings and break fences. Maybe we should praise the lampers for providing a valuable public service and in time, it might reduce the price of venison.'

'I don't eat meat so it wouldn't affect me.'

He read the report. The lamper concerned was a gun enthusiast and claimed the discharge he heard came from an AK 47, the weapon of choice for insurgents and freedom fighters all over the world.

'Come on,' he said looking up, 'how could he possibly know this?'

'Know what, sir?'

'The shot he heard came from an AK 47. Why not a shotgun or an L85, or whatever assault rifle is being used by the British Army nowadays?'

'I was a bit sceptical myself, so I spoke to PC Wallace at Billingshurst, the officer who wrote the report. This lamper convinced him he can tell the difference between many guns from the noise they make as he's been lamping for years, and he's a member of a gun club.'

'Mmm. Now I think about it, I imagine with a bit of knowledge, it might not be a difficult thing to do.'

'How?'

'Well, if you think these guys are out in the middle of the night and so they're not bothered by the sounds you might hear during the day such as cars, scarecrow bangs, a farmer shooting rabbits, or someone banging in a fence post with a sledgehammer. Also, I would imagine the lampers themselves use different weapons and after a time the noises they make are probably discernible to their mates.'

'Makes sense.'

'Although I don't know how he knows it came from a particular rifle unless he used to be in the army. It's not the sort of weapon you would find in the average gun club. Did Billingshurst investigate the incident?'

'They took it seriously, from what I understand. They conducted door-to-door inquiries in the area but they couldn't find anyone to corroborate it, so they didn't take it any further. I suppose most people were asleep when it happened.'

He put the report down on the table and looked at Graham. 'What does this tell us? A former soldier likes shooting at night?'

'A bit more than that, I think. Look at the place where they said they heard it,' she said, pointing at the map attached to the report. 'In a field near Adversane Lane.'

The name rang a bell. 'Isn't that the name of the road where James Archer's got his furniture business?'

'Yes.'

He leapt up and pulled an Ordinance Survey map of Sussex from the unstable bookcase and opened it out across the table. The cop who wrote the Incident Report did a good job as Henderson easily pinpointed the place where the lamper heard the shot. He traced the distance he and Walters had travelled along Adversane Lane to meet James Archer, and could see three properties within a half-mile radius of where the shot was fired. Smack in the centre was James Archer's furniture business.

'Wait a minute though,' he said, 'could there be a more, let's not say innocent, but reasonable explanation for owning and discharging an assault rifle in the middle of the night?'

'You mean rather than shooting innocent women?'

'I mean, say some guy sets up a couple of targets in his back garden and does some shooting practice when it's dark so no one can see what he's doing.'

'Wouldn't he be better shooting during the day when the noise he makes might be confused with all the other daytime noises you mentioned before?'

'Could be.'

'What if the shot was by the kidnapper executing his victim or shooting her when she tried to escape. Maybe, he plays a game with them and lets them run away before hunting them down like rabbits. I saw it in a movie once.'

He stared at her. She looked so sweet and innocent, no way would he take her for a fan of horror or slasher movies. 'Wouldn't it be a bit risky though, with all those twitchers walking around with their night vision goggles and bright lights?'

'Lampers.'

'Eh?'

'They're lampers not twitchers. Twitching is what we bird fanciers do.'

'My apologies for slighting your hobby but take my point. If Rambo and his mates are out there and they can tell the difference between an AK47 and an L85 simply by hearing it fired, wouldn't it be a bit risky to be out there executing women? They probably carry light-enhancing video cameras to record their every kill.'

'I agree, but maybe something out of the ordinary happened. Maybe someone came too close to discovering what was going on, or she escaped.'

'An interesting theory and one we might be able to verify when we catch him. This might sound like a stupid question, but do we know if lampers are regular users of illegal weapons like the AK47?'

She shook her head. 'No. PC Wallace at Billingshurst said they carry shotguns, .22 rifles and airguns. These guys are legal by all accounts and the animals they're after don't require anything more powerful.'

'I suppose so. Using an assault rifle would run the risk of the bullet going through the head of a deer, then someone's bedroom window or killing one of their buddies when it ricochets off a rock.'

'So we're back to an unknown discharge.'

'When did it happen?' Henderson asked.

'Monday 17th October. Just over a week ago.'

He picked up his Operation Condor file and leafed through the papers until he found the document he wanted. 'Roughly eleven days after Amy Sandford went missing. Now isn't that interesting?'

THIRTY-SIX

'Coincidences, coincidences,' Henderson said, as he paced up and down in the lounge of his flat in Vernon Terrace. In one hand he held a large glass of whisky and in the other, a copy of the AK47 gunshot Incident Report.

He accepted the word of the lamper, but why wouldn't he? In the silence of the night he reckoned he would be able to tell the report of an assault rifle from a shotgun, air gun, or .22 rifle, and even if it was not an AK47, it was still an illegal and dangerous weapon fired by someone close by James Archer's furniture workshop. The question remained, why?

For hundreds of years, soldiers returning from conflicts overseas had brought back souvenirs; for some it meant beads, clothes, or sexually transmitted diseases, and for others, captured knives, handguns, grenades, and rifles. Even without the recent conflicts in Syria, Iraq, and Afghanistan, millions of assault rifles were available for sale in Africa, Asia, and parts of the former Soviet Union, especially after their failed invasion of Afghanistan when many thousands of disillusioned and unpaid soldiers sold their weapons to the highest bidder in order to raise enough money to buy food and the train fare home.

The problem for anyone waking up in a hotel room or military barracks after a drunken night out, only to find they now owned a well-used assault rifle with a full clip of ammunition, was how to bring it back to the UK. For a civilian, it would be a chastening experience and the best they could hope for was not being spotted when they consigned it to the nearby skip after taking a vow to limit alcohol consumption in future. A soldier wouldn't experience any such problems. They were part of a vast military transport machine, designed to move weapons and equipment to any part of the world and any soldier with a good understanding of the checks made by Customs and Military Police, could soon spirit the weapon into their own private arms cache.

The discharge of an assault rifle in the towns and fields of Afghanistan or Iraq was dangerous, but to do so in West Sussex, in places often appearing uninhabited when it was nothing of the sort, could only be seen as irresponsible and stupid. Unless of course, something out of the ordinary had happened as envisaged by the vivid imagination of DC Sally Graham.

He tossed around the notion that perhaps a fellow lamper used such a weapon, but the coincidences seemed too great to ignore. Archer was a strong and capable guy and may even have been ex-forces, the shooting incident took place no more than a half-mile from his business, and Amy Sandford disappeared only eleven days before. He put the whisky glass down untouched, grabbed his jacket and headed out to the car.

When he reached Dyke Road, he called Walters, but after five or six rings was diverted to voicemail. He then remembered she was going out tonight with her mates, the witches coven he called them, as even she, often the calmest and most level-headed member of the team, needed a blow-out now and again. He didn't think she was ignoring him, but more likely sitting around in a noisy pub or jumping around to banging music in a club and couldn't hear it ring.

On the point of hanging up, he decided to leave a message. 'Hi Carol, it's Angus. I'm on my way to Archer's place to take a look around. Sally showed me a gunshot discharge report and I think it shows him in a different light. Don't get too drunk as we've got a lot to do tomorrow. If you get into the office early, fat chance I know, I'll bring you up to date before the team meeting. Bye.'

By the time he reached the A23, heading north towards Bolney, he became engrossed in a programme on Radio Four about gambling. He didn't gamble much himself apart from the odd game of poker where his 'winnings' were in the red, which he wrote off as the cost of an evening out.

His father had never gambled in his life, not even to enter a sweepstake for the Grand National, but his father's brother did, and in common with a couple of the radio interviewees, spent every penny passing through his fingers on the habit and lost all contact with his wife and children as a result. After about ten minutes, it became too depressing and he changed to Radio Sussex for some light relief.

Few cars passed by as he drove along Adversane

Lane, but it was after eleven o'clock and most sensible people were in bed. He reached the track leading up to Archer's business, stopped and stared hard at the shadowy forms at the top of the bumpy drive. Archer's wife had told them her ex-husband spent a lot of his time there but as far as he could see, the buildings were in darkness.

A quarter of a mile down the road, he pulled into a siding beside a farm gate. He doused the lights and removed a pair of walking shoes and a waterproof jacket from the boot. He looked up and down the road for approaching cars, and satisfied that a curious farmer was not monitoring his nocturnal activities, he climbed the gate and began walking across the field.

The ground was uneven and full of rabbit holes and mole hills and he needed to be careful where he put his feet, as he didn't fancy a twisted ankle and being forced to explain to his boss his reasons for being there. In his jacket pocket, he found his trusty Maglite and true to form, it still worked. It was a clear, crisp night and he switched it off to save the batteries as he could see fine without it.

In his mind he tried to visualise the Ordinance Survey map he'd looked at earlier with Sally and the first of three houses, all within close proximity to the gunshot discharge, was coming up. From research conducted on the web and using Google maps and satellite imagery, he knew the first farmhouse was occupied and so the field he was walking over probably belonged to them, although he couldn't be accused of causing damage, as nothing much would be planted with winter only a month or so away.

It consisted of a modest house with a couple of barns. The barns lay a fair distance from the house, giving Henderson the confidence to take a good look around without fear of alerting the occupants or waking a sleeping dog. Both barns were open with no doors or windows and one was filled with two tractors, a large tank of red diesel, and various rusting tractor parts and accessories, while the other contained a huge, lethal-looking threshing machine and dozens of sacks of fertiliser. The buildings were old as broad gaps appeared between the panels of each wall allowing the meagre amount of light available outside to pass through.

He walked away, giving the farmhouse a wide berth to avoid any PIRs connected to security lights or an alarm, and headed towards Archer's place. The walking was playing havoc with the joints in his knees and ankles and even though the field appeared flat with only a slight slope moving up to where Archer's barns were located, the terrain was full of ruts and ridges and his shoes frequently slipping on the damp grass. Twenty minutes later he was close enough to make out the nearest barn, the building Archer used as a storeroom, and with no lights or car out front, he was confident Archer wasn't there.

He reached the storeroom, the place he and Walters looked inside a few days before, and walked around its perimeter, staring at the timbers, seeing if he could spot a chink of light. If Archer had kidnapped Kelly or Amy, Henderson felt sure he would hide his victim here, but after a few minutes of methodical walking and searching, he was disappointed not to find anything amiss. He walked across the courtyard to the place Archer used for a workshop and did the same there.

Behind the workshop, he came across a small awning with a wheelbarrow, pieces of off-cut timber, fence panels, and various other bits, but in common with his perimeter tour of the storeroom, he found nothing strange.

Returning here, it reminded him once again what an ideal place it was to hide a kidnap victim and with the fields and woods nearby, hundreds of remote places to bury a body. He couldn't see any lights to indicate the presence of a kidnapped woman and his half hope that Archer had left something incriminating lying around in the mistaken belief that the remoteness of the site exempted him from scrutiny, were dashed like a wooden boat on sharp rocks.

If he could find something to punch without breaking his hand, he would do so and if he could scream without waking every dog in the neighbourhood, he would do that as well. This was it, the card all his money was riding on but it came up a dud.

THIRTY-SEVEN

Henderson walked back to the car, out of luck and out of ideas. The third property, close to the place where the lamper heard the gunshot, turned out to be a smartly presented barn and quite unlike the derelict bundle of rotten wood it looked to be on the web. He wasn't really surprised, as satellite pictures were often several years old and every farmer with an eye on the bottom line and who was fed up looking at the eyesore from his kitchen window, was soon converting old barns and selling them for high profits as upmarket housing.

His search there also drew a blank. It was a big place, clean, and recently renovated, as if about to be put up for sale, evident from close-fitting wood panels, new windows and doors, and a high level of landscaping outside. Looking inside, which he could do through the big picture window in the lounge with the torch, it was devoid of furniture, curtains, pictures on the wall, and carpets on the floor, and more important from his point of view, no kidnap victim.

He walked up a slope, keeping well away from Archer's place, shoulders slumped, heading back to a large glass of whisky and to plan his next move, if there was one to plan although he didn't know what it might be at this precise moment.

It was a lovely clear night, the stars visible in all their glory. He didn't know many galaxies but recognised Orion, The Plough, and the Seven Sisters. In his youth, he'd spent many nights like this, lying on the grass on the outskirts of Fort William, scanning the crisp night sky for shooting stars, planets, satellites, and trying to see as far into the universe as he could, often with his best friend and a couple of cans of strong beer by their side.

A few minutes later, and with his astronomy knowledge exhausted, he carried on walking. The flight of an owl caught his eye: large, silent and utterly majestic. He followed it over the trees until it disappeared into a wood on the far side of the third property, its wings beating casually as it searched the ground for prey. There, high up on the roof of the renovated barn, he could see a light.

He looked again; yes it was a light, he wasn't seeing things or had the starlight of Sirius imprinted on the back of his eye. He walked back to the barn. With the moon at his back, he peered inside but the place was as empty as it had been ten minutes before. He stared hard at the back wall, below the point where he saw the light, but spotted nothing. He walked away and once again, looked up at the roof. It was a steep, sloping roof with a single Velux-style window half-way up, and no, his mind wasn't playing tricks, it was bathed in the glow of artificial light.

He walked back to the building, perplexed. Every school kid who had once endured endless hours in a boring physics lab, knew about light and its amazing capacity for escaping through the tiniest of spaces, and with pitch darkness all around, he should see something. He often caught criminals holed up in empty, deserted properties who were given away by the light of their mobile phone as they tried to call their mates or the flashing of a Bluetooth headset, still attached to their ear.

He was a rational man and the only logical explanation he could think of, was that there had to be a secret room or compartment behind the wall. The design of such a place required the skills of an excellent carpenter and was it too much of a coincidence to find one such individual living next door, albeit four hundred yards away?

He tried the windows but they were sealed double-glazed units and securely locked. The door was wooden and protected by two deadlocks, so much for people in the country being more trusting. He banged the door and windows for several minutes but received no reply. He sighed, there was nothing else for it.

He walked to the back of the barn and bent down to examine a ladder he'd spotted earlier. It was long, probably long enough to reach the roof and most likely used by the owner to make repairs and clean out leaves from the gutters during the autumn. It was tied to a fixed metal pole to stop it moving around in the wind rather than to deter burglars, as they would come prepared with a sharp lock knife, but as a man with skills at tying and untying all manner of wet ropes in the worst possible weather conditions aboard 'Mingary', undoing it was a doddle.

The back of the barn looked a better place to erect the ladder as it could be propped up against a small ridge which would stop the base slipping, but it would put him on the wrong side of the roof and no way did he fancy climbing over the top, thirty feet above the ground with nothing to prevent him sliding down the other side.

The only place it could be anchored was a shallow recess over a drain in the courtyard and while it would position him a touch to the left of where he wanted to be, it was better than giving the base no support at all. As quietly as possible, not wishing to wake sharp-eared dogs and have them howling, he laid the ladder on the ground, extended all the sections and locked them in place. With a heave, he hauled it upright, positioned the base over the drain and slowly let it drop until it rested against the barn roof. After a quick look around to make sure no one was watching, he took a deep breath and put his weight on the first rung.

At the eight or ninth step it creaked and shifted in its rest, causing him to look down, a big mistake as he was in the shadow of the barn and couldn't see a thing, but almost at once his head started to swim and he felt dizzy. He turned around and gripped the sides of the ladder with both hands until his breathing and woozy head returned to normal.

Near the top of the climb, he was pleased to see the ladder rested on a thick, metal gutter, as the more common alternative, UPVC, would bend and flex, making everything move, and depending on the weight placed upon it, might even crack or snap, a sound to wake up even the heaviest sleeper. The heavy gutter offered the added advantage of offering something to hold while he made those final, crucial steps.

He was closer to the window than he thought he would be, which saved some awkward clambering and at this stage of proceedings, any small mercies were gratefully received. Gripping the ladder in his left hand, he leaned over the roof and craned his neck to look inside the window.

It looked to be a narrow room, as long as the width of the barn and secreted behind the end wall. The room was brightly lit and contained a wardrobe, toilet, sink and a chair but not much else, causing his spirits to drop. He was glad he hadn't found a spare room full of dustsheets and overalls, but instead it was probably the temporary living quarters of the owner while he redecorated.

He took a further step up, a point beyond his comfort zone, and now with nothing in front of him now except the roof. He could see slightly more of the room and was shocked to see someone *was* in there. He ducked back. It could be the owner, who might well be James Archer, as Henderson had crossed no fences to get there, or a granny flat for a grizzly, elderly relative. Either way, the sensible course of action was to get the hell out of there, pronto, but curiosity coursed through his veins like a drug and he needed to know more.

He leaned forward and looked again. He could only see a pair of legs, crossed, encased in jeans and ending with bare feet. The jeans were tight and on shapely legs with slender feet, and they sure didn't belong to a man or an old woman.

Using the window for grip, he eased further up the glass. The woman's legs were no longer crossed but spaced apart and he could now see they were slim and long with small feet and toenails painted in a bright purple colour. He rapped his knuckles on the glass. His knock sounded flat and dead, the glass thick and double or triple-glazed, with reinforcing wire between the panes. He waited but it made no impression on the woman inside, she didn't move a muscle.

He repositioned and started hammering on the glass with the heel of his hand. Now he got a reaction. The legs suddenly moved and planted themselves on the floor and the shocked face of a young woman stared back at him. She looked tall and slim with short dark hair. In an instant, her face changed from one of surprise to one of shock and moments later, she started screaming.

He couldn't hear her at all, suggesting the room might be soundproofed but he got the message. He'd experienced similar situations in the past, mainly with jumpers and illegal aliens and often the production of the police ID was enough to assure the person he was part of the solution and not an extension of the problem. He reached into his jacket to retrieve it.

The sudden, jerky movement caused his right foot to slip from the rung. For a second, he recovered his balance but the ladder started to move towards him and he lost his grip of the window and began sliding down the rungs. He tried to slow down by gripping the sides but he was falling too fast and the friction between his hands and the cold metal burned his skin.

When ten feet off the ground, the ladder slid from the roof and with nothing else for it, he jumped. For several moments, time seemed to stand still and in an instant he could see his surroundings: the ladder falling beside him, a bird rising from a tree, a car moving on the road below, and the ground rushing up to meet him. He thumped into the courtyard, his legs folding under him. He heard a loud crack.

An involuntary scream escaped from his mouth as intense pain coursed through his body with the stabbing sensation of a dozen kitchen knives. Out of the corner of his eye, the ladder clattered into the ground in an awful cacophony of clanking and crashing, the noise of a metal monster emerging from a crypt in a horror film.

He lay there for ten or fifteen minutes, half-dreaming, half-sleeping and despite the chill of the night, his brow felt hot and sodden with sweat. He tried to stand but couldn't as the burns on his hand wouldn't allow him to apply enough pressure to lever his body up.

He reached into his jacket for his phone, but it didn't look good when he finally managed to pull it out as the screen was smashed and the case cracked in various places with small bits of plastic falling off in his hand. It was on and working before the fall, but the screen was now blank and when he tried to switch it back on, his fears were realised when it refused to respond.

The sharp pain in his left leg was gradually subsiding to be replaced by a deep throb, as rhythmic as the bass player of a rock band, and endurable until he tried to move, when the sharp pain returned a hundred times more intense.

Only then did he realise his leg was broken.

THIRTY-EIGHT

The note on the bed informing Elaine Chivers she was a kidnap victim did little to calm her. What Steve Egan, or whatever the hell his name was, didn't realise, was that she was a highly trained security expert with expertise in handling weapons, unarmed combat and survival.

She and her colleagues at Gatwick Airport were instructed never to reveal the true nature of their role to even their closest family members and not to any of the millions of passengers who passed through the place every year. She could be one of the most annoying people at the airport, rummaging through personal belongings when the X-ray machine operator became suspicious of what she saw inside someone's bag, making the owners feel as guilty as hell for being singled out. To them, she was a low-paid bag-searcher, but to Gatwick Security, she was one of their key front-line troops in a daily battle against terrorism and illegal smuggling.

One day in this place and she was already forming plans for her escape. It did not take long to realise he was drugging her with some form of date-rape drug, as she tasted its bitterness on her lips when she woke up, but she was at a loss as to why she had been selected. She didn't earn a lot of money and spent most of it on clothes, her expensive flat in a new development close to Three Bridges station, and in socialising. She didn't come from a rich or famous family, her dad worked as a planning official with Crawley Town Council and her mum owned a hairdressing business in the town.

On the first night, she'd sat in the corner ready to defend herself if he came in to rape her or to perform some strange sadistic act. Her job was intensive while on duty, but for long periods she often lazed around with nothing to do and used the time to text friends, flick through magazines, talk shop with colleagues, and read loads of books.

She avoided chick-lit and vampire novels but adored authors such as Brent Easton Ellis and Thomas Harris, and she'd read *Silence of The Lambs* three times, but if re-covering the hall table lamp was part of her kidnapper's plan, her skin was staying exactly where it was, thank you very much mate.

To her surprise, the attack didn't come, but after the first meal and her subsequent vague recollection of what happened afterwards, she knew she was being drugged and already thinking of ways to combat it. She suspected her clothes were being tampered with and maybe he came in to have sex with her, but she couldn't be sure until the end of the following day.

She planned to get to know his routine over the next day or two and exploit any weaknesses she could find. She knew how date-rape drugs worked and suspected the kidnapper used to be in the army, but on a one-to-one, his faded military combat training would pull up short against what she was trained to do. Confidence was everything and so it was important for her to keep her spirits up.

Day two, and things were going as well as she expected, but then she saw the face at the window. She felt spooked, but what girl wouldn't be surprised with a strange man peering into her bedroom window? It didn't take long to realise he was most likely a policeman or a fireman or some other rescue service, as who else would be clambering over the roof at this time of night? If so, why didn't he and his buddies kick the door in?

She didn't panic as she remembered her training but she started to scream at the top of her voice to try and tell him to get her out. She knew the room was soundproofed, as she couldn't hear birdsong or passing cars, and he wouldn't be able to hear her unless she screeched as loud as possible.

Later, she chided herself for overdoing it and coming across like a hysterical teenager, freaked-out by a hideous face at the window, as featured in a thousand horror movies, but it was reassuring to know he was there at all. It proved someone was looking for her and his sudden departure would be to summon additional help. If Gatwick Security had called it in, she was impressed by their rapid response, as she had only been missing a short time.

After the strange encounter with her window visitor, time moved slowly and it took the passage of a couple more hours before she felt tired enough to lie down and sleep. Even though nothing indicated the imminent arrival of the cavalry, difficult to assess with any accuracy on account of the high level of soundproofing, it didn't stop her glancing up at the window every ten seconds or so and lying as far from the door as possible, just in case it flew open and a SWAT team barged in.

The darkness made her feel despondent, as she knew even on the busiest nights, the police would never take this long to respond to an emergency. She began to doubt if the man at the window was from the emergency services at all, but instead a burglar, shocked to find someone at home, before scarpering. No, even though she only saw him for less than a minute and only from the shoulders up, her knight in shining armour didn't look like a burglar, he looked like a cop. She'd met plenty of them in her job and could recognise one at a hundred paces.

She'd been such a fool to fall for the suave, good looking and tanned Steve Egan. He didn't look like the usual sort of guy she went out with, but all his fine talk of deals and contracts seemed to be so exciting. Working at an airport, all they discussed in the staff room was far-off destinations, lying in the sun and sightseeing, and it only succeeded in making the people who worked there, long to visit such places themselves. When the seemingly rich Mr Egan promised her the lot, she fell for it hook, line and bloody sinker.

She now realised he was sham and all the profiling and psychological techniques she used on passengers should have been applied to her personal life, as he didn't wear expensive clothes or drive a smart car and anyone could say the fine words he spoke. She felt a fool for not sussing it earlier and cursed herself for dropping her guard.

When, not if, she got out of here, her boss, far from being pleased at her return, would give her a serious bollocking for getting snatched so easily. He was her guiding light and mentor and paid for all the expensive training courses she attended and maybe when the heat died down following his arrest and she learned to live with the 'survivor' tag, she would be transferred into a back-office position or fired, as who would have any confidence in a member of airport security staff if they could be seduced by a smooth talking dude with fine words and empty promises?

Her training taught her to assume the worst and in this case, to assume the kidnapper would kill her, if he wanted a ransom paid or not. Time now became an important issue too. The longer it went on, the more it would suggest negotiations between the kidnapper and her employer were not progressing and with food rations less than she would like, in a week or two her main weapons, strength, confidence, and energy would start to deplete.

Tiredness took over and with reluctance she resigned herself to the disappointment of no one coming tonight. Forever the optimist, she felt comforted by the thought that perhaps the delay was deliberate, leaving everything in place so as not to alert the kidnapper and wait for him to show up in the morning and nab him.

When they did, she would be the first to kick him in the balls and scratch his face with her short, but tapered nails. He didn't have any right to lock her up like this and deprive her of her liberty and she would make it her mission to ensure the story was told to every newspaper and television station in the land. Doing so might save her job and ensure the twisted bastard spent the rest of his miserable life in jail.

THIRTY-NINE

It was a beautiful crisp late-October morning, a sharp morning chill to be followed by clear, blue skies and unbroken winter sunshine, according to the weather report, but Max Baris, aka Martin Swift, Steve Egan, and a few other names he used when it suited him, didn't believe in the tooth fairy either and always trusted his own judgement.

He shut the door of his flat and heard the Yale make a satisfying click. Despite living on the third floor of a modern block of flats in Horsham, with a stout front door and a keypad entry system, he locked the deadlock.

His car was parked in Bay 4 out back, as even though it was an expensive apartment block, it didn't stretch to underground parking, but being rich, he owned another flat in the building and so had two parking slots. Today he would take the Defender.

'Mr Baris, I'm so glad I've caught you.'

He turned, his face frowning at the approaching figure of his neighbour, Victoria Larchwood, a sixty-plus retiree with nothing to do with her time but to annoy her fellow flat dwellers.

'I would like to complain about the noise from your stereo system.'

'When?'

'The night before last.'

'I had guests.'

'It's not the first time you know. Only last week...'

He tuned out. He had been smoking some fabulous weed and had turned up the sound of the stereo to drown out the strange voices which scrabbled around his head like a family of mice in the loft space whenever he took dope.

'I can't put up with it any more,' she said, 'I need my sleep and it disturbs Buggles. The poor dog hides under the bed.'

'I'll do what I can.' If it means drowning the dog, he would do that too.

'You'll need to do more than that,' she said as she walked away. 'Next time, I'm calling the police.'

He slammed the car door and started the engine. His lips moved, not in time to the Taylor Swift song on the radio but running through a list of kill scenarios he would exact on old Mrs Larchwood at the first whiff of police darkening his door.

Driving always calmed him down and by the time he arrived at the barn in Adversane Lane, he looked forward to breakfast, followed by sex with his new friend, Elaine. He reached for the key to switch off the engine when he spotted a body, lying against the wall of the barn. Good job he'd chosen to drive in the Defender, as he kept a couple of guns in a secret compartment in the back. He removed the handgun and exited the car cautiously.

It was a stupid thing to do, to confront a council official or a bloke from the water company with a loaded weapon, if he didn't want to spend a long time in jail, so he kept it down low, but not out of sight as there wasn't an election on, his community charge was up to date, and the water meter was half-way down the driveway.

The man lay against the wall of the barn, soaking up the morning sunshine, but he knew from his awkward posture he wasn't a lost hiker, but someone who'd used his ladder, only to fall off and break something. Who the hell was he and what did he want around here? Did he know what went on inside the barn? If so, he might not realise it but he wasn't long for this world.

He kicked the nearest leg and the man woke up with a start.

'Hey.'

'What the fuck are you doing here? This is private property.'

'What...what? Who are you?'

He kicked him again. 'I ask the questions. Who are you?'

'Detective Inspector Henderson, Sussex Police.'

Fuck, police. 'What are you doing here?'

'I'm,' he said, shifting his body position, 'looking for some missing women.'

'Well, you won't find them here.' He smiled, a private joke. Henderson shivered. 'You been here all night?'

'No.'

'Liar. It's bad luck for you but good luck for me eh? What were you doing with my ladder?'

'Don't come the innocent with me mate. You're

Martin Swift, aren't you? You've got a woman locked up in there.'

He kicked him again, harder this time. 'Shut the fuck up. You've said enough.' He levelled the gun at his head. 'C'mon get up.'

'I can't. I broke my leg. I can't walk otherwise I wouldn't be lying here.'

'Why didn't you call for help, or are you coppers so strapped for cash they don't give you radios any more?'

'I called for reinforcements, they'll be here any minute.'

Baris leaned over and reached into Henderson's jacket and pulled out his phone. The case was smashed, the electronic circuits visible and the screen broken as if it had taken a smack when he fell. He tried to switch it on and when it wouldn't, he lobbed it into the long grass.

'Ha.' Another piece of good luck. 'Listen to me copper. I'll help you move inside, but if you try any funny stuff, I'll blow your fucking head off. Understand?'

Henderson grunted.

He pulled him to his feet and put his shoulder under Henderson's right arm to take the weight off his broken leg and led him into the barn. He dumped the dishevelled DI into a chair and walked into the kitchen and filled the kettle. When it boiled, he made two mugs of coffee. He handed one to Henderson and drank his own while standing close to the cop.

'How did you find me?'

Henderson told him the story about the AK47

gunshot discharge and after asking a couple of questions of his own, it didn't take long to realise the copper had come here under his own initiative. Christ! The third piece of luck this morning and it wasn't even nine o'clock.

In his current state, Henderson didn't threaten him but he couldn't kill him here. He was a tidy and disciplined person and nothing around here or in the surrounding fields could tie him to any of the missing women and it would remain that way. He would take him to the woods where he took the others. It would be risky in daylight but to delay might encourage more of his ilk to come snooping.

'What do you intend to do now?' Henderson said.

'I'm still thinking about it.'

'You're finished. You made too many mistakes.'

'Mistakes?' He leaned over, putting his face close to Henderson's. 'The only mistake I made is talking to you, copper.'

'What about Amy Sandford and Kelly Langton, two similar looking women from the same type of school?'

'Is this how you found me?' Damn, he knew he shouldn't have done it. He used gyms, cafes, and nightclubs to meet women, but Jimmy told him about all the fine looking women at his kids' school including a couple of celebs, and it didn't disappoint.

'More or less.'

'You got lucky, mate.'

Henderson shifted in the chair, pain etched on his face. 'Tell me one thing.'

'What?'

'Where did you bury them?'

'Bury who? You got it all wrong mate. Try Archer over the field, he's the strange one.'

'The women, the women you kidnapped. Like the woman you've got in there,' he said, pointing towards his secret room, 'behind the wall.'

Baris picked up a slat of wood, a sample from the company who laid the flooring, and whacked him on the side of his face.

'Shut the fuck up, I've heard enough from you.'

He turned away and headed into the kitchen and packed some of his things into a large sports bag he used for his gym kit, something to eat and drink later, as he hadn't eaten breakfast and wanted the copper to think they were evacuating the place.

He carried the bag out to the car and after making sure the shovel, rifle, and gloves were in the back, he reversed it towards the door of the barn. He walked inside and grabbed Henderson. He could feel it in his bones. Today was turning into a great day.

FORTY

The shrill whine of the Sony radio alarm clock penetrated deep into her skull, despite being buried under the duvet and holding it tight around her ears. It was no use resisting, her brain rattled to its awful sound.

Carol Walters could not get up this morning, or any morning come to that, and in order to make it into work on time, she used several alarm clocks, all set at their highest ring volume and hidden in awkward places at the far side of the bedroom, impossible to find unless both eyes were open. No matter how hard she tried, it was never enough and she turned up late for more meetings and more appointments than anyone else in Sussex House. The boys in the fingerprint unit, misogynist, sexist pigs to a man, called her 'late-note' but that was preferable to any nickname making reference to her legs, bum, or how she performed in bed.

She drove carefully through town, feeling certain the bottle of wine and a couple of vodkas drunk last night while enjoying a good natter with some of her mates, would still be in her system and take her over the drink-driving limit. Most civilians believed that coppers were immune from prosecution, a sort of perk of the job like the discount card given to Marks and Spencer employees, but traffic cops enjoyed nothing better than arresting a drunken detective. It would make their day and give them something special to regale their mates with back at John Street canteen and after the case went to court, she would be lucky to be in there with them, back in uniform, her career path blighted.

She parked the car at the far end of the Sussex House car park in a row of empty spaces. No way would she try and fit her car into a tight space near the entrance, as knowing her luck, the cars either side would belong to a visiting Chief Constable and a minister from the Home Office.

Several coffees and paracetamol later, she felt well enough to switch on her computer and phone. Unlike many of her friends who loved their mobiles and swore they never switched them off, she had a love-hate relationship with the thing. She loved sending texts to new boyfriends and family members and receiving messages back in text-speak which took her ages to decipher, but she hated the frequent interruption of banal work messages, telling her to submit her expenses or requesting her attendance at a tedious meeting.

She started reading a report from the forensics boys about Amy Sandford's car, found two days ago on a quiet road in Burgess Hill, close to the railway station when the phone beeped, indicating four messages. The first was from her neighbour Jon asking if she would like to come out for a drink this evening. She replied 'ok', a fair reward for helping him to repair a leaking tap, but did it make sense to go out with a man who couldn't do DIY?

The second message was from her mum, bemoaning the fact she never called. In fact, she'd called her several times over the last few days but the daft old bat often forgot to switch her phone on and when she did, it usually didn't have any battery power.

The DNA lab left the third, informing her the investigation into the flat in Richmond Road was complete and a copy of their report was on its way to her. She knew most of the findings already, but it often paid dividends to read the report in detail later as something that first appeared trivial, might well be important to the investigation. However, she hoped it wouldn't arrive today, as there was a time for staring at hair samples, fingernail fragments and the contents of the vacuum cleaner bag, but this wasn't it.

DI Henderson left the fourth, informing her he was heading out to Archer's place to have a look around and advising her of a meeting first thing this morning. She looked at her watch, 8:00am and an early meeting for him meant 7:30am. So where the hell was he? And why did he go over to Archer's place?

She dialled his mobile but it diverted to the answering service. She tossed the phone into her in-tray and spent a few minutes opening post and checking emails, in case he'd sent her something late last night. A few minutes later, she called his mobile again followed by his home phone. They both defaulted to their answering services.

A few members of the Condor team sat in huddles, working at computers or standing by the window having a natter with colleagues and sipping coffee. She cleared her throat. 'Does anybody know where DI Henderson is?'

'No, no idea, sarg,' DC Phil Bentley said. 'I haven't seen him this morning.'

'Nope,' DC Steve Evans said, 'I ain't seen him around. Have you tried his office?'

On another day, such a stupid comment would be slapped down with a cutting riposte but instead she threw Evans a dirty look and returned to her computer screen. She knew Henderson's girlfriend Rachel worked for *The Argus* but not if the relationship was on or off, as Henderson had said they fell out big-time a few weeks back. She drummed her fingers on the desk, debating the issue in her mind for several minutes before exclaiming, 'what the hell,' and picked up the phone.

'Hello Rachel, it's Carol Walters.'

'Hello Carol, how are you?'

'I'm fine, I—'

'Last time we met, you were looking for a sports top. Did you get it?'

'I did, in a mountaineering shop, if you can believe it, and now I've joined a gym. I did my first spin class this week.'

'Well done you. How did it go?'

'Knackering. It's the hardest work I've done for ages.'

She laughed. 'I'll stick to Pilates.'

'Did you see Angus last night?'

'No, I told him I was staying in to wash my hair. Only partly true as I was also finished off an essay for

332

my Open University course.'

'How's it going?'

'Like your spin class, it's knackering.'

'Ha. It'll be worth it in the end. You don't know if he got called away to a meeting or something?'

'No, I don't. He didn't show up at the office this morning?'

'No, but I suspect it's nothing. More than likely there's a meeting in his diary he forgot to tell me about.'

'You know what he's like.'

'I sure do. Talk to you later. Bye.'

She walked through the double doors and opened the door to Henderson's office. If he'd been inside and the door closed for a while, a wave of coffee and the aroma of Paco Rabanne would flood out, or closer to lunchtime it might change to egg and cress or tuna, but instead it reeked of cleaning fluids and furniture polish.

She thumbed through his desk dairy but found nothing unusual and no urgent notes were lying on the desk or stuck to the monitor screen. She walked out and headed downstairs. Huddling close together and sheltered from the wind by the side of the building, she joined a small throng of ardent smokers.

It was true of Sussex Police and every organisation she had ever worked for, but this strange cabal of nicotine addicts, standing out in all weathers and braving a barrage of insults from a growing band of former smokers who sneered with an elevated sense of smugness, were often better informed and more savvy about what went on inside the building, than either the senior management group or the Human Resources department. In the past, she'd learned about organisational changes, disciplinary action and affairs between colleagues, before everyone else in her team, but this time they were as devoid of information about DI Henderson's whereabouts as everybody else.

Suddenly, as if struck by an idea or an impulse, she shouted a hasty 'bye' to the curious onlookers, before running into the building and dashing upstairs, two steps at a time. At her workstation, she grabbed her jacket and car keys and commandeered, rather than requested, DC Phil Bentley to accompany her, his punishment for not helping earlier.

Walters didn't hesitate this time as she guided the car through lines of parked cars to the exit. When they arrived at Seven Dials, the area looked devoid of commuters, now on their way to offices and shops in London, but busy with the arrival of mums for a spot of retail therapy or a coffee after dropping the kids off at school. Whatever the reason, free parking places were as rare as hen's teeth.

The only space available close to Henderson's flat wasn't a space at all, painted with a set of double yellow lines, but knowing the bulldog-like tenacity of Brighton traffic wardens, Walters left her 'Police Business' sign visible on the windscreen. It wouldn't stop them issuing a ticket but it would buy her some time as they dithered about what to do.

Henderson lived on the top floor of a renovated Edwardian terrace, the front door secured by a phone entry system. After pressing Henderson's bell several times and calling his home phone and mobile without reply, Walters rang the bell of his ground floor neighbour, Mrs Grant. Walters didn't know the woman but Henderson told her she was a nosey old bat who spied on everyone who lived there, as he would often see the curtains twitching late on a Friday or Saturday night when he and Rachel stood by the door fumbling for the keys, and one another most likely, while they tried to open the door.

She cursed as a heavy lorry rumbled past, just as a response squawked from the metal box. She leaned closer to the wall.

'Hello, can you hear me? Hello. Is that you Mrs Grant? This is Detective Sergeant Walters from Sussex Police.'

'Oh, Sussex Police you say? We've got one of them upstairs, a policeman I mean. Detective Angus Henderson, he's called. He's a nice man, a very nice man.'

'I know Mrs Grant, he's my boss and I'm trying to reach him. I'm getting no reply from his buzzer. Can you please let me in so I can knock on his door? I need to speak to him urgently.'

'Oh, oh, I'm not sure. How do I know you are who you say you are? There's been burglars and all sorts around here lately, yes there has.' The box went quiet for several seconds. 'Oh, I don't know. Hold your warrant card up to the window so I can see it. Angus said I should always ask.'

Walters pressed her ID card to the window and a few moments later the lock on the door unlatched with a light 'clunk.' The two officers raced inside and ran upstairs. Outside Henderson's flat, Walters banged on the door with her fist in a succession of short bursts, pausing for several seconds in between to listen for any signs of movement.

A sudden noise made Walters jump but it wasn't the DI returning with an empty bin or a bag of shopping in his hand, wondering what they were doing there, but Mrs Grant, wheezing and grunting as she wearily climbed the stairs. Walters stopped banging, pulled out her phone and called his landline followed by his mobile. She heard the muffled ring of the house phone but despite putting her ear to the door, she couldn't hear his mobile.

Mrs Grant coughed and wiped her mouth with the paper handkerchief she carried. 'He went out last night sometime after ten o' clock, but now I think about it, I don't believe I heard him come back in.'

'He might have returned while you were asleep,' Bentley said.

'Oh, no, no, no, young man. I'm sure I would have heard, yes I definitely would. I don't sleep well you see, never have.'

'Think carefully, Mrs Grant,' Walters said, 'it's important. Are you sure he didn't come home?'

'I go to bed late, after midnight most nights,' she said, 'and the slightest noise wakes me. No, no, he didn't come back. I'm sure of it now. Positive, in fact.'

The detectives dashed to the car leaving Mrs Grant standing at the door, wondering what all the fuss was about. Walters made up for her slow driving earlier in the day by gunning the Golf through the gears as they made their way out of Brighton; if traffic cops wanted to pull her over, they would need to catch her first.

FORTY-ONE

The back door of the Land Rover Defender slammed shut and the man DI Henderson knew as Martin Swift walked back into the barn. Henderson was dozing in the chair and was woken up suddenly when a boot whacked the side of it.

'Let's go Henderson. We're getting the fuck out of here. I want no funny stuff, remember?' He tapped the pocket of a smart leather jacket where the bulge of a gun spoiled the shape.

Swift grabbed Henderson's arm and in a sort of hop-hop dance, they made their way to the car. The pain had eased off while he sat in the chair but he suspected he was getting used to it. The height of the passenger seat presented a bit of a challenge and by the time Swift pushed him in, the daggers in his leg returned with a vengeance; he began sweating and his leg throbbing like the ticking of a grandfather clock.

'Where are we going?' he asked when Swift climbed in behind the wheel and started the engine.

'We're going to a place I know and when we get there, I'm going to fuck-off and leave you behind and you'll never see or hear of me again. You'll be left in the middle of a big field with a phone nearby, but not so close it won't take you a couple of hours to reach it.'

The lying bastard. Having killed three, maybe four women already, why would he stop there? If he'd killed Kelly Langton and Amy Sandford with impunity, why not him? He shuddered at the thought and the helplessness of his situation; he felt so useless. His thoughts were interrupted when the car bounced over a bump on the uneven track and a fresh bolt of pain shot up his left leg.

While Swift had been packing his things, Henderson spent time examining his injuries. Until the excruciating move to the car, his right leg gave him less bother than before and only appeared bruised, but the left, the one which took the impact of the fall, was fractured in a couple of places and the edge of a bone could be seen pushing out against the skin.

In all his training and experience he'd always regarded the inside of a car as a weapon and not a cage, a major failing in many popular crime dramas on television and thriller movies. If he was in the driving seat, and even if the passenger had a gun, there were several options. He could drive fast and attract the attention of a passing patrol car or CCTV camera. If out in the country with no cameras or police cars, he could drive fast and suddenly stamp on the brakes, and hope the rapid deceleration would dislodge the weapon or confuse the passenger. A third more drastic course of action would be to crash the car.

As a passenger, his aim would be to grab the wheel, keys, knock the car out of gear, easy to do in an automatic, or pull up the handbrake; any combination of these would most likely stop the car. This was the position he found himself in now, but he was unable to do any of these things or in any way take Swift on, as he was young and fit and would be a formidable opponent, even if Henderson himself were not so incapacitated. He realised he had no choice but to follow whatever plan that occupied a space in the twisted man's head.

At the bottom of the driveway, they turned into Adversane Lane and the car slowed as Swift reached over to the low shelf beside Henderson, the Defender's poor excuse for a glove box, his eyes straying from the road as he did so. The car wobbled a few times and Henderson couldn't help but think it presented the ideal opportunity for him to attack. A few moments later, he found what he was looking for: sunglasses, and soon the car started moving once again to his destiny.

Up ahead, Henderson spotted something he thought he would never see again. A police patrol car headed towards them. His sense of elation fell flat when he realised no one knew where he was last night and with the patrol car showing no lights or urgency, it was more likely they were answering a local call about a stolen wheelie bin or a faulty burglar alarm. He waved to try and alert the two officers inside, despite the distance between them, but stopped when a forearm smashed across the chest, leaving him doubling up in agony.

To his relief, the officers in the Mondeo did spot him and the car swung across the carriageway, blocking the road. Swift muttered profanities under his breath, his neutral expression turning malevolent and steely and for a moment, Henderson was convinced he was about to ram them. Instead, he braked sharply and executed a three-point turn, some twenty yards from where the two officers were sitting in their car, and sped off in the opposite direction.

Henderson was puzzled and annoyed by the police tactics. Neither officer got out of their vehicle and tried to approach the Land Rover, nor did anything to stop them turning and driving away. If this was their idea of a rescue, they failed at first base.

He tried to recall details from the OS map that he and Sally Graham had looked at. He knew a main road lay a couple of miles ahead after they got through the village of Adversane, but he also remembered a number of smaller roads leading off towards little villages and hamlets. If Swift knew the area well, he could hide out in the heart of the countryside and elude them for weeks.

In places, the road was narrow and twisting with open fields on one side and a high wooded bank on the other. They were fortunate it was quiet, as the car was being driven fast and close to the centre of the road and the lack of any manoeuvring space on either side would give an oncoming driver little chance of avoiding them.

They drove past a small collection of houses, the pace unrelenting and Henderson winced, fully expecting a car to come out of a driveway or a side road at any minute. They approached a steep bend, forcing him to slow down, but before accelerating into the straight that followed, a red VW Golf came rushing towards them. DS Walters owned a red Golf; surely not?

Confirmation arrived seconds later when it made the same manoeuvre as the patrol car had done earlier when it turned across the carriageway and blocked the road. Remembering the patrol car, he glanced in the wing mirror to see if it still was following and there it was, keeping its distance and instantly he knew their tactics were to box them in. It was a risky thing to do, as none of the officers knew Swift was armed and how he would react when cornered.

The speed of the Land Rover decreased and Swift appeared to be caught in two minds, whether to carry on and try to force his way past the Golf or turn and take his chance with the patrol car which took up a position some distance behind, giving him a longer section of road to build up speed.

'You devious bastard, Henderson. You told me no one knew you were at my place last night. I ought to shoot you right now.'

'I didn't organise this, how could I? You saw my phone, it's busted.'

Swift accelerated hard and headed straight for the Golf. Up ahead, Walters, and a male figure looking a lot like DC Phil Bentley, abandoned the car as if it was full of wasps, and dived into a nearby hedgerow. On either side, Henderson could see a profusion of green leaves and a blur of bushes and up ahead in the windscreen, the bright red bodywork of a VW Golf looming larger and larger.

He gripped the upper handrail and was about to clamp his eyes shut when the Land Rover swung to the right and clipped the rear end of the Golf, shunting it to one side. The bang pushed the Land Rover off course and Swift wrestled with the wheel to correct his position and stay on the road; he succeeded and soon they accelerated away.

A quarter of a mile later, close to Adversane village, the main road not far beyond it, and with no sign of the rescue posse, Henderson felt sure Swift was getting away. Without warning, he stamped on the brakes and the car slowed. He hauled the steering wheel and turned into a gap between the trees where they bumped down a path before smashing through a gate into a field.

At first, Henderson thought he had lost control of the car or panicked, but he soon realised it was a pre-planned move as the Land Rover was better equipped at driving over the uneven ground of a field than either the Golf or the Mondeo patrol car and in a matter of minutes, he could see the broken gate diminish in size in the wing mirror. With an open field up ahead and only flimsy fences to stop him, Swift would be long gone before the Sussex Police helicopter could make its way from Shoreham Airport, providing of course, Walters had the sense to scramble it.

FORTY-TWO

The noise the Defender made when it smacked the rear end of Carol Walters' recently purchased VW Golf sounded like a sonic boom, as she hunched down in the briar and nettles. They were trying to untangle themselves from the stinging and scratching vegetation when the police patrol car came alongside and asked if they were ok. She replied they were, and they headed off in hot pursuit.

She said she was ok, but underneath she seethed. It wasn't because she loved the car but over time it had become her saviour. If she was ever late for work in the morning, which happened about ninety per cent of the time, this car got her there on time, so even though they didn't share a huge amount of love, she had grudging respect, and felt livid if anyone damaged it.

With a level of grit and determination surprising DC Bentley, who at 27, was ten years her junior, she clambered her way out of the ditch, grabbed his arm and hauled him up the slippery embankment to the road. Rather than cry about the damaged rear end, the smashed light cluster, and one of the wheels stuck in a ditch, she set about removing the loose pieces of plastic and metal and instructed Bentley to push from the front while she got it started and tried to reverse out.

To her surprise the car started first time but it took three attempts to remove the front wheel from the ditch as the tyres struggled to grip the damp grass. Before getting back inside, Bentley used his foot to sweep small bits of debris into the roadside while Walters revved the engine, her impatience and anger evident.

Before the door closed, they roared off in the same direction as the patrol car, the accelerator pedal not far from the floorboards. They were travelling so fast, she almost missed the turn, difficult to do as the site was marked with all manner of splintered wood and broken fence posts and the road splattered with mud. After a hard stab of the brakes, she made the turn.

The Golf charged through the gap in the gate into the large field and at once, a violent shaking reverberated throughout the car and inside the bodies of both occupants, as the wheels hit furrow after furrow.

'Slow down sarg,' Bentley said, his voice a strange, shaky warble as his hand held a firm grip on the upper handrail, 'you'll knock something else off the car, or my bloody fillings out.'

They could still see the Land Rover as it ascended a small hill, the police patrol car some way behind but the space between them widening.

'I hope to God,' she said through gritted teeth, not so much the result of dogged determination as violent vibration, 'Lewes are sending some 4x4s and not another Mondeo as the one up ahead seems to be having the same trouble we are.'

'Do you think we'll get the 'copter because if we don't close the gap on him soon, he'll disappear.'

'I hope so but we've only got one and if it's being used for something else, we're stuffed.'

'Yeah?'

'One thing bothers me though.'

'What?'

'Did you clock the guy driving the Land Rover?'

'You mean when I was diving into the nettles to avoid being flattened? Not bloody likely.'

'I only caught a glimpse myself, but he looks nothing like James Archer. It's not just the hair but the build, and he looks younger.'

'I dunno. I didn't get a good look.'

Halfway up the small hill, The Defender suddenly lurched to the right. It continued to lean further and further before completely tipping over and rolling down the slope. It came to a juddering halt at the bottom lying on its side.

'Did you see that?' Bentley said, his voice incredulous. 'Did that really happen or am I dreaming?'

'You're hallucinating from having your brain rattled around so much in this field,' Walters replied, but she had trouble believing it herself. Each time she looked out over the bleak, vibrating landscape, the blue Land Rover lay on its side, the driver's door facing skywards.

The cops in the patrol car were aiming for a position to the Land Rover's left and it would be stupid, not to mention embarrassing, if they were to collide out here in a vast, empty field and so she guided the Golf over to the opposite side.

The driver's door of the Land Rover opened and a man climbed out but it wasn't Henderson. He stood for a few seconds doing nothing, as if trying to clear his head and regain his balance, or trying to comprehend what had happened, when he dipped back into the upturned vehicle and pulled out a rifle.

'Fucking hell, sarg he's got a gun!'

'I know son, I know.'

'Slow down, no stop! He's got a bloody assault rifle. He could shoot us from there.'

'No, we're going to stop this bastard.'

She kept going, her eyes fixed on the gun. Her car and the patrol car were in easy range, sitting ducks in a fairground attraction. She once won a teddy bear at a fairground, *pop, pop, pop, pop*, knocked down four ducks in rapid succession with an air rifle. Maybe she should have joined the firearms unit and been given the chance of shooting armed evil bastards like this guy.

He shouldered the rifle and fired a rapid burst at the Mondeo. If he'd aimed for the windscreen, the driver and his passenger would be dead by now, but he fired lower, and immediately a plume of steam shot out from the radiator and the Mondeo slowed to a halt.

Like the poor fairground duck, they were next. She tried to blot out the anxious bleating of the quivering heap of blubber in the passenger seat, tensing all her muscles and trying hard not to pee herself. She was ready to swing the car to the side and duck, although a

0.6mm Golf body panel wouldn't do much to stop a rifle bullet, but with no rocks or woods to hide behind, she couldn't think of doing anything else at the moment. She kept going with a gritty determination that came from God knows where because if they were in the firing line, where did that leave Henderson?

He raised the rifle, about to shoulder it again when he looked up to the sky. They could barely hear it with all the rattling going on inside the car, but it would be the police helicopter. She felt happy they'd responded to her request but how irrational was that? It was an unarmed, MD Explorer civilian helicopter and not a Longbow Apache equipped with a chain gun and Hellfire missiles. It could track suspects but not shoot them, leaving the crew in as much danger from a gunman with an assault rifle as those on the ground.

The clatter of the rotor blades seemed to change the mind of the gunman and he forgot all about shooting them and took a kneeling position ready to aim at the helicopter, still out of range.

She tried to cajole Bentley into calling Lewes Control to tell them to send a warning to the helicopter crew but his hands were shaking so much at the sight of the gun that he couldn't grip the handset, and she couldn't as she was doing all she could to keep the car going in the direction she wanted. She could see no sign of Henderson, he was either incapacitated or bloody useless at getting out of upturned cars.

She imagined the gunman would pull his hostage from the car and try to make their escape on foot, but he started shouting something at Henderson and his body language suggested he was angry at something as he raised the weapon. The going was faster now as the ground was flatter with less teeth-shaking furrows and the distance between them was closing fast.

Henderson appeared to be giving as good as he got and they seemed to be arguing like an old married couple and, strange in the circumstances, thoughts of her ex-husband, Gary, popped into her head. Thirty yards. The gunman turned and spotted them and made to raise the rifle but turned back to face the upturned vehicle, to respond to something Henderson must have said.

Ten yards away, she floored the accelerator. The gunman turned again, but became distracted by the helicopter and a suicidal copper in the Mondeo, exhorting him through a loud hailer to throw down his weapon. He raised his rifle into a firing position.

The Golf smacked him hard in the lower midriff and he crashed against the windscreen, the rifle flying over the roof of the car. She stopped the car and got out. It felt surreal, standing there and surveying the scene, an upturned Land Rover, a helicopter clattering overhead and a man lying lifeless on the grass; but one she would remember forever.

FORTY-THREE

Soft pillows were being plumped up by a pretty young nurse with short black hair and flat shoes that did nothing to detract from long, slender legs, tantalisingly encased in black nylon. DI Henderson relished the inconvenience.

'There you are now, Angus,' she said in a sweet Irish voice. 'You're all ready to receive your visitors.'

'I don't need any visitors when I've got you Mary. Two hours with you messing about with my pillows would suit me just fine.'

'Away with you, you smooth talking Scotsman,' she said, turning to go. 'Don't forget I've seen you naked and if I get any more cheek from you, your bath night will appear as a video on YouTube,' she said with a wink as she walked away.

It was the day after the 'Siege of Hillcrest Copse' as the newspapers were calling it, but as yet he'd not had a spare moment to mull over the events of that eventful morning, as no sooner did he arrive in hospital, than he was rushed into theatre for an operation to set his broken bones. He still felt groggy from the anaesthetic, and it was only now, seeing Walters walking towards his hospital bed, that the memories came flooding back.

'Good afternoon, Angus,' she said, a wide grin on her face. She leaned over and gave him a big hug and a kiss before putting a half bottle of Glenmorangie in a drawer and placing a box of Roses chocolates on top of the unit. She threw a copy of *The Argus* on the bed.

He bent forward gingerly and picked up the paper. The headline read, 'Hero Cop Stops Sussex Serial Killer.'

'Well done, Carol,' he said. 'Fame at last.'

She shook her head. 'No way, Angus. The story is about you.'

Henderson looked closely at the paper and as he did so, tears welled up. He wasn't feeling emotional at all the praise being heaped upon him for being a hero, or the suggestion that he would be commended by the Chief Constable, if not promoted, but by the profiles of each of the killer's five victims. The Forensic team found DVDs in a second flat he owned in Horsham with recordings of all the women he'd once held captive. The thought that he and his colleagues might have done more to catch him sooner, was one he couldn't shake.

'Those poor women,' he said.

'Don't be so down Angus, Martin Swift or Max Baris as he is more commonly known, left enough clues. We should be able find out where he buried the bodies and give them a proper funeral.'

'Make it a priority.'

'Already in motion.'

'Is James Archer still around or did he scarper?'

'I think he's still around.'

'Good. Bring him in before he decides to make a

run for it. I think he knows more about Martin Swift's activities than we thought.'

'Why do you say that?'

'The secret room where he kept the women was a clever piece of carpentry. I'm betting Archer was involved in making it.'

'I'm forgetting your dad worked as a carpenter, some of it must have rubbed off on you, but consider it done. Something is still bothering me. Why did the Land Rover overturn? The papers are saying you hit a log or something.'

'We went over a slope at quite a steep angle and I grabbed the steering wheel and turned it down hill. The weight of the two of us leaning to one side and the lack of traction on the other side of the car did the rest.'

'Ingenious.'

'Not really. In the Highlands, I've seen many tourists do it by accident, those labouring under the false assumption that a 4x4 can go anywhere. How is Swift? Is he here? I'd like to talk to him.'

She shook her head. 'He didn't make it. After my car hit him, he fell back and smacked his head on a rock. Died where he fell. I didn't mean to kill him, obviously, but I can't say I'm sorry he's gone.'

'Has any flak come your way?'

'Nope. The ACC is robust in my defence and telling all who ask that I stopped him killing a police officer, namely you, and prevented him shooting down a police helicopter.'

'Excellent. You did a marvellous job. It's you who should be getting a commendation, not me and I will be saying as much to Lisa Edwards when I see her.'

'Thank you. One last thing and I saved the best for last.'

'There's more? I don't think I can take anything else.'

'You'll like this. You saved a woman called Elaine Chivers.'

'Who's she?'

'The woman being held captive in the secret room in the barn.'

'The one I saw before I fell off the roof? Is she all right? I mean, he didn't harm her, did he?'

'No, she's fine. She's a strong lady, a survivor if ever I saw one. Says she's coming here to thank you personally.'

Henderson sat up and reached unsteadily for the side cabinet. Walters put a hand out to stop him. 'What do want Angus? You only need to ask and I'll get it for you.'

'I'm after the bottle of hooch you put in the drawer. You can use the water glasses,' he said, as he lay back on the bed. 'For the first time in this investigation, I think we've now got something to celebrate.'

ABOUT THE AUTHOR

Iain Cameron was born in Glasgow and moved to Brighton in the early eighties. He has worked as a management accountant, business consultant and a nursery goods retailer. He is now a full-time writer and lives in a village outside Horsham in West Sussex with his wife, two daughters and a lively Collie dog.

His two previous books, *One Last Lesson* and *Driving into Darkness also* feature DI Angus Henderson of Sussex Police, the Scottish detective with the calm demeanour and hidden ruthless streak.

To find out more about the author, visit the website:

www.iain-cameron.com

ALSO BY IAIN CAMERON

Driving into Darkness
They Don't Take 'No' For An Answer

Vicious car-thieves are smashing their way into rural properties and stealing expensive cars. Their violence is escalating and detectives at Sussex Police are fearful they will eventually kill someone.

Their fears are realised when Sir Mathew Markham is killed. Everyone assumes his murder was the work of the gang but DI Angus Henderson is not so sure.

He tenaciously pursues his own theory, bringing him face to face with two killers...one who will stop at nothing to avoid going to jail, and the other equally determined to wreak his own brand of vengeance.

One Last Lesson

University Has Just Become a Dangerous Place

The serenity of a rural golf course is shattered when a popular university student is found murdered.

There are few clues, leaving DI Angus Henderson of Sussex Police frustrated and angry, until he finds out the victim was a model on an adult web site, run by two of her lecturers.

It is a difficult case for the DI and brings him into confrontation with two dangerous animals - but only one of them is human.

Printed in Great Britain
by Amazon